D1252178

THE MAIDEN VOYAGE OF THE
DESTINY UNKNOWN

THE MAIDEN VOYAGE OF THE
DESTINY UNKNOWN

NICHOLAS PONTICELLO

BOOLEANOP, WOODLAND, CALIFORNIA

To my therapists: Doctor K. S., Doctor E. P., and Doctor K. M.
If this book makes me sound crazy, just imagine
what I'd sound like without your help.

Inspired by all that has come before and guided by clear objectives, today we set a new course for America's space program. We will give NASA a new focus and vision for future exploration. We will build new ships to carry man forward into the universe, to gain a new foothold on the moon, and to prepare for new journeys to worlds beyond our own. ...Today I announce a new plan to explore space and extend a human presence across our solar system. ...As our knowledge improves, we'll develop new power generation propulsion, life support, and other systems that can support more distant travels. We do not know where this journey will end, yet we know this: Human beings are headed into the cosmos.

—President George W. Bush
AD January 14, 2004

As our business expands, we intend to make Koffee Brothers coffee available to everybody, even astronauts and space explorers. Moon be damned! It is our aim to open a Koffee Brothers on Mars or Pluto, or another planet orbiting another sun, so long as we're the first ones there.

—Jim Furlong, CEO, Koffee Brothers Inc.
AD April 9, 5988

Man does not belong in space. He can barely walk on two feet without squashing something. Sending man into space is like wishing the plague on all of the universe's inhabitants.

—The Dalai Lama Drukpa Gyatso
AD March 6, 12986

Contents

AUTHOR'S NOTE

A GREAT DEAL OF RESEARCH went into this book. I have taken great pains to throw out as much of it as possible. I *did* make an effort to honor the most fundamental and popularly recognized laws of physics—I don't want to come off as a complete fool.

Epsilon Eridani is a real star. The degree of time dilation experienced by the passengers on the spacecraft is based on complicated Lorentz transformations that I solved on the back of an envelope in the year AD 2008 while I was living in a shabby seven-hundred-square-foot apartment in Burbank, California, with a mousy roommate from New Jersey. I cannot reproduce those calculations today as I have only gotten stupider since I started writing the story of the *Destiny Unknown*.

Hydrazoic acid *is* highly explosive—don't ask me why or how. And our sun will die in the pitiful manner that I have described, more or less.

Aside from these few veracities, and a couple of other minor details that are based in scientific fact, I have made a point of dispensing with reason in favor of creating a more colorful world for my fifty space travelers, among which are a dog, a parrot, and a chimpanzee.

Why a space captain would waste valuable cargo room on a dog, a parrot, and a chimpanzee, I do not know. But there they are: a dog, a parrot, and a chimpanzee. Perhaps they are there because *I* cannot stand to have a cast made up entirely of members of the *Homo sapiens* species. So they are there for me.

The other forty-seven space travelers aboard the ship are there because they are human. And humans are bound to be just about anywhere. The characters in this book represent the hodgepodge of humanity you might encounter in rush-hour traffic on the southbound 101 Freeway between Agoura Hills and the Cahuenga Pass on a balmy Friday evening. These unlikely heroes are just as likely to be texting while driving seventy-five miles per hour on the freeway as they are to be bickering over kitchen duty on a space vessel traveling 0.876 times the speed of light, sixty-one trillion miles from Earth.

That is to say, the humans in this story are universal.

—N. P.

BOOK ONE: NISSAN SENTRA

CHAPTER 1
YEAR ZERO

FOUR AND A HALF BILLION YEARS ago, a greenish G-type star called Sol was born out of a cloudy mass of hydrogen, helium, carbon, oxygen, and nitrogen. With it came eight planets and a puny little ice cube called Pluto, now known to be an afterthought of the initial formation and, hence, not a planet at all—a fact that for many thousands of years eluded even the most big-brained, upright-walking inhabitants of the little water-filled planet Earth.

Five and a half billion years later, the sun would die a rather unimpressive death, swelling like an overripe peach to an unmanageable size and shedding its gaseous outer layers like an onion being peeled—essentially burping and farting itself into oblivion.

But some billions of years before this rather unextraordinary end to the source of all life in the solar system, a small crew of brave voyagers from the insignificant but determined planet Earth set out in search of a new home. These voyagers, though mere carbon-based beings, were the pioneers of an until-then-unexplored universe.

The crew consisted of fifty passengers, nearly all of them from the *Homo sapiens* species. There were a few others as well: a chimpanzee named Bobo, a great African grey parrot called Bill, and a yellow cocker spaniel named Dog.

Their ship, the *Destiny Unknown*, was a state-of-the-art space vessel built to endure the harsh extremes of deep space and equipped with all the essentials needed to support life for upward of fifty years. There were replenishing supplies of oxygen and water and enough food to last half a century—that is, assuming there were no greedy overeaters among the fifty passengers, an assumption that, given the history of humankind, was extremely optimistic.

The sorry truth of the matter was that several aboard the *Destiny Unknown* were greedy overeaters, but none so greedy as Bartholomew Barbate, a three-hundred-pound electrician from Cape Trafalgar. Not only would Bartholomew Barbate eat more than his fair share on the *Destiny Unknown*, he would also ceaselessly annoy the other passengers by forever emitting thick, vaporous gases from his tail end, much like the ill-fated sun just before its death in the year AD 5.52 billion.

The captain of the *Destiny Unknown*, a well-known astrophysicist and space pilot named Marcus Fincus, would deplete fifty years' supply of air freshener in the first six months of the journey trying to eliminate the odor of Bartholomew Barbate, to no avail. Despite his PhD from the California Institute of Technology and years of research in the fields of astronomy, chemistry, and math, he would be unable to render Bartholomew's gaseous fumes inert, no matter how much pine-scented aerosol he sprayed into the air.

There was a surgeon aboard the ship—Dr. Myles Jamison, from Minnesota—who, at the urging of the crew, drugged Bartholomew in his sleep, turned his belly inside out, and tried to surgically shrink his stomach. But the doctor did not administer enough anesthesia to this three-hundred-pound whale of a man; Bartholomew woke in the middle of the surgery and screamed so loudly that the doctor jumped back, slipped in a puddle of blood, and fell facedown on the hospital floor, slicing his own jugular vein wide open with his scalpel, consequently slaying the one qualified surgeon aboard the ship.

It took three other passengers, all trained in various medical fields, to readminister the drugs and patch Bartholomew back up the way he was before, excepting the thick, badly sewn scar across his abdomen. They must have accidentally kinked Bartholomew's intestines in the process, because after that, he farted just as much—but louder and more violently.

The space vessel, the *Destiny Unknown*, took off from Earth at a time when the sun had expanded to a size hot enough to burn off all the oceans and lakes and rivers. Where at one time the majority of the water was on the surface of the Earth, forming oceans and rivers and ice, now it was in the sky, forming hot, humid clouds. The average surface temperature had risen to about 245 degrees Fahrenheit, and the atmosphere more closely resembled that of its sister planet, Venus, than it did the Earth of the twenty-first century, when humans still lived above ground.

Scientists long before had predicted this fiery end to life on Earth, but humans proved to be more resilient than expected. Still they survived on this hell of a planet, deep, deep underground, where they could filter water and oxygen out of the soil and where temperatures were more bearable.

Only a few other animals were spared extinction. Dogs survived because they were smart enough to befriend humans back at the beginning of time, winning themselves a place among the underground colonies of men. Chimps had their place among humans, too, because chimps so closely resembled humans in behavior and DNA that they made perfect subjects for scientific tests. And the African grey parrot, Bill, was one of the thousand or so parrots that had remained among humans because bird lovers continued to breed them, even in such dire conditions, and because the greys were smart enough to do menial tasks on command, such as set the table or line up matchsticks.

Incidentally, cockroaches, rats, and fleas persisted despite the heat and despite humans' repeated efforts to exterminate them. They had evolved considerably: roaches were bigger now and had long burrowing tusks for living underground, rats were hairless and spindly to avoid overheating, and fleas had become increasingly immune to insecticides and pest removers.

It so happened that the fleas made good fodder for the chimpanzees and the African grey parrots and the dogs made good fodder for the fleas—the last remaining food chain on Earth.

***

NASA bankrolled the mission, with Marcus Fincus at the helm. The selection process for the passengers of the voyage of the *Destiny Unknown* had been quite simple, really. A committee of geneticists took applications from around the globe for positions necessary on such a mission: doctor, engineer, electrician, veterinarian, and so on. With their resumes, applicants were asked to include a hair follicle from their own heads. Once the committee members had chosen the most qualified people out of the thousands of applications they had received, they analyzed the genetic makeup of each candidate using the hair follicle provided and then correlated and cross-correlated the data until they could determine a set of fifty applicants with the most distinct genetic identities.

In an interview for a French radio program, Captain Marcus Fincus postulated: "If we are to leave the planet Earth for another planet, and we are to populate that planet using only fifty people, isn't it in our best interest—in the best interest of the human race—to have as many genetic variations as possible in the genetic pool to prevent domination of any one genetic trait, such as baldness or sleep apnea? Or suppose that every person ends up creatively minded but they're all duds at math, or vice versa. What then?"

So even if a pair of identical twins applied, one a world-famous surgeon and the other a celebrated poet, the committee could take only one. Such was the case of Earl Updike, a recent poet laureate from Manhattan. His identical twin brother, a doctor in Los Angeles, was turned away from the program with a line that simply stated, "Thank you for your interest in NASA's New World Population Project. We regret to inform you that your application has been declined." Meanwhile, his brother, a quarter of the way around the world, received the notice, "Congratulations! You have been accepted into NASA's elite New World Population Project. Please join us in Washington, DC, this fall for orientation and training."

Forty-three other acceptance letters, each saying the same thing, went out to forty-three other soon-to-be passengers of the *Destiny Unknown*. Six passengers did not receive such letters but were admitted nonetheless: Captain Marcus Fincus, his wife, his son, Bobo the chimpanzee, Bill the African grey parrot, and Dog.

Orientation and training were held in an underground government facility in Washington, DC, where the *Destiny Unknown* was docked and ready for launch. Each passenger underwent extensive protocol training and was subsequently issued a badge that designated the level of access he or she was to have on the ship. Captain Marcus Fincus and his first mate, Johannes Levi, were granted level-A access, which meant they could go anywhere on the vessel at any time. Others, such as Bartholomew Barbate, the ship's key electrician, and Melanie Lorne, the ship's chief engineer, were granted level-B access, which gave them access to all of the ship's inner workings, but not, for example, to the captain's stateroom or any of the other passengers' private quarters.

Fifteen children were aboard the ship at the time of take-off. They were given level-E access, which basically meant they couldn't go anywhere or do anything much at all. On the role of children in NASA's New World Population Project, Captain Marcus Fincus told a Nigerian radio correspondent, "Even with a fast ship and the finest instrumentation, we still can't be sure how long we'll be out in space. Our ship is equipped with enough supplies to sustain fifty-plus people for fifty-plus years. In fifty years, surely, many of the adult members of the crew will be dead or nearly so, and it will be up to the children to do the repopulating of a new planet."

Fourteen of the children were orphan savants—gifted boys and girls with no family to miss them when they were gone. The one exception, and the only child genetically linked to any other passenger in any way, was Jason Fincus, the captain's son.

***

Orientation and training lasted a period of seventy-two weeks, at the end of which the fifty selected passengers could successfully live and survive on the ship without help from NASA or anybody else from the outside world. By then everybody was intimately acquainted with everybody else, and they all got along famously, so much so that the people at NASA were patting themselves on the back and giving one another high fives for doing such a bang-up job of everything so far.

What they did not know was that among these fifty agreeable passengers were a number of ticking time bombs, as is often the case with any randomly selected group of human beings. The Spertzhung-Platz rating for humans is relatively high—about thirty-five—which means that out of any given sample of one hundred human beings, thirty-five are likely to be certifiably crazy.

At an American press conference, a reporter from the *New York Times* asked, "Why choose so many nobodies for a mission of such great importance?"

Marcus Fincus replied, "It takes all kinds. It takes all kinds."

Really it takes one kind—the explorer kind—and in the many millions of years since the long-forgotten days of the Vikings, conquistadors, silk traders, and American pioneers, true explorers among the human race had become exceedingly rare. What may not be evident to the average Djoran[1] reader—since our species is a nomadic one, naturally predisposed to risk and adventure—is how little any human being in his or her right mind would want to take part in such a perilous adventure. This little band of humans was to travel for years and years in deep space, heading for an uninhabited planet, void of all human life, to begin a new colony far from anything familiar. They would never see their loved ones again, never go to another baseball game, never see another summer blockbuster at the theater, and never hear the latest hit on the radio. They were leaving all of human civilization behind, and that is a difficult thing for a human being to do.

Humans are among the most homesick creatures in the universe—and they are the only species known to shed H_2O tears due to extreme emotion.

Sure, it was hot as hell on Earth, and nobody went above the ground long enough to see anything of interest, but most people were fine in their underground lairs. Yes, in a billion years or so, it would be even hotter and perhaps unbearable. And surely the sun would burn out by AD 5.52 billion. But none of the people alive at the time of the launch of the *Destiny Unknown* were going to be around for any of that; right

---

[1] Pronounced "Joh-ran."

now, even though it was pretty damn hot, most people were certain to live full and happy lives.

So it was that the fifty passengers aboard the *Destiny Unknown* were called many things by the press. "Selfless Pioneers of Mankind!" exclaimed the *Hollywood Reporter*. "Narcissistic Self-Martyrs on a Suicide Mission," wrote the *Toronto Sun*.

Marcus Jay Fincus was the mastermind of the whole enterprise, and although the people at NASA thought the New World Population Project was a great idea and, if indeed successful, a good way to ensure the survival of the human species, they were all perfectly content to see Marcus Fincus and his crew on their merry way. Nobody alive on Earth at that time, not the members of NASA or anybody else, would ever see or hear from any of them ever again. But it would always be nice for everybody on Earth to think that somewhere out there humans were populating the universe, whether or not it was true.

CHAPTER 2

YEAR ZERO

THE SHIP WAS DIVIDED into three areas. They were commonly referred to as the main deck, central command (CC for short), and "down below."

The main deck consisted of five levels of private cabins, each complete with a washroom and kitchenette. The walls and floors were carpeted to muffle the rumble of the ship's engine. Clam-shaped light fixtures hung on the corridor walls, emitting warm natural light. The starboard staterooms had small round portholes, dressed with velvet curtains that could be drawn tight to shut out the view of the endless night. The cafeteria on level three was open from six to eight in the morning, from noon to two in the afternoon, and from five to seven in the evening. The kitchen staffers were a sour bunch, each assuming the attitude of the brazen high-school lunch ladies of yore, and they doled out strictly regulated portions for breakfast, lunch, and dinner to the passengers in their time, in their turn. Snacks were carefully measured out and weighed to conserve food, and each passenger had his or her own snack locker with a key.

The long corridor on level five opened onto a grand library with a clear-glass ceiling that bellied out into deep space like the giant eyeball of a watchful Cyclops. The library was stocked with enough books to last a lifetime, even if one were a voracious and speedy reader, as was Amanda Sphinx, a fifteen-year-old piano prodigy from Saskatchewan, Canada. If Amanda wasn't in the library, then she was in the music room one floor below (accessible by a long spiral staircase), practicing or composing on the grand piano. Her music was a thing to marvel at; when she played, the sound of it would drift up the spiral staircase into the library and float right up to the glass ceiling as if to serenade the stars.

Her best friend on the ship was a boy named Austin Ibsen, an autistic twelve-year-old savant with an IQ to rival anyone's on planet Earth.

There was also a media center on level five, adjacent the library, with a digital archive of more than fifty-seven million video files, thirteen billion music files, and another eleven trillion image and text files. These were stored on a megacomputer that could be accessed with the code word *diverticulitis.*

The code word was meant to keep the young children from browsing through material meant for mature audiences only. Dr. Myles Jamison chose it as a sort of inside joke since nobody really knew what *diverticulitis* meant. But Dr. Myles Jamison got a kick out of it because he knew very well that diverticulitis is the condition of having small swollen pockets in the colon—a condition that, incidentally, more than half the population of the *Destiny Unknown* would suffer from before the end of the journey.

***

Central command was the brains of the ship. Accessible only to level-A and level-B badge holders, CC housed the offices of the captain and his crew. The captain had his station on the foredeck with the sailing master, Howard Oppenheimer. Howard Oppenheimer was a distant relative of Robert Oppenheimer, the man largely responsible for the creation of the atom bomb. Much less controversial was Howard Oppenheimer's job of navigating the *Destiny Unknown* through deep space, a job in which no unwitting civilians were to be blown to smithereens (that is, except for one, as we shall see later).

The other crew members present on the ship's main deck were the first mate, Johannes Levi; the chief mechanical engineer, Melanie Lorne; a French signals specialist named Maurice Yanne; and a collection of technicians and engineers who assisted the others wherever they could.

Bartholomew Barbate, the electrician from Cape Trafalgar, had level-B access, which meant he could be on the foredeck with the captain if he liked. However, Bartholomew was most often scrambling about down below, working and reworking the electrical wiring of the *Destiny Unknown*'s air and lighting mechanisms, which were faulty from day one.

The *Destiny Unknown* was a beautiful ship, and like all beautiful ships, it had a personality of its own. From the very moment the ship launched into space, it began to exhibit signs of stubbornness. Within the first six hours of leaving Earth's hot, stormy atmosphere, a ship-wide power outage was made all the worse by the fact that the shivering passengers were spiraling through space 3.5 billion miles from civilization, with no sun or moon to offer comfort or solace. Bartholomew Barbate was immediately called into action to fix the problem; he clambered down to the giant fuse box located in the hull of the ship and, with a little fiddling, restored light to the *Destiny Unknown*. But power outages would be a frequent occurrence during their many years in deep space—so frequent, in fact, that the passengers began attaching little flashlights to their belt loops, mimicking the fashion of humans back on Earth who needed the flashlights to navigate the dark tunnels of their underground lairs.

Then there were the issues with the water and air. The ship's water and oxygen supply was regulated by a brilliant machine called a moleculator, originally designed to filter the H_2O and O_2 out of the deep soil of the planet for the underground colonies on Earth. Aboard the *Destiny Unknown*, the moleculator was tasked with filtering water and oxygen out of the very barren interstellar medium. If no such substances were in the interstellar medium, the moleculator could break down other substances—such as CO_2 from the ship's cabin or water vapor in the air—to create fresh water and oxygen for the passengers. In this way, the moleculator served as a recycler and reuser of gases aboard the *Destiny Unknown*, converting useless fumes into drinkable, breathable substances.

And so the passengers never lacked for air to breathe and water to drink—unless the moleculator malfunctioned, which it inevitably did more than a handful of times.

Fortunately Bartholomew Barbate was an excellent electrician and, more important, one of the designers of the moleculator. He could usually bring the fickle life-support system back online within a few hours—or days, at most—and the passengers suffered only a little, if any, hypoxia of the brain.[2]

The moleculator was just one of the mechanisms aboard the ship that was designed to recycle and reuse waste products. There was a greenhouse run by a handsome woman—a biologist from Seattle—named Ginger Martin. She held a

---

[2] Hypoxia of the brain is a condition in which the brain does not receive enough oxygen to remain operative. This, you might imagine, is the number one leading cause of brain damage among oxygen-dependent trans-solar species such as space-traveling humans.

PhD in plant and cell biology from Stanford and was in charge of tending the greenhouse, which processed human feces, as well as dog feces, chimp feces, and even parrot feces to fertilize a vegetable garden that supplemented the ship's already large supply of canned, dried, and freeze-dried goods.

Ginger was also responsible for maintaining, in a large laboratory freezer, the cell cultures that were destined to spread life to whatever planet the little band of humans happened to settle on.

Yes, they had cell cultures ready for the harvesting, cell cultures that they could drop into any ocean anywhere in the universe and—*BAM!*—primordial soup. They also had buckets and buckets of seeds from all earthborn plants imaginable.

All of this in the storage facilities in the hull of the ship. *Down below*, as the crew would say, meaning the place where all the food was kept, along with spare parts, clothing for any climate, all-weather tents for cold nights on potentially barren planets, enough pills and medication to stock a small pharmacy, and vaccinations for smallpox, polio, and rabies—because who knew what they would meet out there in the great unknown.

The food stores were categorized and divided into three groups: the perishables from the greenhouse garden, fertilized with human feces, which were always eaten first; the canned, jarred, and dried goods, used to supplement the perishables; and last, far, far away, buried under everything else because everyone hoped it would never come to this, the freeze-dried goods—the astronaut food, bland and tasteless—at least thirty-three years' worth of nutrition for fifty people, compressed into tiny airtight plastic bags, to be eaten only in emergencies.

***

When the *Destiny Unknown* took off from Earth, it knew exactly where it was going, despite its ill-fated name. Where it ended up is another matter entirely.

The ship and its crew were headed for a nearby star known to astronomers as Epsilon Eridani—a star similar in size to the sun, a bit smaller and much dimmer, but very young and certain to live a long and happy life.

To understand the vast difference in the ages of the dim young star known as Epsilon Eridani and the ancient, dying star known as the sun, you might make this comparison: if Epsilon Eridani were in the first grade, then the sun could be its great-grandfather. That's how young Epsilon Eridani was in the world of stars. This, Marcus Fincus decided, was a very good thing since the last thing anybody wanted to do was travel tens of trillions of miles—which was how far away Epsilon Eridani was from Earth—only to find the star on its deathbed, just like the soon-to-be farting, burping sun.

More important, a young astronomer working long hours

at the Jet Propulsion Laboratory in California had discovered a small terrestrial planet (70 percent the size of Earth) orbiting Epsilon Eridani at a distance just far enough away to allow for liquid water to exist on the planet's surface. Further studies of the planet's atmosphere indicated a 97 percent chance that liquid water existed somewhere on the planet's surface—and not just a little water but oceans and oceans of the stuff. Moreover, astronomers found evidence to suggest that the atmosphere contained oxygen, loads of it, surely enough oxygen to last fifty people, their children, and their children's children thousands of millions of years.

This little Earthlike planet was called Nissan Sentra, named after a model of car popular at the time of its discovery. The man who discovered the planet was named Ernest Glump. On the morning of the discovery of this little water-filled planet, Ernest Glump was making the three-mile commute to his laboratory in the hills of La Cañada Flintridge when a tabby cat leaped into the path of his fossil-fuel-guzzling vehicle. Ernest, being a cat lover (and *not* a dog lover—always an important distinction among humans), swerved to avoid the cat and went barreling down an adjacent hillside toward a low stone wall bordering a mud flat. The expert brakes on his little Nissan Sentra stopped Ernest from ramming headfirst into the stone wall.

And because nobody wanted to hear about a planet called Glump, Ernest named the planet after the car that had saved his life. Newspapers reported the sensational story, practically giving full credit to Ernest's Nissan Sentra with the expert brakes for the ultimate discovery of Nissan Sentra with the oceans and oceans of water.

Nissan Motors Company, Ltd., a Japanese automobile manufacturer, was thrilled. So was the tabby cat.

This all happened way back in the twenty-first century, when humans were still driving gasoline-fueled cars that spouted CO_2 into the atmosphere—back when it was still cool enough to go outside for prolonged periods without risking first-degree burns.

For a time, this little water-filled planet called Nissan Sentra became the topic of much discussion in scientific communities around the world. And then, like most information of no immediate import, it was buried under tomorrow's headlines and forgotten. Interest in the planet Nissan Sentra was revived only when, millions of years later, humans finally developed the moleculator and the multitude of other advanced technologies that would take them to it.

***

Here's the thing: Epsilon Eridani and its little planet Nissan Sentra were very, *very* close to Earth—only sixty-one trillion miles away, a short distance, astronomically speaking. Epsilon Eridani was, in fact, one of the closest stars neighboring the sun, and light traveling at 670 million miles per hour could get there in a mere ten and a half years.

Alas, an object with mass—such as a spaceship—cannot travel at the speed of light. Only light can travel at the speed of light. Albert Einstein theorized this way back in AD 1905. He happened to be spot-on, which is saying a lot for any human in the year 1905, when one of the most advanced nations on the planet still had separate drinking fountains for people with dark skin and people with light skin.

Nevertheless, and in keeping with Einstein's theory, the *Destiny Unknown* could travel up to 0.876 times the speed of light, or 587 million miles per hour, record speeds for a ship of that size.

What did this mean for the fifty passengers aboard the *Destiny Unknown*?

Taking special relativity into account and allowing for occasional fluctuations in speed, they would be traveling in deep space together for exactly twelve years before finally reaching Nissan Sentra, the planet that was to be their new home.

***

Twelve long years in deep space—that was how long Bartholomew Barbate would have his diet regulated by a lockbox in the pantry. Twelve years was how long Ginger Martin would be tending a vegetable garden fed by human feces. Twelve years was how long Marcus Fincus would have to sleep every night in the same tiny cabin with his pampered, snoring wife. Twelve years was how long Howard Oppenheimer would have to sit at the same set of controls and navigate the *Destiny Unknown* through the unchanging darkness of deep space.

Twelve years—the time it takes Jupiter to make one trip around the sun. Twelve years—the gestation period of the black-billed Filitian marsalk.

In this field report, filed on UT43:65:19342177003, I aim to prove one thing: a lot can happen in twelve years as far as humans are concerned.

CHAPTER 3

YEAR 1

THE NIGHT OF THE LAUNCH of the *Destiny Unknown* was a very important moment for the committee at NASA. This was to be the last they would ever see of their beloved New World Population Project and its fearless director. Years of planning and calculating and engineering and designing and training had come to this moment—the most publicized moment in NASA's history since Neil Armstrong first set foot on the Moon. Every human eye was fixed on a live broadcast of the event.

As luck would have it, I had my eye fixed on Earth at that particular moment, too.

On the eve of the launch, NASA threw a big party at the base of the launch pad, with guided tours of the space vessel departing every hour. The guests were pleased to be above ground in the bearable nighttime climate—a mild 125 degrees Fahrenheit—flaunting their fancy suits and gowns.

Everybody who was anybody was in attendance: celebrities, politicians, military leaders, and the greatest minds in art and science. A few nobodies were in attendance, too: the bedraggled friends and families of the fifty never-to-be-seen-again passengers.

The celebrity guests greeted and congratulated the crew while stuffing large handfuls of crackers and cheese into their faces. Meanwhile, the families and friends of the fifty passengers sniffled and sobbed and stuffed large handfuls of crackers and cheese into their pockets.

After a final inspection, the passengers took their seats on board the ship. The administrator of NASA said a few words, and then, with a *BANG*, the passengers took off, peering and waving through the small round portholes at the farewell party below.

***

The *Destiny Unknown* was fueled almost entirely by solar energy or, in this case, by stellar energy. Almost the entire expanse of the ship's surface was lined with solar paneling that could absorb light, no matter how faint, and convert it into usable energy. NASA had unveiled its new supersolar cells, which could convert light in any form, whether infrared or visible or ultraviolet, to electrical energy at about 98 percent efficiency, something that had never been done before. So as long as there were stars in the universe, the

Destiny Unknown would never want for power.

But stellar light was not the only thing that the supersolar cells absorbed and coughed out as usable energy. Way back at the beginning of the universe there was a big bang. This bang was so big that even today, billions of years later, there are faint traces of heat from the explosion known as cosmic microwave background radiation, measured at a temperature of approximately *negative* 454 degrees Fahrenheit. A very faint source of energy, indeed, but absolutely necessary for reaching top speeds of 0.876 times the speed of light.

In this way, by using thousands of supersolar cells aligned in energy-efficient arrays, the *Destiny Unknown* was able to career through space at record speeds, gathering starlight and leftover energy from the big bang for storage in a megabattery called Axon 5.

Axon 5 could store up to five gigawatts of power at any one time, hence the name. It was responsible not only for power to the engines, but to every light bulb, coffee maker, electric fan, alarm clock, and electric razor on the ship. The battery was so powerful that it was locked in a bombproof, airtight room with walls thirty-two inches thick, far from any place an ordinary passenger might wander unwittingly.

Axon 5 had a sister called Axon 4, also aboard the ship. Axon 4 was a less-powerful replacement battery, kept unplugged in the storage facilities with the other spare parts in case Axon 5 ever decided to give up.

Had the *Destiny Unknown* been built in the twenty-first

century, the designers might have used gasoline-fueled engines instead of super-solar-cell-powered battery-operated engines. But at the time of the launch, there were no more fossil fuels to be found anywhere on Earth.

***

When the *Destiny Unknown* took off from Earth, there was plenty of solar energy to go around. The sun's hot rays had charged the Axon 5 to maximum capacity. When the ship first left the ground, it bolted like a racehorse out of the gate. The ship was out of the atmosphere so fast that the boohooing families and friends below saw the passengers' faces in the windows one minute and a cloud of water vapor and hot, sticky air the next.

Then it was time for the members of the farewell party to go back underground. The sun was rising, and nobody ever stayed above ground during the day. Not if they wanted to live, anyway.

***

In space the passengers of the *Destiny Unknown* were getting their last glimpse of the sun as they zoomed past Mars and Jupiter and Saturn and Uranus and Neptune, and finally beyond the nonplanet Pluto, covering 3.5 billion miles in just six hours. From then on, the sun would become just another star in the night sky, shooting little photons into the supersolar cells like every other star.

***

In space there is no sun and thus no way to measure time. The twenty-four-hour day is something inherent to the ever-rotating Earth and, hence, is completely meaningless when hurtling through darkness at 587 million miles per hour in a solar-paneled spaceship. In space there is no difference between day and night—no sunrise, no sunset, no morning, no afternoon—no nothing. All these things are arbitrary in the near-total darkness of space. Nevertheless, the *Destiny Unknown* was chock-full of standard twenty-four-hour clocks that regulated the days and weeks and months and years for its passengers. And so it was that a clock somewhere chimed noon on the first morning of their departure, moments before the *Destiny Unknown* had its first power failure.

When this happened, every single passenger on the ship was certain he or she was a goner. Done. Finished. Kaput. Certainly some screw had come loose somewhere on the ship, and the whole thing was about to rip apart. Not only had the lights gone out, along with the clocks and the coffee makers—a sudden lurch also tossed everybody and everything that wasn't tied down up into the air like a blast of confetti. And none of it, not the people nor the books nor the berries on the commissary table, came down again.

When the fuse or whatever it was that controlled the lights and the clocks and coffee makers had blown, it had taken down the gravity simulator as well. No light. No gravity.

Luckily, Bartholomew Barbate was an excellent swimmer. In a gravity-free world, he and his three-hundred-pound frame were as graceful as a dolphin in the sea—when there were still dolphins and seas to speak of. The electrician butterfly-stroked his way down below and set to work immediately fixing the fuse box.

Meanwhile, upstairs in the library, Amanda Sphinx found herself engulfed in a sea of floating books. When the power had gone out and the gravity simulator had lurched, she had lost her place in *Atlas Shrugged* and was trying to find it again by the light of the flickering stars shining through the glass ceiling above. Then she realized that she wasn't alone in the library. Someone else was struggling through the maze of floating books, his breathing heavy and uneven.

"Who's there?" she asked sharply.

Austin Ibsen's face emerged from between a copy of Newton's *Principia* and George Orwell's *Animal Farm*.

Amanda Sphinx extended her small pale hand, and Austin grabbed hold of it as if it were a life buoy. Amanda pulled him up to the glass ceiling where it was light enough to see the broad expanse of his forehead and the squat, ruddy tip of his nose. And there in a starlit sea of books, she opened up to

Austin Ibsen and told him about her parents, what she could remember of them anyway; the foster homes; and the Program for Orphaned Geniuses. Austin just listened, nodding his addled head and counting silently how many times she used the word *actually* in each sentence.

"I was actually born in Saint Paul, Minnesota," Amanda said, "which is actually the same place F. Scott Fitzgerald was born, and it's funny because I recently discovered that I am actually a distant relative of Ernest Hemingway, who was a big fan of Fitzgerald's work."

To which Austin replied, "Three."

They were both orphaned geniuses, and even though their conversation leaped here and there like a grasshopper on hot pavement, they understood each other perfectly.

***

Downstairs Marcus Fincus was making love to his wife on a king-size canopy bed in the large captain's suite. The sudden lurch and consequential loss of gravity hastened the captain's climax as both he and his wife were propelled into the air.

Marcus had left Johannes Levi alone at the helm of the ship so that he and his wife might christen their quarters.

"Don't kill us," were the captain's last words to Johannes Levi.

"Aye-aye, sir."

The captain's first thought when the ship bucked and the lights went out was "Aye-aye, my ass," which he sputtered into his wife's ear on climax.

After the initial jolt and the consequential loss of gravity, it was clear that Johannes Levi had not killed them. He had merely blown a fuse. The captain, who was not a delicate lover, heaved Esmeralda off his dwindling erection, pulled his pants up to his waist, and blindly felt his way into the hall.

The ship was pitch black except for the twinkling emergency lights that lined the corridors like blinking eyes. When the captain first saw Bartholomew Barbate swimming toward him, he was sure he was seeing some enormous airborne ghost in the darkness.

"Is that you, sir?" came Bartholomew's voice. "We've blown a fuse. Should be no more than fifteen minutes. Everybody needs to be in position when the gravity comes back online, like we practiced."

They had indeed practiced for just such an occasion. In their training they had perfected drills for a good many things, including oxygen deprivation, extreme climate change and, thank goodness, gravity loss.

On the deck, Johannes Levi was fiddling with the control panel, wishing for a way to go back in time and undo this horrible mistake, the likes of which would surely result in his eventual demotion. When the captain burst in, Johannes was hovering over Howard Oppenheimer as they tried fruitlessly to hit any combination of buttons to get the ship back online.

Much to Johannes's relief, the captain did not single him out. Rather, Marcus Fincus barked orders to Johannes and the eight other people in CC to sweep the ship and remind everybody what to do in the event of gravity loss.

Here Johannes felt another cold pang of guilt. *He did not remember what to do in the event of gravity loss.*

The drill Johannes did not remember was simply this: lie close to the ground and keep your head covered.

There was another problem: Johannes couldn't remember which part of the ship he was supposed to patrol in just such an emergency.

So this is what Johannes did: he hid in the service closet.

Surely enough, at precisely fifteen minutes past the hour, the lights in the ship flickered on, and, a second later, there was a giant suctioning sound as everything crashed to the ground.

Part of Johannes's neglected patrol included the library where Amanda Sphinx and Austin Ibsen lay floating on their backs amid the clutter of books, staring out of the glass ceiling at the starlit heavens. When the gravity simulator hummed into action, they were both awakened from their reverie by the sudden sensation of having weight after having none, which can only be likened to the sensation of floating in a pool and then being dropped on your head. They slammed against the library floor and were buried amid an onslaught of heavy hardbacks, one of which cracked

Austin Ibsen's glasses in two.

Johannes's patrol also included the starboard corridor and adjoining staterooms, where, incidentally, Esmeralda Fincus was floating naked in the captain's cabin, examining the smooth contours of her body by flashlight in the mirror of her vanity table. She particularly liked the effect weightlessness had on her sagging breasts. So when the gravity came back on quite suddenly, Esmeralda collapsed right on top of her vanity, literally and figuratively, breaking not only several vials of perfume but also two ribs and a pinky toe.

Deidre Hundt, one of the engineers from the bridge, who had been sent to retrieve the captain's shoes, found Esmeralda nearly an hour later, bruised and naked on the stateroom floor.

Deidre wrapped a towel around Esmeralda and went to get Dr. Myles Jamison, who hadn't yet killed himself with his own scalpel. Poor vain Esmeralda lay there in the nude, unable to move while Dr. Jamison examined her ribcage and administered various anesthetics to ease her pain. Marcus Fincus had not yet received news that his wife had been injured, and when Deidre Hundt returned with his shoes, he was chatting up one of the midshipwomen, a pretty young brunette called Edith Young.

Deidre informed the captain that his wife was injured and receiving care in the infirmary. Marcus Fincus took his hand off Edith Young's elbow, winked, and rushed out of the room—again forgetting his shoes.

Amanda Sphinx and Austin Ibsen escaped unharmed. They were children and still quite indestructible.

Everybody else on the ship had managed to duck and cover before the gravity came back online, and except for Esmeralda Fincus's broken ribs and pinky toe, there were no serious injuries.

The *Destiny Unknown*, on the other hand, was a mess, with odds and ends scattered all over the place. Everything had shifted during the power failure, and for years the passengers would find pens and nail clippers and brushes in the most unlikely of places.

***

What the passengers aboard the *Destiny Unknown* did not realize then, six hours out of port on the first day of what was supposed to be a twelve-year journey, was this: the sudden power failure at twelve o'clock noon was a harbinger of a thousand little tragedies that would befall the ship and its crew over what would be more than four decades in space.

If they had known this, had known that their plan was full of tiny little holes just like the ship's battery, surely they would have turned the ship around and taken it back to Earth, where they were all certain to live happily until the ends of their days.

But a power outage is just a power outage, and although Esmeralda Fincus would never be the same again, forever complaining of pain in her side and constantly tripping over what was to be a badly healed pinky toe, the *Destiny Unknown* stayed its course, with Marcus Fincus at the helm, determined as ever to ensure the survival of the human species.

***

When the power went out, the only passenger not concerned solely with his own safety was the ship's veterinarian, Elijah Borges, a selfless, animal-loving graduate of the School of Veterinary Medicine at the University of California, Davis. His first responsibility was the well-being of the animals on the ship: Bobo, Bill, and Dog.

Bill, the African grey parrot, was the most at ease in the gravity-free environment. He fluttered from perch to perch, a little unnerved but otherwise very much himself. Bobo, on the other hand, clung tightly to Elijah's back and chattered his teeth nervously as he and Elijah drifted through the dark cabin.

Dog was the most uncomfortable, having no opposable thumbs and hence no means of holding on to anything. He floated and bobbed through the air, unable to steer a course. Elijah tried to get a hold on him, but Dog wouldn't have it. The normally agreeable cocker spaniel growled and snapped every time Elijah tried to pluck him up.

Elijah stayed with the animals until the gravity came back

on, his great big heart breaking every time Dog collided with a wall.

While Elijah was getting the animals settled after power had been restored to the ship, Esmeralda was causing a ruckus in the infirmary. She was still naked, covered only by a bath towel, and was demanding that Deidre Hundt and the rest of the bridge crew come down to apologize for their incompetence.

Johannes Levi was still sequestered in the service closet.

Marcus Fincus, who always did what his wife said, accompanied the midshipmen and midshipwomen down to the infirmary and ushered an apology out of them. Then they all watched wincingly as the doctor administered care to the raging woman, who was just as dangerous in a hospital bed as she was on her own two feet. Throughout the whole procedure, Marcus Fincus cowered in the corner like a frightened field mouse. The crew later joked that Esmeralda outranked the captain and, in the privacy of Deidre Hundt's cabin that night, as they relived the whole episode over a bottle of Scotch, they gave Esmeralda a new nickname to be used whenever the captain wasn't around. They called her *Admiral-da*.

From then on, Esmeralda took her meals in bed and hardly left her room. Within the first weeks of the injury, Dr. Myles Jamison suggested a regime of simple exercises to help with her recovery. However, Esmeralda Fincus complained of stabbing pains in her side and back that kept her from standing.

During the next few months she gained upward of thirty pounds, which gave her a matriarchal appearance, like a well-fed lioness in her den. She was still beautiful, but she had the weight of a woman in charge, and it became increasingly apparent that even though Marcus Fincus was captain of the ship, Admiral-da called the shots.

CHAPTER 4

YEARS 1-2

AT DINNER THAT FIRST DAY, after everything had been set right following the gravity lurch, all of the passengers finally gathered together in one place for the first time since takeoff.

The tables were crowded and warm, and the room had a lively sense of camaraderie about it, an artificial camaraderie fostered by the strangeness and isolation of space and of having survived a traumatic experience together. The energy was very much like the prickly excitement of the first day at summer camp or a freshman dormitory on move-in day. The sense of camaraderie that they all shared that first night would evaporate over the months and years to follow and be replaced by a cold formality more befitting the passengers of an airplane or guests in a hotel lobby. If you walked into the commissary forty years from then, you would get the sense that the passengers knew nothing about one another, or that perhaps they all knew one another too well and had nothing left to say.

But tonight a collective adrenaline was running through the veins of these fifty survivors of the Great Gravity Lurch of the *Destiny Unknown*, and everyone wanted to tell his or her own version of the story—how he had been chopping onions in the kitchen, how she had been napping in bed, or how he had been sitting on the toilet (a grotesque but hilarious account by one of the midshipmen).

In this way, news of Esmeralda's injuries spread among the crew. Hers was a juicy story, and humans are suckers for juicy stories. The story was this: Esmeralda had been found naked in her room with two broken ribs. The part that made it all the juicier was this: Deidre Hundt had noticed scars under the folds of Esmeralda's well-rounded breasts, suggesting that Esmeralda Fincus had at some point in her life injected silicone implants into the muscle and fat around her mammary glands.

A naked woman with fake breasts can almost always be counted on for a juicy story.

***

You might ask: How do you feed fifty passengers three times a day?

There was a kitchen staff consisting of two sous chefs, supplemented daily by four or five civilian volunteers, all of whom were under the instruction of the head chef, Barbary Montclair, a classically trained culinary genius from Niger.

Everybody had to cook aboard the *Destiny Unknown.* Voluntary cooking duty was voluntary only in name. In fact, Barbary Montclair kept a strict ledger of which passengers volunteered, when, and how often. Cooking duty might have been a lovely way to pass the time aboard the *Destiny Unknown.* The human brain is a sucker for mindless tasks like cooking. But Barbary Montclair was anything but a mindless cook. He barked orders to the staff as if every sprinkle of pepper or turn of the ladle was a matter of life or death. Consequently, every meal served on the *Destiny Unknown* was fit for a king, and cooking duty became the most dreaded task aboard the ship and could be traded as the highest form of currency.

That was how Bartholomew Barbate managed to acquire the universe's largest collection of candy bars, which he kept locked in his private toolshed in the tiny, almost uninhabitable office he was afforded as the ship's chief electrician. He offered to cover cooking detail in return for simple carbohydrates.

Making a meal for fifty people three times a day is no easy task, but Barbary made full use of the efforts of every single sous chef in his kitchen, from the youngest child (Hannah Montgomery) to the most arthritic old man (Arthur Stanton), from the greatest dunce (Jason Fincus) to the greatest genius (Austin Ibsen). In the galley, the hierarchy of the vessel changed dramatically—if you held any authority elsewhere on the ship, it didn't matter in the kitchen. Barbary was king.

So it was that under the leadership of Barbary Montclair—head chef and, as far as anyone was concerned, king of the kitchen—that the members of NASA's New World Population Project became master chefs, trained in the arts of seasoning, stirring, baking, boiling, chopping, dicing, filleting, frying, flipping, toasting, buttering, battering, and so on—skills they would later pass on to future generations of humans, giving birth to one of the finest culinary civilizations in the universe.

And get this:

When the canned and jarred and dried food became scarce in the decades to come, and when the crew had nothing left to eat but gooey astronaut food (which eventually gave many of them that rare condition diverticulitis), the members of NASA's New World Population Project would sit around the commissary tables and reminisce about the "golden years" when Barbary Montclair used to scold them for every charred piece of toast and every poorly diced pepper.

And get this:

Barbary Montclair would not be there to join in the reminiscing. When finally nothing remained in the pantry cupboards, the master chef would cook the only thing left to cook.

Himself!

The cook was cooked.

***

If we could sit down for a one-on-one interview with the ghost of Barbary Montclair, we might ask him to look back on his life—way, way back as far as he could remember—and to recall a moment when he felt he had been grievously wronged. He would trace a line through the chutes and ladders of childhood and, finding only the innocuous insults of other children, continue on to adulthood. In culinary school he would recall only the competitive mind games of his peers, games that ultimately shaped him into a ruthless cooking machine. And he was thankful for those experiences. And at the Chez D'Extase, where he worked up until the day he decided to take a one-way trip into space, he was shielded from the outside world by a waitstaff so completely devoted to him that nothing but praise ever made it into his bubble of consciousness.

So we would ask the question to the ghost of Barbary Montclair again: *When in your life were you most grievously wronged?*

And he would think for a moment and then say, "It was the time I was blamed for that little girl's death."

He would, of course, be talking about the time a little girl named Brandelyn McCormack died after eating Barbary's eggplant soufflé. "That night I served heirloom tomato salad, followed by couscous and stuffed zucchini," Barbary Montclair's ghost would explain. "And one of the little children didn't like zucchini. So she had my eggplant soufflé. The next morning she was dead."

***

The initial diagnosis was food poisoning because Brandelyn was found dead after dinner in a puddle of feces and vomit. However, later that evening, Martha Marigold recalled that Brandelyn had been coughing in class that same morning.

"Could that have had anything to do with her death?" Martha asked.

"Naturally!" Barbary said.

"Unlikely," Dr. Myles Jamison said. "You don't die of a cough."

But the cough spread quickly among the other children and, pretty soon, among the adults, too. Then they were complaining of headaches and muscle cramps and nausea. Nine of the children had fevers. Then the vomiting began. All the beds in the infirmary were occupied. Dr. Myles Jamison had to quarantine the overflow of patients in the library. There he began a series of flu vaccinations with the assistance of the vaccination specialist, Richard Park.

However, when Richard Park finally got a look at Brandelyn McCormack's gaunt corpse, he pulled Dr. Myles Jamison aside and hissed, "This, Myles, is not the result of food poisoning, and it is not the common flu."

Richard Park conducted a detailed autopsy of Brandelyn McCormack's tiny body and found a series of fleabites on her scalp. Richard Park then traced the fleabites back to her longtime playmate Dog, who, despite Elijah Borges's careful attention, was a flea metropolis.

The fleas were put under a powerful microscope, and it was then that Richard Park identified a strain of bacteria called *Rickettsia typhi*.

These little bacteria had another name, too. They were called typhoid fever.

Acting swiftly, Richard Park prescribed the antibiotic chloramphenicol to the suffering patients and was rewarded with a 100 percent recovery rate almost immediately—except for poor Brandelyn McCormack, who was already dead. The rest of the passengers were vaccinated against typhus. And poor Dog was drenched in Flea-B-Gone for five days straight until everybody could be certain the fleas were as extinct as poor little Brandelyn.

How had the fleas come to be carrying that rare bacteria *Rickettsia typhi* in the first place? wondered Richard Park. He knew very well that typhoid fever spreads through fleas that feed off rats, not through fleas that feed off cocker spaniels. *So*—Richard Park surmised—*there are rats on the ship!* Or so it would seem.

Many refused to believe that they had somehow carried an undetected stowaway population of rats with them for two years. Nobody had seen anything even remotely rat-like so far. And Esmeralda Fincus refused to believe that rodents had somehow passed unnoticed under the watchful eye of her husband, Captain Marcus Fincus. Furthermore, she proclaimed, NASA would never be so careless as to let rats on a spaceship.

But Richard Park wasn't convinced. He advised Elijah Borges to watch Dog carefully to see if the cocker spaniel turned anything up.

From then on, the ship was divided. There were those who sided with Richard Park and believed they were sharing their food and air and water with a colony of rats. And there were those who thought, as Esmeralda did, that Richard Park had it in for the captain.

"He has a mutinous look about him," Esmeralda would say of Richard Park. "The look of a real mutineer."

Indeed, Dr. Richard Park was a real mutineer. Decades earlier, he had led a revolt on a US supply shuttle during the Moon Wars. His mutiny, however, was sanctioned and approved by the US Space Corps. The supply shuttle was involved in an illegal arms heist, and Dr. Richard Park was given a shiny brass medal commemorating his bravery and leadership.

They had a proper sendoff for poor dead Brandelyn McCormack. She was eight when she boarded the *Destiny*

Unknown. She was only ten when they dumped her dead body out into space.

Even Esmeralda Fincus attended the funeral. Captain Marcus Fincus made a long speech about sacrifice and tragedy and other generalities that are meant to comfort the living. He concluded by saying what a shame it was that the thing Brandelyn loved most—playing with Dog—was the very thing that killed her in the end.

That was enough to make most of the passengers steer clear of Dog forever.

Others were more forgiving. Maisey Perkins still let Dog sleep at the foot of her bunk every night, and Martha Marigold, the in-house schoolteacher, regularly took Dog on long walks around the ship.

Nobody knew Brandelyn well or had much to remember her by—she was only ten years old, after all, and an orphan at that. All that could really be said of her was that she loved Dog very much and didn't like zucchini.

They hadn't packed a casket, so they just wrapped Brandelyn in a white sheet and fired her body into space, where it quickly swelled to twice its size and bobbed up and down like a party balloon.

After Brandelyn McCormack died, the other children were given two weeks off from school, not only to recover from typhus but also to attend grief counseling with the ship's psychiatrist, Barbara Chatsworth. It was believed that the sudden death of their classmate would have a profound effect on their developing psyches. But what Marcus Fincus and Barbara Chatsworth did not realize was that the adults on the ship were more rattled by Brandelyn's death than any of the children.

The children knew Brandelyn McCormack only as the girl who liked to play with Dog. Two girls on the ship about Brandelyn's age, Kelsey Holmes and Margaret Frost, knew her a little better than everybody else—but how much do ten-year-olds actually know about other ten-year-olds? Studies suggest very little.

So the children on the *Destiny Unknown* got over Brandelyn's death pretty quickly, and by the end of their two-week hiatus, they had forgotten her completely.

The passenger who took Brandelyn's death most to heart was her teacher, Martha Marigold, a devoted instructor who had, in two years' time, come to know and love each of the fifteen children as her own. All the children, with the exception of Jason Fincus, had been selected specifically for their blossoming talents. Some were gifted mathematicians, like Austin Ibsen, while others, like Amanda Sphinx, could play the piano better than Rachmaninoff or Little Richard.

Jason Fincus, with his measly IQ of eighty, had no talents to speak of.

***

Brandelyn McCormack was a gifted painter. She produced thirteen watercolor landscapes of their new home on Nissan Sentra: beautiful sweeping rock fields and blue-green oceans, cratered plains and jagged snow-crested peaks. She envisioned a sky made bright by two moons, one small and elliptical and the other large and round.

Nobody actually knew how many moons orbited Nissan Sentra or what they looked like—there still wasn't a telescope on Earth powerful enough to see things that closely. But the crew of the *Destiny Unknown* would soon find out that Brandelyn McCormack, by divine foresight or just dumb luck, had depicted the moons of Nissan Sentra almost exactly as they were: one large and round like Earth's moon and the other oblong and small, like a shelled cashew.

Martha Marigold would later suggest that they name one of the moons of Nissan Sentra "Brandelyn" after the girl who had first prophesied their existence. But the others would end up calling the moons Ralph and Alice after the beleaguered married couple from the 1950s sitcom *The Honeymooners*, a show that had become a favorite diversion for the passengers on the ship during their long, long journey through space.

CHAPTER 5
YEARS 2-6

EVERY EVENING AFTER DINNER was served in the cafeteria, most of the passengers had the night free to do with as they pleased. Even Captain Marcus Fincus, Johannes Levi, and Howard Oppenheimer had evenings off. They would put the ship on cruise control and leave it to fate to carry them the next couple of billion miles without incident. They never had to worry much about steering because the vessel was on a direct route headed straight for Nissan Sentra—the coordinates were already programmed into the supercomputer, the brains of the ship.

Most of their evenings were spent in the theater watching films and reruns of old television shows on a digital projector that cast lifelike semiholographic images onto a narrow stage. The kids usually sat up in front, lying on their bellies or sitting cross-legged on the carpet. The adults lounged in couches and armchairs scattered around the room at various angles. Austin Ibsen usually ran the projector—he was a whiz with technology. Sometimes they even let him pick the show.

That was how they all ended up falling in love with *The Honeymooners*, a comedy starring Audrey Meadows and Jackie Gleason. It was just another night, and Austin Ibsen was perusing the thousands of terabytes of media when he stumbled across an episode of *The Honeymooners* called "Jellybeans."

On Earth, jellybeans were Austin's favorite food, and it had been some time since he had seen a jellybean—not since leaving Earth. So, naturally, when Austin Ibsen saw the episode of *The Honeymooners* called "Jellybeans," he instinctively pushed play, and the passengers on the *Destiny Unknown* got their first taste of Ralph and Alice Kramden, the classic television couple who would later serve as the inspiration for the 1960s cartoon couple in *The Flintstones* and, even later, as the inspiration for the names of the two moons of Nissan Sentra, Ralph and Alice.

The Honeymooners was such a hit among the passengers that future generations of the *Destiny Unknown* would still be watching episodes millions of years later on cathode-ray-tube boxes that looked very much like old television sets, and they would even erect a monument to Ralph and Alice Kramden in the city square of the first extraterrestrial human colony.

***

Around the same time as the typhus outbreak, Amanda Sphinx, age seventeen, graduated from her studies aboard the *Destiny Unknown* and was given her first job as an assistant to Chef Barbary Montclair. Barbary had the insane notion that because poor little Brandelyn McCormack had died, he could suddenly ration out the food in larger portions because they had one less mouth to feed. When Amanda Sphinx started her internship with Barbary, she took an inventory of their stores and did a few calculations on a piece of paper in her bunk one night, and she quickly discovered that Barbary had been using too much food too quickly. In fact, Barbary had been depleting their stores so rapidly that within thirteen years they would be left with only tasteless astronaut food.

When Amanda Sphinx delivered this sobering news to the chef, he nodded and replied, "Naturally! You don't expect me to skimp, do you?"

Amanda, who knew what diverticulitis was and how it came about, cautioned Barbary, saying it would be very bad for their intestinal tracts if all they ever had to eat was astronaut food.

But, of course, Barbary Montclair, like Marcus Fincus and Johannes Levi and almost everybody on the ship, truly believed their journey would end on schedule. They imagined crops of corn and potatoes and carrots within the decade. So they swept Amanda's warnings aside and went on using far too much far too soon—just as all humans have done for millions and millions of years.

Amanda Sphinx grew ornery and sullen, which didn't much suit Barbary's flamboyant style, and before she could have a say either way, Amanda was stationed somewhere where her intellect couldn't be a nuisance to anyone else. She was given custody of the old library and was charged with organizing the books—a job she had been doing all along.

***

By this time Austin Ibsen was fourteen and fully experiencing all the embarrassing symptoms of puberty. His face was freckled with pimples. Hair sprouted all over the place like weeds. He smelled like a gym sock. It was around this time, the very same time that Amanda Sphinx—a late bloomer—grew a foot taller and sprouted breasts, that Austin began to have sexual fantasies. These fantasies naturally featured Amanda Sphinx and her breasts in the leading roles. There was also a robust supporting cast made up of several other women on the ship, including Esmeralda Fincus and Austin's schoolteacher, Martha Marigold.

Austin did not know what to make of these vivid imaginings. He kept a flip-book of words matched to pictures of faces to help him identify the emotions his fellow passengers were feeling at any given time. The flip-book had proved an essential player in the development of his and Amanda's relationship. But there simply weren't enough pages in the flip-book to help him make sense of all the different feelings he was experiencing now.

During one of his routine psychiatric evaluations with Barbara Chatsworth, Austin finally confessed in embarrassing detail everything that was going on in his mind, much to Barbara's mortification. Austin was promptly dismissed and left to wander the corridors of the *Destiny Unknown* alone with his insufferable thoughts. It wasn't until their next session together that Barbara Chatsworth was finally able to regain her composure. She assured Austin Ibsen that what he was going through was perfectly normal for a boy his age. There was no reason to be ashamed, she explained, so long as he kept his thoughts and hands *to himself*.

Had Austin Ibsen confessed these things to a priest, there might have been a whole lot of Our Fathers and Hail Marys bouncing around the confessional box. But believe it or not, by the time the oceans boiled off the face of the Earth and the *Destiny Unknown* shot into space with its fifty passengers, there were no longer religions of any kind left anywhere in the world. So there couldn't have been a priest aboard the ship, or a confessional box for that matter, even if Captain Marcus Fincus and the committee at NASA had determined such things to be absolutely essential for the well-being of deep-space explorers. They had Barbara Chatsworth and a whole lot of medication instead.

From then on, Austin Ibsen, trusting fully that all the bending, twisting, pulsing images in his brain were perfectly normal by-products of his hormonal development, drooled over Amanda Sphinx and her new breasts without guilt or shame. And it was around this time, while she was busy organizing the books in the library, that Amanda noticed how tall Austin had grown and how wherever he went he trailed the hypnotizing scent of sweat and musk behind him.

And so there was hope of human repopulation in NASA's New World Population Project after all.

**

A crowded spaceship is no place for young teenagers in love. So poor Austin Ibsen and Amanda Sphinx had to conduct their romance in the secrecy of service closets and storage bunkers and other hideaways aboard the *Destiny Unknown*. Their love affair was very innocent for the first few years—a touch here, a kiss there, nothing more than the sweet nothings of a couple of kids in the first stages of pheromonal attraction. And nobody was around to tell them they were being stupid or naïve or to forget such foolishness. They had no one to describe for them all the millions of ways a heart can break. All they had to worry about was each other. And they did a fine job of that. Austin Ibsen was always checking on Amanda Sphinx in the library, making sure she didn't need help reaching books on the highest shelves. And Amanda Sphinx was always double-checking Austin's homework to make sure he had the highest marks in his class. They were a fine pair, with a combined IQ of 383 and the kind of bond that can only form between two lonely people stranded in space for many, many years.

Their relationship developed over the years, and when Austin Ibsen was eighteen and Amanda Sphinx was twenty-one, neither of them could claim to be virgins anymore. Still, whenever the power went off in the *Destiny Unknown*, they both stopped whatever they were doing and, in the fifteen or twenty minutes it usually took Bartholomew Barbate to get the ship back online, they joined each other in the library, floating quietly on their backs and looking out through the glass ceiling at the millions of stars.

During one of these moments, while they gazed out into deep space together, holding hands side by side, Austin Ibsen shared a poem he had written for Amanda:

> Every morning I rise and think:
> Never before have I seen a girl
> Play piano quite so well
> As Amanda Sphinx

Amanda carried the worn-out transcript of Austin's poem in her pocket wherever she went until the day she died.

***

While Austin Ibsen was losing his virginity to a piano prodigy in the downstairs service closet, another romance was blossoming elsewhere on the ship. Maisey Perkins had noticed a discoloration in Dog's gums the previous evening as she rubbed him down before bed. Being the ship's primary dental physician, Maisey immediately recognized all the symptoms of periodontitis, including a fairly progressed infection in the fourth and fifth mandibular incisors. That morning, as Austin and Amanda were going at it downstairs, she brought the infection to the attention of the beloved veterinarian, Elijah Borges.

Together, Maisey and Elijah experienced the rare pleasure that only medics and sadists share of cutting up and taking bits and pieces out of a living body. In other words, Dog was cured. From then on, Maisey would conduct weekly checkups on Dog's teeth and report the results to Elijah Borges, which led to an established pattern of communication each of them anticipated with eagerness as the slow, unchanging weeks marched on.

Soon Elijah and Maisey were seen eating together in the cafeteria and snuggling on the couch with Dog as they watched episodes of *The Honeymooners*. They were even caught snogging in the animal clinic while Bobo, Bill, and Dog looked on.

Eventually, Maisey Perkins moved into the same cabin with Elijah, displacing the belching, farting Bartholomew Barbate, who had been Elijah's roommate—much to Elijah's displeasure—since their departure from Earth six years earlier. Bartholomew squeezed into a cabin with Howard Oppenheimer, making what was already a tight space infinitely tighter.

Howard, however, was glad for the company. His time at the navigation controls, with little or nothing to think about except for the vast expanse of space, had led him to develop a paranoid fantasy—he became convinced that he was going to be the lone survivor of some catastrophic space tragedy, the last living creature aboard the *Destiny Unknown*, left alone until the end of his days. The sound at night of Bartholomew snoring from the adjacent bunk calmed Howard's fraying nerves and helped lull him to sleep.

Elijah Borges and Maisey Perkins were married on the ship two months later. Unfortunately, their wedding, which was to be a cause for celebration, took a tragic turn when, during the reception, Esmeralda Fincus realized with horror that young Jason Fincus was missing. Search as the wedding party might, Jason Fincus would not turn up again for twenty-one long years, or forty-three long years—depending on your frame of reference.

By the time Jason Fincus reappeared, Elijah and Maisey Perkins-Borges had four growing children of their own.

***

Unbeknown to the rest of the ship, Marcus Fincus and a young member of the janitorial staff named Emma Greene were actually the first humans to make a contribution to NASA's New World Population Project. Even before Amanda Sphinx had Austin Ibsen's child, and before the births of the Perkins-Borges girls, even before Jason Fincus went missing for twenty-one years—forty-three years afor[3]—Marcus Fincus impregnated twenty-six-year-old Emma Greene.

He had a good excuse: over the last six years Esmeralda Fincus had grown portly, temperamental, and lazy in bed. Marcus and Esmeralda hadn't had sex in over eight months, so when Emma Greene burst into his cabin one morning with her janitorial cart just as he was getting out of the shower, he took the opportunity, because his wife was away for one of her biannual checkups, to experience another

---

[3] The English word *afor* originated in the early thirty-first century when NASA spacecraft became capable of traveling at relativistic speeds. To account for relativistic time dilation, NASA coined the phrase *alternate frame of reference*—AFOR for short—when referring to the discrepancy in timeframes reported by astronauts traveling near the speed of light. Over the latter part of the thirty-first century, the use of the acronym AFOR became popularized by the mainstream media, and eventually morphed into the word *afor*, colloquially meaning "depending on how you look at it."

woman. He had nothing to hide his rising interest but a flimsy white towel, and she, having always imagined herself the mistress of the captain, accepted his invitation eagerly.

That was the only time Marcus Fincus and Emma Greene ever consorted in the captain's quarters. That was like pissing all over the den of the lioness. The captain's quarters were the admiral's lair. Esmeralda was too often brushing her hair in the vanity mirror or languishing in bed to ever afford Marcus Fincus and Emma Greene that luxury again. Instead, Marcus Fincus and Emma Greene began frequenting the very same service closet that was home to the exploits of Amanda Sphinx and Austin Ibsen. It is a wonder both couples could share the same love nest for weeks without ever crossing paths. The same cannot be said for poor Jason Fincus, who discovered his father with Emma Greene in the service closet on the eve of his sudden disappearance.

What Captain Marcus Fincus did not know the first time he slept with a woman who was not his wife was that Emma Greene had intended it to happen as much as he had *not* intended it to happen. From the very first, Emma Greene had been scheming to catch the eye of the illustrious captain of the *Destiny Unknown*. The fact that he had a wife and a son on the ship did not inhibit her ambitions in any way. She would be content to be his mistress if that's what it came to. You see, Emma Greene was very much like Esmeralda Fincus in that they were both attracted to men in positions of power, and from the first moment Emma laid eyes on Marcus Fincus in a televised broadcast promoting NASA's New World Population Project, she aspired to be his lover.

Fortunately for her, she worked for a janitorial service called Clean Space that had been servicing NASA space missions for over one hundred years, and Emma had been on fifteen missions during her eight years with the company. Her extensive experience in spaceship janitorial services won her a prized position on the *Destiny Unknown*, along with Anita Lund, her best friend, and Albert Morris, their manager.

On each of the fifteen previous space missions to which Emma Greene had been stationed, the captain had been a middle-aged man with a wife and family, and on each of those fifteen missions, she had succeeded in seducing him.

The only reason it took Emma Greene so long to seduce Captain Marcus Fincus—six years, to be exact—was that his wife was actually with him on the ship. That was not usually the case on long space flights. And Esmeralda proved to be formidable competition for Emma Greene. Not only was Esmeralda beautiful, even after her injury and subsequent weight gain, but she was also very watchful of her husband and kept him on a tight leash.

When Emma Greene burst into the captain's quarters, she knew Marcus and Esmeralda had not had sex in many months. She knew that Esmeralda had gone in for a mammogram and that the captain was alone in his room. And she knew that he was just getting out of the shower because she had heard the pipes running while she was cleaning the bath-room next door.

So it came to her as no surprise to find the captain in his towel, his member rising to greet her. But she played it off as though she were shocked and embarrassed and shaded her eyes with her hand so as not to see him. But she did not run out of the room and close the door behind her as she should have done. Instead, she stepped toward him, feeling blindly with her hand for something—the captain did not know what. Emma distracted the captain as she groped along, eyes shaded, hand out, by apologizing with such a degree of urgency that the captain hardly noticed how far she had come into the room.

When her groping hand brushed against the top of his throbbing genitalia, he no longer wondered why she was there and what she was looking for. His towel dropped almost of its own accord, and she stumbled into his naked body, finally looking up to meet his eyes. And so she had her way with him, letting him think all along that some accident of fate had brought them together.

***

When Emma Greene was with Captain Marcus Fincus, or any other space captain for that matter, she felt like the most beautiful woman in the universe. She imagined that if any captain would step away from the helm of a ship to be with her, she must be well worth it. So seducing captains of spaceships had become her way of validating her existence. In a way, she had made a career of it.

Every part of Emma wanted Esmeralda Fincus to find them out. Emma wanted to prove to the matriarch of the ship that another woman was capable of demanding the captain's attention—at least for fifteen minutes a day in the downstairs service closet. Emma would moan loudly when they were making love in the hopes of being discovered, and this little performance only spurred Marcus Fincus onward. Sometimes when cleaning the captain's quarters, she would leave little presents for the captain under his pillow—a pair of lacy panties or a note scented with perfume—in the hopes that Esmeralda would happen upon them one day. But the captain was always quick to root out these goodies and stow them away before his wife could learn of their existence.

It infuriated Emma how much Marcus Fincus talked about his wife. She often tried to steer the conversation away from Esmeralda, but some sort of psychological homing beacon always brought the captain back to the matriarch again. The only time Marcus Fincus forgot about Esmeralda was just before climax when he and Emma were making love, and at that moment, Emma Greene was sure of the path she had chosen as the mistress to a space captain. Just as a stockbroker is sure of his or her path the moment his or her profits double, just as a surgeon is sure of his or her path the moment he or she successfully repairs a broken artery—

Emma Greene felt sure of her path the moment she made Marcus Fincus forget his wife.

Her coconspirator and best friend, Anita Lund, had a different notion of love altogether. Anita believed in a man and a woman devoted entirely to one another till death do them part—an absurd concept, given the long sordid history of polygamy in the *Homo sapiens* species. Anita listened patiently to Emma's accounts of the many captains she had loved, and Anita sometimes envied Emma her liaisons, but she never once believed that what Emma Greene had with any of the captains was actually love.

What made Anita Lund such an expert on love? When she was fourteen, she was in love with a boy for a week. They met at Craighead Caverns Summer Camp in Tennessee and shared their first kiss on the shore of a subterranean lake. Then the boy she loved ventured above ground during the day on a dare and was burned to death by the hot rays of the expanding sun.

Ever since then—and she was now twenty-four—Anita clung to a notion of love that was based on her tragic romance with a fourteen-year-old boy who was stupid enough to go above ground during the day.

Emma and Anita's manager, Albert Morris, didn't believe in love whatsoever. Incidentally, he would be the first to impregnate Anita Lund when it came time to replenish the population of the *Destiny Unknown*. And even though Anita Lund would eventually conceive more children than any other woman on the ship, she would never claim to love again.

CHAPTER 6

YEAR 6

MARCUS FINCUS had a box of Cuban cigars from the year AD 1967, perfectly preserved for hundreds of millions of years and purchased from the Global Heritage Society for $25 million. He bought the cigars after he learned that NASA had agreed to fund the New World Population Project, with him at the helm of a revolutionary new ship called the *Destiny Unknown*. Marcus Fincus, having married into a family of water barons that controlled more than 90 percent of the world's aquifers, was a wealthy man, and could afford to blow $25 million of his wife's inheritance on a box of cigars.

The box originally contained twenty-five cigars—a million a smoke—but already Marcus Fincus had found two occasions to puff some of Earth's global heritage into oblivion. The first occasion was the day NASA gave the go-ahead for the New World Population Project—the same day he bought the cigars. Then he had enjoyed a cigar in the privacy of his home office, looking over the proposal he had submitted returned to him with the big word *approved* stamped across the front page in official red ink.

The second time he smoked a million-dollar cigar was the day the *Destiny Unknown* took off at 0.876 times the speed of light. Fifteen minutes out of Earth's atmosphere, he sat at the controls of the ship and, disregardful of the fact that he was polluting invaluable oxygen, puffed his million-dollar cigar as he watched the planets of the solar system fly by.

The remaining cigars were kept in a cryogenic storage chest in the captain's stateroom, along with a few expensive bottles of champagne. Marcus Fincus intended to smoke another cigar the moment he set foot on Nissan Sentra. But when they eventually reached the planet, he would only manage to smoke half a cigar before a sudden catastrophe would force him back onto the *Destiny Unknown* and into deep space again, leaving five hundred thousand dollars' worth of fermented tobacco in the dirt of an uninhabited planet.

What Captain Marcus Fincus did not know was that the box in the cryogenic storage chest now contained only eleven cigars and that twelve million dollars' worth of Cuban tobacco had been smoked into oblivion by his own flesh and blood, his genetic contribution to the New World Population Project, his son and heir to all his earthly possessions: Jason Fincus.

At sixteen, Jason Fincus was the kind of kid who never washed his hair and sat alone for long hours contemplating his many misfortunes. In his adolescence he had grown bitter and depressed, loathing his lot in life and hating his father for thinking fifty passengers could ever be happy on a ship floating tens of trillions of miles from any sort of civilization.

Barbara Chatsworth concluded that Jason Fincus was chemically unbalanced and prescribed Ritalin to ease his anxiety. But Jason, believing he was being drugged into submission, always flushed his medication down the toilet where it became one more ingredient for Ginger Martin's vegetable garden.

One thing did make Jason Fincus feel better: his father's million-dollar cigars. When he turned fifteen and everybody forgot his birthday, he felt justified taking one of the Cubans from his father's cryogenic storage chest as a present to himself.

He smoked his first cigar in the downstairs service closet while everybody else was upstairs watching *The Honeymooners*. And once every month thereafter, Jason stole another cigar from the captain's stateroom and smoked it in defiance of all those who would keep him holed up forever on a ship trillions of miles from home.

Nobody ever did end up remembering Jason Fincus's fifteenth birthday, and so far as anyone was concerned he was still fourteen years old. And incidentally, the fourth of May, the day of the big Perkins-Borges wedding, was the day Jason Fincus turned sixteen, and once again nobody remembered. Everybody was too busy fussing over the future Mr. and Mrs. Perkins-Borges. And the only cake Barbary Montclair was cooking up in the kitchen was the seven-layer wedding cake that would be smashed into the bride's and groom's faces that evening at the reception.

So Jason, feeling especially low, slipped into his parents' room and took another Cuban cigar from the little box in the cryogenic storage chest. Getting away with at least this much was relatively easy because his mother was in the kitchen barking orders at the sous chefs, and his father was unbuttoning his trousers for Emma Greene in the downstairs service closet.

Had Jason Fincus been counting, he would have known he was about to smoke his thirteenth cigar. And had he been a superstitious person, he might have flushed the unlucky thirteenth cigar down the toilet with his medication. But Jason Fincus had never been good with numbers, and he figured he must have smoked at least fifty of the things by now. So what was one more?

Poor, unfortunate fellow! That thirteenth cigar would prove to cost him forty-three years of his life and—some might argue—his sanity.

You see, in celebration of his forgotten sixteenth birthday, Jason Fincus planned to have a private party in the downstairs service closet with only himself and that fateful thirteenth cigar for company. And as misfortune would have it, a naked Marcus Fincus and his mistress were, at that moment, taking up quite a lot of space in the very same closet. The addition of one more person could prove problematic.

No one could say that Jason Fincus wasn't given fair warning before he opened the door to find his father on top of another woman. Jason heard the moans of Emma Greene as soon as he came into the downstairs corridor, and he correctly deduced that they were coming from the service closet. But it was *his* service closet as far as he was concerned, and it was *his* birthday. So he wasn't easily deterred.

In fact, the sounds of Emma's ecstasy excited him. He was a sixteen-year-old boy after all.

Furthermore, Jason Fincus harbored secret feelings for Emma Greene. He had even made a few pathetic overtures toward her—holding the door open or pushing her janitorial cart down the hall. But Emma hardly took notice of these little gallantries. It was doubtful Emma Greene even knew Jason Fincus from Austin Ibsen, that's how little she noticed him.

When Jason heard *her* voice moaning from *his* service closet, he had an easy time convincing himself that Emma was in there waiting to give him a very special birthday surprise. And instead of heading the other way, Jason did what any other hormonal sixteen-year-old would do: he opened the closet door.

The first thing Jason saw was Emma's contorted face as she lay on her back with a weathered lump of flesh on top of her. Emma saw him, too, and she was glad of it, so glad of it, in fact, that she smiled. She had been hoping to be discovered for many months now. News would spread throughout the ship that she, a mere janitress, had bagged the captain of the *Destiny Unknown*. Finally Esmeralda, that tyrant wife, would know all about their affair, an outcome, Emma believed, that would validate her very existence.

That's how Emma hoped it would go, anyway. But that's not exactly how things played out. Jason Fincus would not have the chance to tell his mother what he saw in the service closet because Jason would disappear into thin air before he saw his mother again. Meanwhile, one of Emma's eggs, which was traveling innocently down her fallopian tube, would be speared by one of the captain's spermatozoa, and the first child to be conceived on the *Destiny Unknown* would spark into existence.

The captain was going at it so fiercely and was nearing climax—at which point he always closed his eyes tight—that he didn't even notice the door open and then slam closed behind him.

But Jason Fincus had certainly noticed the captain. And Jason was furious, not because his father was cheating on his mother but because his father was banging Emma Greene in *his* service closet on *his* birthday.

Jason slammed the door so hard that Emma Greene

jumped. The captain, amid his climax, only noticed Emma pressing harder against him and responded by releasing the spermatozoon that would eventually, when joined with Emma's egg, become Lydia Anne Greene.

After Jason closed the door on a sight he would forever try, with little success, to wipe from his memory, he wandered deeper into the mazelike hull of the giant ship, past the laundry room where Anita Lund was busy doing what Emma Greene should have been doing: ironing clothes. The hum and whir of the washers and dryers disguised the sound of Emma Greene moaning down the hall so that Anita, lost in memories of summer camp at Craighead Caverns, heard nothing.

Jason had the impulse to go in and shake Anita and say, "Don't you know what's going on down the hall? Can't you hear?" And he might have done just that if only Anita had looked up and seen him there. But she was busy folding a pair of the captain's trousers and didn't take notice of him at all. So Jason moved on, rage building inside him.

He didn't really know where he was going. He couldn't possibly face anybody right now, not after what he had seen, not when he was feeling so sorry for himself. He had always thought his father a very selfish man to take him and his mother far away from their friends and family. And now that selfish bastard was making love to Emma Greene in *his* service closet on *his* birthday.

In the muttered words of Jason Fincus, "What the fuck?"

Then Jason came to a door leading off the main corridor labeled "Escape Pod A." There were two escape pods on the ship, A and B, each capable of sustaining fifty passengers for exactly one year or, conversely, one passenger for fifty years. Jason, having just turned sixteen and having passed all his exams, if just barely, was now qualified for level-D access, which would allow him entry into the escape pods, among other things. He didn't know it, but at that very moment, as he stood before the door to escape pod A, the supercomputer that was the brain of the ship was processing Jason's exam scores and could verify that, yes, Jason Harrison Fincus, against all odds and despite his remarkably low IQ, had indeed passed his exams and was eligible for level-D access.

And although every human brain had plumb forgotten poor Jason's birthday, the supercomputer had not. And, working without the assistance of Melanie Lorne or Deidre Hundt or any of the other engineers, the supercomputer upgraded the access level on Jason Harrison Fincus's badge just as Jason himself, downstairs in the corridor, swiped his badge in the air lock of escape pod A.

Much to his surprise and delight, the air lock slid open, causing Jason to wonder if somebody had, in fact, remembered his birthday. It gave him a fleeting sense of comfort to think that at least one of the engineers had remembered and had upgraded his badge. He couldn't possibly conceive that the *Destiny Unknown* had remembered all on its own without any help whatsoever from the scatterbrained humanoids.

Escape pod A was about the size of a basketball court, with fifty sleeping cubbies stacked in columns along the port and starboard walls. There was a control panel set against a large glass windowpane that gaped into deep space. The escape pod was crammed floor to ceiling with cases that held emergency equipment: flashlights, food, clothing, medical supplies, and navigation equipment. A spare moleculator was connected to the pod's air and water supplies, and was ready to go in case of an emergency. All the food was in the form of little freeze-dried packets, portioned out for each of what was supposed to be fifty passengers. Each packet was labeled in the following manner: breakfast day one, lunch day one, dinner day one, breakfast day two, lunch day two, and on and on for 365 days, enough for fifty people.

Jason needed a space to smoke his cigar and think. While he was in the escape pod smoking his cigar and thinking, he had what seemed to him a great idea: He would activate the escape pod and disengage from the *Destiny Unknown*. He would run away!

Surely then they would all remember it was his birthday. Surely then they would regret how they had treated him. Surely then Emma Greene would lament and wonder why she hadn't noticed Jason sooner.

And, Jason concluded, he could fly home to Earth. He knew how to operate the escape pod, or at least he thought he knew. He had learned all about the operation of the *Des-*

tiny Unknown and its escape pods in Martha Marigold's class. Jason could go back to Earth, where there were movie theaters and skate parks and lots and lots of available women. Surely no plan could be better!

What Jason Fincus did not consider at that very crucial moment was that the escape pod could only reach top speeds of forty-four miles per hour, thirteen million times slower than the speed of the *Destiny Unknown*, and that at speeds of forty-four miles per hour it would take Jason Fincus nearly eighty-seven million years to get back to Earth.

Incidentally, Jason had answered that question correctly on one of his recent exams: What is the maximum velocity of escape pod A?

"44 MPH," Jason had written in blue ink.

So perhaps Jason did consider how fast the escape pod could go. Maybe he simply didn't know how to calculate the time it would take for him to get back to Earth. Or perhaps some part of his subconscious did not want him to make it home at all.

Poor Jason Fincus. If only he had taken his medication instead of flushing it down the toilet.

Whatever his reasoning, he went ahead and initiated the launch sequence for escape pod A. Within several seconds, the pod hummed to life like a bumblebee, and with a loud *pop*, it fell away from the main ship. Jason had expected more resistance. Part of him even expected somebody on the bridge of the *Destiny Unknown* to see what was happening and override it with the supercomputer. But unfortunately for Jason Fincus, the only living thing on the bridge at the time was Bobo the chimp, who had escaped his enclosure earlier that day during the commotion of the wedding. Bobo saw what was happening on a flashing monitor, saw the little escape pod count down from ten and then dislodge from the main ship. And Bobo's only response was to chew on a vinyl armrest.

Everyone else was off watching Elijah and Maisey Perkins-Borges shove cake into each other's faces.

And certainly the supercomputer, which had just updated Jason's badge, was not going to do anything to stop Jason. What did it care if Jason Fincus had dropped a few zeros when calculating the time it would take to get back to Earth? What interest did the supercomputer have in sparing Jason Harrison Fincus forty-three lonely years in space?

The *Destiny Unknown* was out of sight before Jason even knew what had happened.

He was exhilarated. He was on his own for the first time in his life. He kicked the escape pod into gear and started back the way he thought they had come, steering the ship along a little digital marker that he assumed, incorrectly, pointed home. In fact, the marker he was following was an oxygen gauge.

After a few hours, it began to get stuffy in escape pod A. Jason switched on the moleculator, and it began rearranging the molecules in the air so that Jason had something to breathe.

Unbeknownst to the ship's engineers, the other spare moleculator in escape pod B was a total dud and would sputter out and die within two minutes of being switched on. Theoretically, had Jason chosen to smoke his father's million-dollar cigar in escape pod B, he would have suffocated on his own CO_2 within three days of disengaging from the main ship.

But because Jason had chosen to take off in escape pod A, he would still be alive twenty-one years later—forty-three years afor—when he was eventually rescued.

Elsewhere on the ship everyone was too busy to notice the distant rumble and the flickering of lights when escape pod A detached from the body of the ship. The only two intelligences that had any idea Jason Fincus was gone were the supercomputer and Bobo the chimp. And neither gave a damn.

***

When the captain finished consorting with Emma Greene in the downstairs service closet, he went upstairs and stole a dollop of frosting off the wedding cake with his index finger.

Esmeralda swatted him away like a fly. Neither of them knew that their son was one hundred million miles away, putting through space at a measly forty-four miles per hour. Nor did either of them suspect that one of the captain's frisky spermatozoa was at that moment burrowing its tadpole head into one of Emma Greene's unsuspecting eggs.

Emma Greene would not reveal that she was pregnant until several months later when she could no longer hide her bulging waist. When asked about the father, she would stick her nose in the air and reply, "There is no father."

Marcus Fincus believed her. It was the easiest thing for him to do.

Regardless of how Emma tried to spin the story, it would eventually become clear to the more suspicious individuals aboard the ship that Emma's daughter shared genetic material with the captain. Lydia Anne—as the child came to be called—would start to look so much like Marcus Fincus, and like Jason Fincus, too, that Esmeralda, who was totally clueless about the whole affair, would often stop short when she saw Lydia Anne, thinking her poor Jason had returned.

No matter how hard Emma Greene was pressed to reveal the father, she would never tell. Emma carried the secret to her grave, which was, incidentally, a hastily dug pit on a far-off planet known as Gzorazki.[4]

---

[4] Pronounced "Zor-az-kee."

CHAPTER 7

YEAR 6

WHEN AUSTIN IBSEN woke up the morning after the Perkins-Borges wedding, he noticed that Jason Fincus was not in bed, which was highly irregular because no matter how late Jason Fincus stayed out wrestling with his moods, he was always in bed the following morning and was bound to stay there until at least one or two in the afternoon.

Austin also noticed a full prescription bottle on Jason's nightstand with the prior day's date stamped across the label. The plastic safety seal on the bottle had not been broken, so Austin knew Jason had neither taken his medication the previous evening nor flushed it down the toilet, as he was wont to do. That should have given Austin pause, if not simply because Austin had previously calculated that it usually took Jason Fincus an average of 2.314 hours to flush away his medication. And it had been nearly twenty-four hours since it had been prescribed.

So Austin Ibsen deserved some blame for not noticing sooner that Jason was missing. As did Esmeralda Fincus who, for many years now, had forgone the traditional good-night kiss and, consequently, could not have known that Jason had never been to bed.

Marcus Fincus might also be blamed—he had very nearly kicked Jason in the shins as he made love to Emma in the downstairs service closet the previous evening. But the real blame fell on Emma Greene, who knew Jason had seen them together in the service closet, and had smiled at him.

Perhaps nobody would have noticed Jason Fincus's absence that morning if it weren't for another power failure. Most passengers were in the cafeteria nursing their hangovers from the previous night's festivities when a great lurch sent everybody spinning into the air. Darkness descended.

Of course, Bartholomew Barbate was the first to do anything about anything. While the other passengers struggled to gain cover under the cafeteria tables, which were the only things in the vicinity bolted to the floor, Bartholomew squeezed out of the cafeteria and butterfly-stroked down to the hull, where the great big fuse box that had given him so much trouble all these years lay smoking. Bartholomew knew the drill pretty well by now, so it was only a matter of time before the power was up and running, and as usual, there was the cacophonous clamor of things hitting the ground as the gravity simulator hummed into action.

It was an unexpected bout of maternal instinct that finally

made Esmeralda Fincus realize she hadn't seen Jason for quite some time now. She was in her stateroom massaging her cuticles when the power went out. Esmeralda cursed the incompetence of the engineers and electricians, who were always the obvious source of all her problems, and set about reorganizing the many lotions and perfumes on her vanity table once the power had been restored. Then Esmeralda did something quite out of character—she thought of someone other than herself. This is what she thought: *My little Jason hasn't had his cuticles massaged in such a long while. Wouldn't it be a nice treat if we massaged our cuticles together?*

She stepped out into the long corridor that ran from stern to aft and signaled the first person she could find. It was the unlucky Deidre Hundt, who had been the first to find Esmeralda lying naked and injured on the stateroom floor so many years ago. Esmeralda did not remember Deidre and summoned her with a shrill and haughty, "Girl!"

Deidre was ordered to fetch Esmeralda's darling little boy, for he was to have his cuticles massaged today. Deidre, who was in the middle of running a system-wide diagnostic assessment following the power failure, simply replied, "Yes, Admiral-da," which was her sneaky way of poking fun at the captain's wife, and went straightaway to the school-room where Martha Marigold kept watch over the children.

Martha Marigold reminded Deidre Hundt that Jason Fincus had recently passed his exams and would be starting his apprenticeship in the kitchen with the sous chefs. Knowing full well that Esmeralda was likely to soon forget about her request and return to her self-care, Deidre let the matter drop and returned to her regular duties.

But Esmeralda did not forget. It had become exceedingly urgent in her mind that her darling Jason have his cuticles massaged right away. When the grease-stained girl from down below did not return, Esmeralda set out in search of Jason herself.

She found Austin Ibsen in his bunk, working out some sort of circuitry calculation for Bartholomew Barbate, to whom he was apprenticed.

"Have you seen Jason?" Esmeralda asked. "We are going to have our cuticles massaged today."

Austin replied without looking up. "Not since three o'clock Eastern Daylight Time." Eastern Daylight Time was the time zone all the clocks were set to follow.

It was still only eleven in the morning, so Esmeralda asked, "Do you mean yesterday?"

Austin nodded.

"Was he not in bed last night?"

"No, ma'am," which is how all the children addressed Esmeralda Fincus.

Now was the perfect time to panic. You see, Esmeralda never missed an opportunity to panic; it made her the center of attention. So she began by hurling herself about the ship in a manic frenzy, asking anybody she could find if they'd seen her darling son, Jason Harrison Fincus, who was, *heaven forbid*, missing.

And when no one could tell her where Jason was, she marched straight up to CC and bellowed into the intercom separating the common folk from those at the helm of the ship.

"Marcus!" she screeched. "It's Jason! He's been kidnapped!"

The captain had to pause a moment and think of which Jason she was talking about, even though there was only one Jason on the ship. And when he realized she meant Jason Fincus, his offspring and heir, his one genetic contribution to NASA's New World Population Project—not counting his and Emma's bastard child, Lydia Anne Greene—Marcus Fincus sounded the alarm and ordered everyone on board to search for his son.

It was a fruitless quest that lasted well into the night. The ship was enormous, and there could be no telling where a young miscreant might be hiding, or where a twisted psychopath, as Esmeralda would narrate it, might stash a child's body. At three in the morning, Deidre Hundt, exhausted and discouraged, sat down at her station on the bridge, rested her chin on her hands, and stared blankly at the little flashing lights on the dashboard. She was still hungover from the Perkins-Borges wedding, and she hadn't brushed her teeth in thirty-eight hours.

It was quiet on the bridge. The ship was on autopilot, as it was more often than not, what with nothing in sight for another twenty-eight trillion miles. All Deidre wanted to do was sleep. They had been searching for hours, and the most they had turned up was Jason's unopened bottle of pills. The *Destiny Unknown* was big—big enough to hide a colony of rats if you happened to believe the immunization specialist, Richard Park.

So when Deidre Hundt put her elbows on the dashboard and her chin in her hands, all she was hoping to accomplish was a little shut-eye. Staring blearily at the dashboard as she had done for the last six years, wishing for sleep, she noticed a blue light blinking that hadn't been there before. Upon examining the little blue light more closely, Deidre Hundt knew everything she needed to know: escape pod A was gone.

***

After six and a half long years of never straying off course, Marcus Fincus turned the ship around to look for his son. Somewhere in the big brain of the ship, the super-computer had noted exactly when escape pod A had disengaged from the *Destiny Unknown* so that Marcus Fincus and the rest of the crew knew exactly where to look.

But the trouble was this: Jason had not simply disengaged from the ship and then stayed in one place. He had motored away from his initial coordinates at a speed of forty-four miles per hour, not very fast but certainly fast enough to get lost in the deep darkness of space.

They retraced their steps to the point where they had left Jason Fincus in the dust of the interstellar medium. It had been over thirty-six hours since escape pod A had disengaged from the ship, so it would take at least that long to make it back. And when they finally did return to the coordinates of Jason's disappearance, he was, of course, nowhere to be seen.

The supercomputer certainly didn't know where Jason was. It had stopped caring all about escape pod A and its pilot the moment they had disembarked.

Howard Oppenheimer used the ship's radar to probe hundreds of cubic miles in every direction. But Jason Fincus was already three thousand miles away, and the radar simply didn't extend that far. When they tried to radio Jason, sending signals out in every possible direction, they were met with silence.

Jason Fincus did receive the radio transmissions—or at least his stalwart ship did—but was fast asleep when the ship's communications dashboard lit up. The escape pod recorded a message and stored it away for later. Jason would never hear it. He didn't know how to work a transceiver any more than he knew how to navigate the stars.

They stayed there, transmitting for two days until finally Marcus Fincus sighed and said, "Well, at least we tried." Esmeralda made a spectacle and then took to her bed. And everybody else got on pretty much as before, except now Austin Ibsen had a room all to himself, which meant he and Amanda didn't need to conduct their consortship in the service closet anymore.

CHAPTER 8

YEARS 6-12

DR. MYLES JAMISON was still alive for all of this. He hadn't yet agreed to perform a guerilla operation on Bartholomew Barbate—the last thing he would agree to before he died an unceremonious death on the point of his own scalpel.

Because he was so big, Bartholomew Barbate was having more and more trouble fitting through the narrow service corridors that led to the giant fuse box and the Axon 5 battery and the gravity simulator and the moleculator. So whenever the power went out unexpectedly, or the moleculator stopped working, or the climate control was being wonky, it was taking Bartholomew longer and longer to get it fixed because he was getting stuck in the corridors more and more often.

The passengers were starting to worry that someday soon Bartholomew simply wouldn't fit down the corridors anymore and that there'd be nobody to fix the fuse box or the moleculator or the climate gauge or the gravity simulator. Austin Ibsen was a good apprentice to Bartholomew, but he simply didn't have the experience or the know-how to take over should Bartholomew become incapacitated.

So that's when a few well-meaning members of *Homo sapiens* species had the idea to install an adjustable gastric band in Bartholomew's stomach.

Well-meaning members of the *Homo sapiens* species have ridiculous ideas all the time. And this particular idea was especially ridiculous. And the well-meaning *Homo sapiens* who first suggested it was a midshipman by the name of George McGraw. George McGraw wasn't particularly bright, and he didn't have much to contribute to NASA's New World Population Project except his spermatozoa, which was nothing spectacular. But George McGraw was a yes-man, and that was exactly what Captain Marcus Fincus valued most in his deckhands. So, having served Marcus Fincus well on many previous space missions, George McGraw was invited to join the crew on the *Destiny Unknown* if only because he always did *exactly* what he was told.

George McGraw didn't usually have many ideas of his own. He was the sort of fellow who got his ideas about things from other people. So when he had the idea to surgically shrink Bartholomew's stomach and everybody went along with it, he felt pretty damn good about himself—that is, until the doctor died.

The surgery should have gone off without a hitch. Bartholomew, of course, did not have a say one way or another about the whole thing because nobody told him he was going to have an adjustable gastric band installed. During the night, he was drugged and brought to the operating table. But Bartholomew was a big man, and Myles Jamison had not administered the proper dosage of anesthesia. So Bartholomew woke up in the middle of the surgery to find his bowels disinterred. That was when Dr. Myles Jamison slipped in a pool of blood and fell on the pointy end of his own scalpel.[5]

The passengers on the ship took the doctor's death harder than they took little Brandelyn McCormack's death, certainly not because they liked the doctor any more than they liked Brandelyn but because the doctor was the one person who could fix their ever-ailing bodies. Dr. Myles Jamison was to the humans what Bartholomew Barbate was to the ship.

***

---

[5] Richard Park and Elijah Perkins-Borges succeeded in putting Bartholomew Barbate back together again when Dr. Myles Jamison expired. Neither Richard nor Elijah had been part of the original coup—they were only called to the scene after the fact. George McGraw spent two weeks in the brig for his part in the crusade. But since he had only *had* the idea and had not played any part in cutting Bartholomew open, he walked away scot-free in the end. Dr. Myles Jamison shouldered the lion's share of the blame, and he was already dead. Humans love to have a dead man to pin things on—it makes things a whole lot easier for everyone.

Bartholomew Barbate was not getting any smaller. And the ship certainly wasn't fixing itself. So Bartholomew promoted Austin Ibsen to first technician, a title that simply meant he would be doing the majority of the work from then on.

Austin Ibsen had already been shadowing Bartholomew for the better part of two years. His big brain could remember details better than any human brain in the universe. However, Austin did not have the intuition of an electrician. And he never would. So he and Bartholomew became partners in crime, so to speak. Austin would descend into the hull of the ship and slip nimbly down the corridors, between pipes and wires, while Bartholomew would lean back in his office swivel chair and guide Austin along on a walkie-talkie.

Austin and Bartholomew made a good team, and the passengers began to worry less about dying of oxygen deficiency and freezing to death. Now they just had to worry about what they would do if they needed a doctor.

***

Meanwhile, a tiny fetus was growing inside Emma Greene, who by now had an idea that she might be pregnant and was trying to hide it for as long as possible behind ironing boards and janitorial carts.

Incidentally, Esmeralda Fincus was the first to notice. She

called Emma Greene in one day to change the sheets and noted Emma's waistline. Esmeralda, never suspecting that her husband was having an affair, was delighted.

"You scoundrel!" Esmeralda scolded. "How long have you known?"

"Known about what?" Emma said, redoubling her efforts to remove the sheets from the bed.

"The baby!" Esmeralda cried. "Surely you didn't think you could hide it from me? You can't hide anything from me. Come now. Who's the father?"

"There is no father," Emma said.

"I bet it's that Albert Morris fellow. All that time in the laundry room *alone*."

Esmeralda could not possibly conceive of any person sleeping with a janitress other than a janitor.

"Uhmph," Emma murmured.

That was enough of an answer for Esmeralda. After that there was no hiding it anymore. Esmeralda was keen on telling anybody who might pass by her room.

"She won't say who the father is," Esmeralda would whisper, "but I caught her blushing when I mentioned Albert Morris."

Captain Marcus Fincus took the news in stride. He was admitted to the infirmary for several days on account of heart pain. When he finally reemerged with a clean bill of health, he pulled Emma aside and called off the affair.

Lydia Anne Greene was born in February, a healthy eight

pounds four ounces—a real screamer. Nothing could shut her up. Not a clean diaper. Not warm milk. Not a little bouncing up and down. Lydia Anne Greene cried and cried all through the day and night, and finally Emma had to consult a medical professional.

Since the doctor was dead, Emma took Lydia Anne to see Elijah Perkins-Borges, the veterinarian. Elijah diagnosed Lydia Anne Greene with infantile colic, all the while saying she should see a *real* doctor.

"I'm afraid I don't know much about human babies," he apologized. "If she were a basset hound or a baboon, I might be of more help."

But that was good enough for Emma Greene, who could have found out as much by picking up any one of the baby books in the library. Elijah told her infantile colic had no cure but would probably subside in three or four months. Emma would have to wait it out.

So would everyone else.

The novelty of a new baby girl wore off pretty quickly. Emma silently cursed the captain for his colicky spermatozoa. And she swore never to have a baby again.

When Lydia Anne got over being colicky all the time, she was absolutely adorable, and finally people on the ship could start thinking about having babies again. The next few years were all about babies. Lydia Anne Greene paved the way for the six most blissful years the ship would ever see, filled with new-baby smell and first steps and first words and all the mushy stuff that humans can't resist.

Elijah and Maisey Perkins-Borges popped out four daughters before Lydia Anne Greene could say her ABCs. Then Amanda Sphinx announced that she and Austin were due the following spring, the same month they were scheduled to set down on the planet Nissan Sentra.

Martha Marigold was delighted! She had graduated the last of her fifteen students and was eager to begin molding the next batch of impressionable young minds. Martha Marigold was fifty-seven years old and knew full well that she would never have children of her own.

Bartholomew Barbate became the go-to babysitter now that he was practically retired. He lounged around all day in his office swivel chair with babies crawling all over him.

Austin Ibsen was still working and reworking the wiring of the ship in Bartholomew's stead while Amanda grew rounder and rounder. Austin was twenty-three. Amanda was twenty-six. Perfect baby-making ages, biologically speaking. Every morning Austin would wake up and report: eight months seventeen days to go, eight months sixteen days to go, and so on, as that was the only way he knew how to be a father.

CHAPTER 9
YEAR 12

NISSAN SENTRA was so close now it hurt. Nobody really knew what to expect, and except for Brandelyn McCormack's watercolors still hanging in Martha Marigold's classroom, the passengers couldn't even begin to imagine a planet that wasn't Earth.

Epsilon Eridani, the star to which all their navigational equipment pointed, shone bright ahead, brighter than any other star—still only a star—but a light at the end of a long twelve-year tunnel.

And already Lydia Anne Greene and the Perkins-Borges girls were calling it *our star*.

"When are we going to get to *our star*?" the girls would ask. Or, "How big is *our star*?"

Lydia Anne Greene and the four Perkins-Borges girls were the first humans ever to be born without a star of their own, and their excitement about *our star* was rubbing off on everyone.

Meanwhile, Austin Ibsen was preparing for fatherhood. In the months leading up to Amanda Sphinx's delivery, Austin practiced his parenting skills on Lydia Anne Greene and the Perkins-Borges girls. The girls were drawn to Austin because he was so peculiar. They would throw out random sums like "What's fifty million times seventy-five trillion?" and Austin would click his tongue and roll his eyes back in his head and then say, "Three point seven five times ten to the twenty-one."

The kids treated Austin like one of them. He had a child-like demeanor, and Austin found he could communicate with children more readily than he could with adults. Amanda would look on while the girls climbed all over Austin like he was a jungle gym, and she would nod and pat her stirring belly.

She was pregnant with a boy. He would be the first boy born to NASA's New World Population Project, and Amanda would call him John Galt Ibsen after the man who stopped the world in *Atlas Shrugged*. And John Galt Ibsen would inherit his father's IQ, his mother's talent, and then something more: he would be born with the sort of commanding presence both his parents lacked.

***

The star—*our star*—was getting closer and brighter by

the day. An endless dawn stretched out over the ship, stirring long-forgotten feelings of home. The sight of Epsilon Eridani billions of miles away warmed everyone to the core.

What would the planet Nissan Sentra be like? Would it be warm in the summertime and cool in the autumn? Would it be blue with oceans and white with clouds? Would it be solid and firm underfoot?

It would be all those things. It would be perfect—but only for fifty-seven minutes. Then it wouldn't be any of those things anymore.

***

It was easy to imagine that the world of Nissan Sentra would be a veritable Eden for the passengers on the *Destiny Unknown*, albeit a treeless, lifeless Eden. But once Ginger Martin had her way with it, it would be swarming with microbes and bacteria and the first of the staple crops: potatoes, corn, wheat, and alfalfa. And, for a while at least, there would be Bobo, Bill, and Dog, too, to add a little flavor to the mix.

Elijah had stepped into the role of chief medical officer following the death of Dr. Myles Jamison. If Elijah were lucky, he would always have Bobo and Bill for company. They were both relatively young in chimp and bird years; they could easily outlive Elijah, so long as they were well cared for, which they were. Bobo was only fourteen years old and could expect to reach a ripe old age of sixty or seventy. And Bill the African grey was only eighteen and had at least forty years to go. Elijah Perkins-Borges was thirty-eight.

Dog was the youngest of them all, having just turned thirteen. Paradoxically, he was also the oldest of them all, roughly seventy-three in dog years. Elijah only hoped Dog would live long enough to set paw on Nissan Sentra.

Dog no longer moved with any speed, but he still played a slow game of fetch with Lydia Anne Greene and the Perkins-Borges girls. They would throw a ratty tennis ball, and Dog would trot over, pick it up in his mouth, and then wander in a lazy zigzag back to where he started, usually getting distracted along the way by some curious odor on the floor.

The girls enjoyed this game. They didn't know that on Earth it was usually played much faster with much younger, stronger dogs. As far back as they could remember, Dog had been slow as dirt.

Dog wasn't the only passenger that was slowing down. Twelve years may be nothing to you and me, but to the average human, twelve years is roughly an eighth of a lifetime. Many of the passengers were getting on in years. Richard Park was fifty-two. Marcus Fincus was fifty-four. Martha Marigold was fifty-eight. Barbary Montclair was sixty but pretended to be much younger. The oldest person on the ship was a man by the name of Arthur Stanton, who during his time on Earth had been a world-renowned composer, songwriter, and producer, composing over two hundred popular songs that were still crowding the airwaves on Earth all those trillions of miles away. He was seventy-two.

Who would guess he'd actually make it to the end of this journey? He did. He does.

Arthur Stanton sometimes played alongside Amanda Sphinx in the music room. She was a much better piano player than he was, but Arthur could make up songs without trying and put words to them just as quickly, so he sang and strummed the guitar while Amanda followed along on the piano.

Together Amanda and Arthur wrote over three hundred songs aboard the *Destiny Unknown*, some of them so good that it was a shame nobody back on Earth could hear them. They imagined most of their songs would be long forgotten after the ship set down on Nissan Sentra.

They couldn't have predicted that one of their songs, a silly ditty they wrote in twenty minutes called "We Come from the Planet Earth," would become the anthem of a brand-new civilization and would be sung by billions of people over hundreds of millions of years.

***

Music was good for the morale of the passengers. Amanda and Arthur did their part to raise the spirits of the crew by holding concerts to debut their new songs. Their winter concert every year became a much-anticipated tradition, and most of the wintertime festivities revolved around the music room where Amanda and Arthur were rehearsing carols for the performance on New Year's Eve.

Anybody with any musical talent whatsoever was invited to join in—Richard Park played the tuba, Martha Marigold took up the flute. Earl Updike was a fine violinist, and had he not been an even finer poet, he would have played for the New York Philharmonic at Lincoln Center. And Austin Ibsen, who had no ear for music, chimed in on the triangle. So it was always a very intimate experience, and very popular, too—standing room only. Even Esmeralda, who generally preferred the confines of her bedroom, would limp down to the music hall on New Year's Eve to hear them play.

Most of the music composed aboard the *Destiny Unknown* went unrecorded. The melodies and lyrics lived on in the heads of the passengers. Arthur Stanton and Amanda Sphinx did record one album, however. It was called "A Boy Alone in Space," and each track chronicled the life of a boy floating through space at a speed of forty-four miles per hour. It was a depressing fictional account of what they thought must have become of poor Jason Fincus.

***

The Christmas before they landed on Nissan Sentra was especially joyful. Nobody could look out the front of the ship and see Epsilon Eridani shining so brightly and not think of the star of Bethlehem, even if he or she thought the whole story of Jesus was a crock of shit.

Barbary Montclair splurged and made an extravagant dinner for Christmas Day, despite the warnings from Amanda Sphinx. Their natural food supply was running dangerously low, and Amanda, with the help of Austin, calculated they'd all be living off freeze-dried goods within three years. But Barbary and almost everyone else figured three years was long enough to get crops going on Nissan Sentra with the seeds they'd transported in the hull of the ship.

They didn't know that it would be thirty-two years before those seeds found their way into the ground. And then several more months before anything edible came of them. Barbary Montclair had killed himself by then.

Except for Amanda Sphinx, everybody very much enjoyed Barbary's Christmas feast. After they finished off the berry pie, the passengers retired to the media center to watch *The Muppet Christmas Carol*, still popular all those hundreds of millions of years later. Everyone loved it because it had snow, and nobody had seen the slightest trace of snow since the year AD 3478, except on distant moons or in labs where it was manufactured artificially.

***

By New Year's Eve, the *Destiny Unknown* was three

months out from its destination. Amanda Sphinx was in her third trimester, and the baby was kicking.

Perhaps the lights strung up in the library for the New Year's Eve concert had made the power go out. Or perhaps it was the fact that Barbary Montclair had all the ovens going at once. Or maybe the ship was just getting old and didn't feel like racing ahead at 0.876 times the speed of light anymore. Whatever it was that caused the power to blow, when it happened this time, everybody knew it wasn't just any old power outage. For starters, the *Destiny Unknown* had never turned over before—and that's exactly what it did. In midair, careening ahead at 0.876 times the speed of light, the *Destiny Unknown* did a somersault through space, coming to rest upside down with its tail end pointing toward the star Epsilon Eridani and its front facing back toward the bloated, farting speck that was the sun.

But this didn't stop the *Destiny Unknown* from pursuing its course. Its engines idled and died; the ship went pitch black except for the faint light from Epsilon Eridani. Yet the *Destiny Unknown* flew onward, upside down and backward, toward Nissan Sentra.[6]

---

[6] The ship did not stop because of Newton's First Law of Motion, which says an object in motion will stay in motion unless acted on by an external force. Because there is no gravity that far out in space and no oxygen or gas of any kind to create resistance, nothing stopped the *Destiny Unknown* from continuing just as it always had, only backward and belly-up. This, by the way, is why it was so easy for the ship to travel at such high speeds through space: The engines were only necessary to get the *Destiny Unknown* up to traveling speed. After that, Newton's first law kept the

When the ship somersaulted, Barbary Montclair, who was dicing onions in the kitchen, hacked off three fingers, sparing only a pinky and the all-important opposable thumb.

He would learn to do many things with just a thumb and a pinky. And he'd be damned if he couldn't still bake the best lemon soufflé in the universe.

---

ship running at a constant speed all on its own. So, except for the occasional hydrogen molecule or dust grain that, in the moment of contact, gave the ship a little bop on the nose, there was nothing to slow them down, and the engines had very little to do but start ovens and supply power to such devices as the gravity simulator and the moleculator and the strings of tiny white lights that decorated the library on New Year's Eve. Why this time, when the power went out, the *Destiny Unknown* did a cartwheel in space is anyone's guess. Perhaps one such speck of dust in space whose bop on the ship's nose at exactly the right moment had proved to be more than the ship could handle. Or, more likely, it was the result of Johannes Levi, who was napping at the wheel of the ship and just so happened to give the control stick a nudge with his elbow at the very moment the ship went dark.

CHAPTER 10
YEAR 12

THIS WAS NO ORDINARY power failure. Austin Ibsen knew it from the smell of smoke that drifted in through the vents. Bartholomew Barbate knew it, too. "This," he said to himself as he hovered over his swivel chair, "is not good."

And then he added, "No, sirree," which was an English phrase he had picked up when he was studying English at the Universidad Politécnica de Madrid, where he had earned his doctorate in electrical engineering.

***

The last words Austin Ibsen said to Amanda Sphinx were "Three. Yes."

This was in response to the last thing she said to him, which went something like this: "I thought we were actually going to bust right through the ceiling. I can't believe the

104

power actually went out again—and on New Year's Eve. Do you think it's actually serious this time?"

He still counted how many times she used the word *actually*, so he said, "Three," and then, in response to her question about it being serious, he said, "Yes." Then he disappeared down into the hull of the ship.

The first thing Austin Ibsen did was check the fuse box, even though something told him this time it had nothing to do with the fuse box. The smell of charred copper was coming from somewhere else, deeper within the ship.

So when Austin found the fuse box entirely in order, he figured it had to be the battery, which up until then had never caused them any trouble before. Austin had only fiddled with the battery a few times before when Bartholomew was teaching him how the ship worked. Nevertheless, he felt like he understood it pretty well—as well as anybody.

What neither Austin nor Bartholomew knew was that Axon 5 was planning to commit suicide. The high-voltage battery had been mulling it over for the last twelve years and was pretty sure it didn't want to turn on ovens or provide heat to cabins or turn feces into fertilizer anymore. And it started thinking about all this very early on because this particular model of Axon 5 battery had been made with a glitch. That glitch being that after twelve years of careening through space at speeds of 0.876 times the speed of light, the Axon 5 battery would explode into a million tiny pieces.

As Austin made his way into the bowels of the ship where

the battery lay tucked away in a steel bunker, Axon 5 was remembering exactly why it wanted to die and was just hoping someone would come along and mess with its highly fragile wiring.

Austen had only a flashlight to guide the way. When he reached the bunker he saw for a fact that the smell of burning was coming from Axon 5. One side of the battery was blackened and charred. And somewhere acid was leaking because little beads of battery fluid were floating in the air like frozen raindrops.

Austin Ibsen set the flashlight down and pried open the blackened side of the battery with a crowbar. The insides were a mess, and Austin felt like a pathologist sifting through the remains of a gangrened patient, pulling out loose wires and broken bits of metallic flesh.

He was amused at the thought of performing an autopsy on a dead battery and was having fun pretending to be a doctor when Axon 5 came to life again. The battery was not dead, as Austin had thought—at least not yet. It had one last act to perform before it kicked the bucket, and that was to explode itself and Austin Ibsen and the flashlight and the crowbar into a million tiny pieces.

**

Austin Ibsen's death was a serious loss to NASA's New World Population Project. Now both so-called doctors were dead: Dr. Myles Jamison, who had been responsible for fixing human bodies, and Austin Ibsen, who had been responsible for fixing the *Destiny Unknown*.

And Bartholomew Barbate was forced out of retirement, which was no easy task since he could no longer fit down the narrow corridors that led to the electrical wiring. Instead, he had to coach Melanie Lorne and a host of engineers through the process of installing the backup battery, Axon 4, via walkie-talkie, as they fumbled around in a mess of obliterated metal and human flesh.

It took the better part of three days to get Axon 4 up and running, and all that time the ship barreled through space ass backward and upside down. This was about the time they realized the spare moleculator in escape pod B was just as much a dud as Axon 5.

***

Escape pod B, just like escape pod A, was equipped with its very own tiny battery and its own gravity simulator and its own moleculator. Because the rest of the ship was offline and running out of oxygen fast, the fifty passengers on the *Destiny Unknown* crowded into escape pod B and stayed there while Bartholomew Barbate and Melanie Lorne and the rest of the engineers worked tirelessly to get the Axon 4 battery up and running.

That first night, sensing that they were liable to run out of oxygen in the next day or two, they switched on the spare moleculator. It sputtered out a few quadrillion molecules of oxygen, which is nothing really, and then breathed its final breath. Bartholomew Barbate, who *could* fit into escape pod B, took one look at the moleculator and pronounced it dead, finished, kaput. And upon the captain's orders to resuscitate it, Bartholomew said, "No, sirree. No can do."

The *Destiny Unknown* was beginning to show signs of her age.

Fearing another tragic explosion, Esmeralda insisted that the dead moleculator be moved somewhere out of sight—she didn't care where, as long as it was far enough away that it couldn't blow *her* to smithereens.

Meanwhile, all those passengers crammed into escape pod B were rapidly exhausting their very limited supply of O_2. They kept the air-lock doors wide open so that all the oxygen from uninhabited parts of the ship could keep their lungs inflated for those three miserable days while they waited for Axon 4 to come to their rescue.

The situation was rather desperate. The O_2 gauge in the escape pod kept creeping ever downward. The temperature was dropping rapidly. And there simply wasn't enough functionality in the rest of the ship to keep the food and water supplies at a stable level. The passengers kept the little furnace in the escape pod running on high at all hours, but with the doors wide open, most of that heat drifted out into the empty ship. No matter how hard the poor little furnace worked, it was as cold as a meat locker in the escape pod and even colder in the rest of the ship. Anytime the engineers ventured into the bowels of the vessel, they had to put on full space suits to keep from freezing to death.

Some New Year it must have been.

CHAPTER 11

YEAR 12

ALL THE WHILE, Amanda Sphinx was mourning the loss of Austin Ibsen, the father of her unborn child. Almost everybody else had forgotten Austin in the panic that ensued when they realized they were running out of oxygen and heat. But no matter—Amanda Sphinx grieved enough for all of them. She held a quiet vigil for Austin, camped out in one of the fifty bunks lining the walls of escape pod B, and stayed up all night hugging her swollen stomach and crying softly into a blanket. After three days of crying, Amanda Sphinx dried her eyes, and thought only about John Galt Ibsen and preserving his little fetal life.

***

The passengers aboard the *Destiny Unknown* had no idea they had flipped upside down. They were very aware that the ship was careening toward Nissan Sentra tail end first. They imagined perhaps that they had spun around like a merry-go-round. They didn't know that they had actually spun head over heels like a Ferris wheel. How could they know? Space has no up or down.

When Axon 4 started pumping oxygen and heat and light into other parts of the ship, and when the gravity simulator hummed into action, their feet hit the ship's floor with a thud, and it was as if they had never flipped upside-down at all. But for those of us who were watching through our superspectrum x-ray telescopes, they were all still standing on their heads.

And because they had no idea that they had somersaulted onto their heads, they did nothing to set the ship right again. Nor did they turn the ship around. They dared not risk the loss of valuable momentum doing a one-eighty at 0.876 times the speed of light. So they continued on as upside down and ass backward as they had been when Austin Ibsen was blown to smithereens.

So now, as interstellar biologists, we must do something tricky: we must turn ourselves on our heads so that we are seeing everything the way the passengers on the *Destiny Unknown* must have seen it, which is right side up.

***

Axon 4 proved to be every bit as effective as the murderous Axon 5. Sure, the lights flickered and dimmed on occasion, and the ovens took longer to warm up, but it was preferable to having no lights or ovens at all.

So the *Destiny Unknown* was little delayed on its journey to Epsilon Eridani. Exactly three days before they came into orbit around Nissan Sentra, Amanda Sphinx went into labor.

Thanks to the handiwork of the ship's sailing master, Howard Oppenheimer, the *Destiny Unknown* had just traversed Epsilon Eridani's massive Oort cloud, a minefield of icy debris left over from the star's birth, when Amanda Sphinx started dripping amniotic fluid all over the cafeteria floor.

The birth lasted a good seventeen hours, stretching across the 7.5 billion miles of empty space between the Oort cloud and Epsilon Eridani's outermost dwarf planet, a little irregular thing half the size of Pluto, which the Perkins-Borges girls named Fluttershy after their favorite My Little Pony. In the time it took John Galt Ibsen to free himself from his mother's womb, he had already traveled farther than approximately 100 percent of all humans who had ever lived.

When John Galt Ibsen popped out of the womb, he didn't cry. He was so silent, in fact, that Amanda Sphinx thought he was dead. Maisey Perkins-Borges, who performed the delivery with her husband, Elijah Perkins-Borges, had to listen very closely to the infant's breathing to confirm that he was indeed fine and healthy—just not much of a crier.

Lydia Anne Greene and the Perkins-Borges girls were in raptures over this little baby boy. They wanted to name him Fluttershy, too. None of them had ever seen anything like him before—he was the only baby boy for sixty-one trillion miles.

Amanda slept with him in her bed—she lay with the baby on her stomach and fell asleep feeling his little body go up and down with her breathing.

He was such an easy baby compared to all the others. Emma Greene was envious. Her daughter, Lydia Anne, had been so troublesome; nobody in any of the adjoining cabins had gotten any sleep in the first few months after Lydia Anne was born. But John Galt Ibsen slept through the night, and Amanda Sphinx always awoke refreshed in the morning.

John Galt was already thinking so many big things; he didn't have time to cry or fuss like other babies—he was a born genius, although nobody knew it yet.

John Galt had only been around for two and a half days when the first full-size planet came into view. The *Destiny Unknown* slowed down so everybody could get a look at it. It was nearly the size of Neptune, a ball of roiling white gas with three silvery rings. Then came another planet, about eight times the size of Jupiter and with at least seventy-two moons, some Earth-size but barren and cold. This was perhaps even more exciting, because nobody, not even the adults, had ever seen a planet of that size up close before. Its surface was a tumult of gaseous storms and violent hurricanes, and the gravity of the colossal thing tugged and pulled at the ship so much that Marcus Fincus had to pull tight on the steering wheel and rev the engines to keep from spiraling into its hungry core.

The star Epsilon Eridani loomed brilliantly on the horizon, growing in size from what was no more than a distant flame to a dazzling orb that shed natural, vitamin D–rich light on the upturned faces of the passengers of the *Destiny Unknown*.

And for the first time in twelve years they could power down the ship's heaters and still be warm.

***

John Galt Ibsen stared out at the approaching star. It was like being born a second time: a bright light was shining at the end of a dark tunnel.

The first glimpse they got of Nissan Sentra was of its dark shadow as it transited Epsilon Eridani, a speck of darkness against the bright sun. It was promising. The planet was a suitable size and distance from the star. And it moved slowly enough with just the right axial tilt that its seasons would match those on Earth.

It was a fine planet indeed—for now. What none of them could see were the thousands of meteoroids hurtling through space en route for this happy, unsuspecting little planet. Nobody realized that Nissan Sentra was only days from merging with this cluster of meteoroids in an episodic meeting of celestial bodies that occurred like clockwork once every two hundred million years.

In about two weeks, Nissan Sentra would resemble Earth in more than its shape, size, and axial tilt—its oceans would be vapor in the air, kicked up into the atmosphere by high-impact strikes of meteoroids from space, and the average temperature on the surface of the planet would reach a scalding three hundred degrees Fahrenheit, not much different from the temperatures they had escaped on Earth twelve years ago.

Captain Marcus Fincus couldn't have known this—it was hard enough detecting a planet the size of Earth all those trillions of miles away and even harder still to learn that it was covered in liquid oceans. No technology known to humans was sophisticated enough to see the relatively tiny little meteoroids spinning around in the dark.[7]

***

---

[7] If only they had had our superspectrum x-ray telescope, then they could have seen the meteoroids twelve years ago. They could have looked around for a better planet, preferably one such as our own, with intelligent life and the capacity to invent a superspectrum x-ray telescope, and with relatively friendly inhabitants, too. But that's like the question of the chicken or the egg, neither here nor there. As it was, the humans did not have a superspectrum x-ray telescope and wouldn't still for millions of years.

It took thirteen days to land the *Destiny Unknown*, with all crew on deck and a slew of anxious passengers standing at every porthole to watch. Nobody had ever landed the vessel before, and it took some time to work out a feasible trajectory that would put the ship down on Nissan Sentra safely.

As they orbited the planet in search of the perfect place to start a new civilization, they were impressed by the vast oceans and the plentiful inland seas the planet had to offer. It was a wonder life had not found a way to exist here yet.

None of them had ever seen an ocean before, except in pictures and on TV. Amanda Sphinx felt a pang of regret, knowing Austin Ibsen hadn't lived to see the deep blue of an ocean.

They chose a spot just north of the equator, where the days were nearly as long as the nights, and where the temperatures suited crops of corn and wheat and tomatoes.

The planet was divided into three large continents, each about the size of South America, and populated with rivers and lakes and freshwater springs. Their projected landing site was on the largest of these continents. They chose a coastal region at the mouth of a freshwater tributary, on the very southern tip of a long peninsula about the size of Florida. Here the terrain was flat, and the soil was rich and damp, and they could be sure to reap an abundance of food from the seeds they had brought along with them.

It was a rough ride to the ground. And it took a good sixteen hours, which was about the length of one day on Nissan Sentra. The *Destiny Unknown* entered the planet's atmosphere and experienced a great deal of turbulence but nothing unexpected. Howard Oppenheimer gave instructions to the captain, shouting numbers and coordinates as they glided into the stratosphere.

They set down lightly, like a parachutist, and everyone experienced some level of disbelief. After so many little disasters along the way, it was hard to believe they'd actually made it to Nissan Sentra. All the instruments promised that the atmosphere was nontoxic and had enough oxygen to sustain carbon-based life. But just to be sure, they sent Bobo the chimp out into the balmy weather first.

Bobo took three steps on solid ground and then defecated. Everybody was watching from the portholes, and when Bobo didn't die or turn blue or fall over within three minutes, they figured it was okay.

The passengers came streaming out of the *Destiny Unknown*. Some of them kissed the ground, others did jumping jacks, and others just cried and cried like babies. As for Amanda Sphinx—she changed John Galt's diaper and then put on a pair of khaki shorts and a Hawaiian shirt. She said a quiet prayer for Austin Ibsen, who she felt inhabited the walls of the ship, and then stepped slowly onto the hard ground with John Galt Ibsen in her arms.

When she was on the ship, Amanda always felt Austin Ibsen wasn't far away. Now, on a strange planet, with nothing but earth and sky for as far as the eye could see, nothing at all reminded her of him.

Stepping onto Nissan Sentra was a strange feeling, mostly because the gravity wasn't quite as strong as it was on Earth, which is to say the gravity wasn't quite as strong as it was on the *Destiny Unknown*. They could jump a few inches higher here. John Galt was easier to carry. Amanda tried to show him everything—the oceans, the spire-like mountains in the distance, and the rivulets rushing out of the tributaries. She wanted him to always remember his first moments on this new planet.[8]

Captain Marcus Fincus first suggested the names Ralph and Alice for the two moons. Martha Marigold hoped to call one Brandelyn for little Brandelyn McCormack. Nobody else really cared what the moons were called. They were busy drinking freshwater from the tributary, and smelling the ocean breeze and marveling at the total lack of life anywhere on the planet. How could such a beautiful place not have grass or bugs or seagulls or even fish in the sea?

Elijah let Dog loose on the beach. He didn't think the

---

[8] Because John Galt Ibsen's brain was so advanced, he would indeed remember all these things many years later, when the *Destiny Unknown* was once again wandering through space, its disheartened passengers suffering from diverticulitis and in desperate search of another habitable planet. He would remember the fifty-seven minutes he spent on a beautiful oceanfront with the two moons, Ralph and Alice, hovering overhead, and it would inspire him to keep searching, on and on, for a new home.

aging cocker spaniel would get very far. But Elijah was wrong. In all his excitement to be outside, Dog started sprinting up and down the oceanfront with the speed and energy of a dog half his age.

And fifty-seven minutes went by like that. Captain Marcus Fincus lit a million-dollar cigar, and then a burning chunk of rock streaked across the sky.

CHAPTER 12

YEAR 12

DOG SEEMED TO THINK the universe was playing a giant game of fetch. He chased after the meteor and disappeared out of sight over a rocky hummock.

Elijah called after him, but the roaring of several more meteors and the subsequent crashes drowned out every other sound.

This was about the time Captain Marcus Fincus dropped the remaining half of his cigar on the ground, where it smoldered and smoked like the distant craters made by the fiery space debris.

Lydia Anne Greene and the Perkins-Borges girls started screaming. Bobo the chimp clambered back onto the ship with a shriek. And everybody else stood stricken. Was this it, then? Were they going to die fifty-seven minutes after setting foot on the planet of their dreams?

Nobody was quite ready to believe this world was coming

to an end. They stood for a long time and watched the meteors enter the atmosphere, burning fiery white and then plummeting to the ground, sending up huge mushroom clouds of dust and rock. The heavens were ablaze, and it looked like a thousand Maseratis had left smoky tire tracks across the blue sky.

Then Johannes Levi tugged on the captain's sleeve and said, "Uh, sir? I think it's time to go."

The captain merely nodded and mumbled something incoherent. Then a large meteor, maybe a mile in diameter, struck somewhere out in the ocean.

The shoreline receded nearly a mile, which could only mean that somewhere off the coast a huge volume of water was gathering into a giant tidal wave.

"Everyone back to the ship!" the captain cried. The command was useless because every passenger was already sprinting for the open air lock where Amanda Sphinx stood cradling John Galt Ibsen in one arm and ushering the passengers in with the other.

The only person lagging was poor Elijah, who called desperately to Dog. He could see Dog; the cocker spaniel had reemerged one hundred yards off, on the edge of the receding shoreline, and was barking madly at the thing that had struck the ocean many miles offshore, a thing poor Dog mistook for a giant tennis ball.

Dog's hearing was nearly gone, which was common in cocker spaniels of his age, and so he did not hear Elijah calling for him, offering him treats, and begging him to come back to the ship. Maisey, with the help of Deidre Hundt and George McGraw, dragged Elijah on board, and the *Destiny Unknown* took off like a bat out of hell, leaving Dog behind.

As they ventured skyward, they could see the tidal wave smash against the peninsula and devour it completely so that every inch of land, every rock and tributary, every hummock and hill—including Dog and the remaining half of the captain's cigar—disappeared under water.[9]

***

Elijah mourned the death of Dog more than he mourned the loss of Austin Ibsen—nearly everyone did. To the addled humans, it seemed unjust for any creature with such a fledg-

---

[9] Future space explorers would visit Nissan Sentra and find a world turned on its head, scarred with craters, with all the dirt in the sky and all the oxygen polluted with dust, and a dull red haze where the sun barely shone through the clouds. Yet there was still hope for Nissan Sentra. The tiny microorganisms that had been living in Dog's intestinal tract would begin to repopulate the oceans of the planet, taking occupancy in the energy-rich hydrothermal vents on the sea floor. And within several hundreds of millions of years, Nissan Sentra would be a world rich with vegetation, tiny little creatures in the sea, and a handful of intrepid land dwellers—all descended from the microscopic bacteria that had been a part of Dog. And except for the periodic meteor showers that arrived at the same time every two hundred million years, causing global mass extinctions, evolution would proceed unimpeded, and life would go on evolving on Nissan Sentra for several billions of years, until Epsilon Eridani, too, burned out like the withering, fading sun.

ling intellect to be left behind simply because it had mistaken a meteor for a giant tennis ball. Austin Ibsen had, at least, had a chance—he was one of the smartest humans in the universe. Dog, on the other hand, was only doing what he had been programmed to do: go fetch.

Elijah would have gladly traded his own life for Dog's. But unless you are a three-toed septenium from Sarakis, the universe doesn't work that way.[10]

***

Howard Oppenheimer did the best he could to escape the atmosphere of Nissan Sentra before everything went up in smoke. He managed to dodge the most deadly meteors on his way up, but he was helpless to avoid the myriad pea-size meteors that rained down from the mesosphere. The ship rattled like a tin roof in a hailstorm. This was, of course, very alarming to all the passengers of the *Destiny Unknown*, who had never experienced a hailstorm, much less a mesospheric

---

[10] Not every passenger who dies on this journey deserves the epitaph I have just given Dog. But Dog died in such a way as to give birth to a whole world of living organisms: the Nissan Sentrans. This makes Dog infinitely more significant than many of the others who die in this story—from an evolutionary standpoint, that is. Many important dissertations have been written on the subject of Dog and his role in populating a barren world. The Nissan Sentrans were not an intelligent bunch. Thanks to the mass extinctions caused by periodic meteor showers, life would never evolve to be quite as complex on Nissan Sentra as it had been on Earth—but it would be life, after all, and that alone is quite a miracle.

meteor shower.

Just as they cleared the worst of the storm, a meteor the size of a Volkswagen Beetle struck the *Destiny Unknown* on the starboard side where Howard Oppenheimer was sitting at the navigation panel and contemplating their haphazard trajectory through the riddled atmosphere.

The digital display above the navigation panel read 61,724,248,329,453—the number of miles they had traveled thus far. When the car-size meteor struck the side of the ship, all the little dials and meters on the panel started spinning wildly, and the digital display blinked to zero.

When the ship recovered from the blow and Howard was sure they had exited the thermosphere of the planet, he tried desperately to recover the navigational data from the past twelve years. Every coordinate, every odometer, every trajectory had been reset. It was as if they had never left Earth—which meant Howard Oppenheimer had no idea where they were relative to the rest of space or which distant star was their dying sun. They might as well have been sailors at sea on a starless night with no compass. Or ancient Mayans dropped into the snowy plains of Antarctica.

In three words: they were lost.

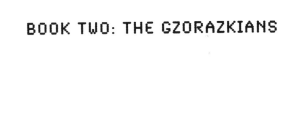

BOOK TWO: THE GZORAZKIANS

CHAPTER 13
YEAR 12

THE PASSENGERS clamored to return to Earth now that Nissan Sentra was done for. Gone. Finished. Kaput. They had no plan B. NASA protocol simply stated that should Nissan Sentra prove uninhabitable for any reason, they had better turn the fuck around and fly the twelve years back to Earth. There wasn't another planet nearby that any of them knew of that could sustain life. Nissan Sentra had been their one and only shot. And now Nissan Sentra was a hot, smoky cloud of dust and vapor. Earth was pretty much all they had left.

If only they knew which way to go.

You see, they didn't know where Earth was anymore because everything that could tell them where they were and how'd they gotten there had gone up in smoke when the meteor struck the starboard side of CC. They didn't have a superspectrum x-ray telescope, so they couldn't see Earth from where they were in space. All they could see was an unfamiliar map of stars that all glowed with the same apparent brightness and had about the same general look. Any one of them could have been the sun.

Howard cursed the goddamned navigation system for abandoning him at a time like this, then he cursed the meteor shower for causing all this trouble, and then he just cursed and cursed and cursed. This was about the worst thing that could happen. Until now, no matter what happened all those trillions of miles from home, they had known how to get back to Earth. Now they were marooned in space without hope of ever finding habitable soil again.

The *Destiny Unknown* orbited the desolate planet for three days. Everyone was in a foul mood, especially Captain Marcus Fincus. He ordered people left and right, up and down, and out of his way. He had never been so angry in all his life. Who would have thought a meteor shower with a period of two hundred million years would have been their undoing? Surely nobody had seen it coming, not from sixty-one trillion miles away.

While the captain was storming about, the deckhands were busy checking the gear on the bridge. Their collision with the car-size meteor had done a lot of damage to the hardwiring of the ship. The supercomputer was confused. It suffered memory loss. It couldn't keep track of the time. It forgot how many passengers were aboard the ship. Melanie Lorne and Bartholomew Barbate had to remind the supercomputer of these things over and over again before it could get anything straight. Even then, it still had no recollection of the past twelve years. For all it knew, it was still sitting in the underground hangar on Earth.

While Deidre Hundt was recalibrating the super-high-frequency radio, she suddenly heard a sound that gave her some inkling of hope: a series of short regular beeps followed by a string of garbled noises that sounded vaguely humanoid. She adjusted the dial left and right until the message came through clear as a bell—it was as though someone were standing right in front of her reciting the Gettysburg Address, except it wasn't the Gettysburg Address. It wasn't anything Deidre recognized. She signaled the captain.

"We're receiving a transmission from Earth!" she shouted.

Marcus Fincus couldn't make heads or tails of the transmission, either. He summoned Maurice Yanne, the signals specialist from France. There were guesses as to what language was being spoken so many trillions of miles from home: Chukchi, spoken by fewer than eight thousand people in Russia, or perhaps Dolgan, also from Russia, or Cashinahua, known to about one thousand people in Peru, or maybe Washo, a Native American language known to as few as seven people in Washo County, Nevada.

But when Maurice Yanne arrived on the scene, he listened to the message for fewer than ten seconds and concluded the foreign speaker wasn't even human. What they were hearing was an alien signal from an alien space vessel or perhaps an alien planet.

After a stunned silence, George McGraw said, "I don't see how that's going to help us get home."

He was right, of course. An alien signal would not point them in the direction of Earth, even if Maurice Yanne could figure out what the alien was saying.

Deidre Hundt was the first to offer a sensible reply. This was a signal from somewhere, she reminded them, somewhere capable of sustaining life.

Perhaps there was hope after all.

CHAPTER 14

YEAR 12

WHETHER THE TRANSMISSION was coming from a planet down the block or from a star millions of light-years away, Maurice Yanne could not tell—at least not yet. He hoped—and it was worth hoping—that the message contained some information regarding the source of the signal. And if the source was close, then perhaps they would indeed find habitable land again before the food supply was exhausted.

Maurice Yanne and a bevy of deckhands listened to the signal for several days, everybody crowded around the radio. Every seventeen minutes a series of beeps was followed by a seven-minute monologue spoken in the alien language and a nine-minute concerto much like the symphonies back on Earth. And every seventeen minutes, it was a new monologue and a new concerto.

After several hours, the transmission terminated with a

long, piercing buzz, and the recordings started over from the beginning.

Listening well into the third day, Maurice Yanne concluded that sixty-three distinct messages were rotating on an eighteen-hour cycle.

On the fourth day, Captain Marcus Fincus fired up the ship's PA system and addressed the anxious passengers: the *Destiny Unknown* would remain in orbit around Nissan Sentra until Maurice Yanne could decipher the mysterious signals and determine the distance to their source. If the source was close enough, they would then set off in search of the nonhumanoid beings that had sent the signal.

***

The weeks slid by, and Maurice seemed to be getting no closer to decoding the message. The speech patterns were unlike anything he had ever heard, the dialogue garbled and multilayered, with more than one intonation built into every sound. It could take years to decode a language such as this, with no basis in Arabic, Slavic, Scandinavian, or Latin.

It occurred to Maurice many weeks later—after poring over phonetic transcriptions of the mysterious messages, after replaying each transmission at various speeds and frequencies, after banging his head against the wall—that perhaps the concertos were related to the transmissions somehow.

He did not like to admit it, for he was not used to being stumped, but he—the expert signals specialist from France—needed help. And when it came to interpreting music, only two people on the ship were qualified for the job: Amanda Sphinx and Arthur Stanton.

Maurice Yanne confessed to them that he had overlooked one very likely possibility: that the music held the key to deciphering the alien language—that the music *was* the code.

Amanda Sphinx and Arthur Stanton set to work immediately. Meanwhile, John Galt Ibsen lay wrapped in a cocoon of swaddling and watched placidly from the crib they had set up for him on the bridge. Neither of them knew it then, but his brain was absorbing everything they said and did. He watched closely as Howard Oppenheimer guided the ship in wide circles around Nissan Sentra. He fell asleep to the lull and lilt of the alien symphonies. And he listened to his mother repeat words in the alien tongue and then read them back as best she could in English while Arthur Stanton took notes.

So it shouldn't come as a surprise, given his nearly constant proximity to the alien transmissions and his mother's active role in translating them, that many months later, when they were already on their way to the source of the signal on the planet Gzorazki, John Galt Ibsen uttered his first word, *Mgu*,[11] the Gzorazkian word for yes.

---

[11] Pronounced "Moo."

***

Maurice Yanne's hypothesis turned out to be correct: the music accompanying each transmission was the key to decoding the message. Once Amanda Sphinx and Arthur Stanton figured out how the music correlated with the speech patterns, they could understand what the aliens were saying in the first of the sixty-three recordings:

> We are the Gzorazkians, a race of intelligent beings inhabiting the planet Gzorazki. If by chance you get this message and happen to have a super-high-frequency radio transmitter, please respond, for we are ever so lonely in this great big thing called the universe and would be glad to have a neighbor.

The second of the sixty-three recordings included a description of the Gzorazkian people: "Long-headed with smooth round backs for rocking back and forth. Friendly eyes, not unlike the eyes of a cocoyucan, but with far greater intelligence. White hair behind the ears that turns blue with age. Dark folds around the waist for attracting a mate."

Some transmissions included jokes: "How many Gzorazkians does it take to screw in a light bulb? Two—one guy to screw it in, and another to eat the first guy for lunch."

And then there was the common Gzorazkian adage: "All

intelligent creatures are fools in space. All intelligent creatures in space are fools. All fools in space are intelligent creatures." That much the passengers of the *Destiny Unknown* had learned for themselves.

The Gzorazkians claimed to live on a planet orbiting an M-class star at the vertex of a teardrop-shape supernova remnant halfway between one pulsar with a period of 0.012 seconds and another with a period of 6.238 seconds. Pairing this essential data with the very rudimentary telescopic technology on the ship, Howard Oppenheimer was able to track the radio signal back to its source. After about six weeks of figuring, he could confirm that the signal was coming from a point five and a half light-years away, originating in the vicinity of a shiny white star visible to the naked eye. It was one of a thousand shiny white stars in the sky, and if not for Howard Oppenheimer, they would have never been able to tell which shiny white star was home to the long-headed, round-backed Gzorazkians.

When all sixty-three Gzorazkian transmissions were decoded, their content evaluated, and the star located, Howard Oppenheimer typed the relative coordinates of the planet Gzorazki into the supercomputer and the *Destiny Unknown* sped off, leaving Nissan Sentra far behind.

CHAPTER 15

YEARS 12-14

PLANETS CAPABLE of sustaining life—for all humans knew at the time of the maiden voyage of the *Destiny Unknown*—were rare. A human looking at the relatively few planets he or she could observe from Earth might have concluded that the universe was a hostile place. Look at Mars, for instance. Its atmosphere was so thin that a cup of coffee poured onto its rocky surface would have evaporated within milliseconds. And Venus was a hellhole of suffocating gases and sulfuric fumes—not unlike Earth at the time of the ship's launch. Then there were the nearby gas giants— Saturn, Jupiter, Uranus, and Neptune—all of which had atmospheres so great they could have crushed a military tank as flat as a sheet of tissue paper. And Pluto—well, Pluto was hardly anything. And at one time there had been a planet called Mercury, but it had been swallowed by the ever-expanding sun about three million years before our story begins.

Naturally, Captain Marcus Fincus and the passengers aboard the *Destiny Unknown* would conclude that their chances of stumbling upon a life-sustaining planet all those trillions of miles away from home were impossibly low. They couldn't have been more surprised to find a race of beings known as Gzorazkians inhabiting just such a planet a mere thirty-two trillion miles down the block. It was exactly what the Neanderthals must have felt when they were wandering through the forests of Pangaea and happened on the Cro-Magnons. It was nearly impossible to believe that intelligent life had developed elsewhere, much less right next door.

But what the humans didn't know—and what they couldn't have known, given that they had yet to invent the superspectrum x-ray telescope—was that their coveted solar system is no more extraordinary than the common cold. About a quarter of the solar systems in the Milky Way Galaxy contain habitable planets, and approximately 90 percent of those actually harbor some form of life, whether it be microbial or more advanced. And, as it turns out, about a millionth of a percent of those life-sustaining, life-harboring planets are home to intelligent life—beings capable of understanding their universe.

So, yes, it was serendipitous that they happened to stumble across super-high-frequency radio waves from another planet inhabited by sentient beings. But in the universe as we know it—those of us with superspectrum x-ray telescopes, that is—it's not unheard of.

***

The first transmission they sent back to the Gzorazkians was a simple message composed entirely of musical notes. It said, using only seven chords played over and over again in varying arrangements, "We are here. We can hear you. We are coming."[12]

Later, when Amanda and Arthur had mastered the musical language, they sent a more detailed message describing who they were and where they came from. In part it said, "We are fifty-odd passengers lost in space. We need a place to live. We are scheduled to arrive in 6.283 years, or, more universally (since we assume you do not measure time in Earth-years), the time it takes for a sample of cesium-134 to decay to 12.138 percent of its original mass."

Then following the Gzorazkians' lead, they described themselves. "We are, for the most part, long-armed, long-legged bipeds with large brains and relatively hairless bodies. We are mostly pink and brown, and we have opposable thumbs on each hand."

It seemed appropriate, too, to add a little human wisdom: a stitch in time saves nine. And a joke: How many humans

---

[12] Because the message could not travel any faster than the speed of light, it would not reach the Gzorazkians for another five and a half years.

does it take to screw in a light bulb? Three—one to screw it in, one to switch it on, and one to forget to turn it off.

Altogether, the message sounded a little like Dvořák's Piano Quintet No. 2 in A Major. And that was it. They wouldn't hear back from the Gzorazkians for nearly six years—five and a half years for the message to reach Gzorazki and then another nineteen weeks for a response to reach the approaching ship. When they finally did hear back from the Gzorazkians, they were just over two trillion miles away and, having depleted their natural food stores, were surviving on freeze-dried astronaut food.

**

By the time John Galt Ibsen uttered his first coherent word—the Gzorazkian word for yes—Esmeralda Fincus, fifty-two, was spending upward of six days a week confined to her bed. The distress of being lost in space and her ever-worsening arthritis had made her sickly, weak, and virtually unable to stand or move without jolts of electric pain shooting through her bones.

She still had her opinions though. No matter what happens to them, human beings somehow manage to retain their opinions. One of Esmeralda's opinions was this: the Gzorazkians must be a race of brutes. Esmeralda didn't like the sound of them one bit. Anybody who couldn't pronounce their *R*s properly—which was something everybody noticed about the Gzorazkians, who pronounced their *R*s like *W*s, as in "I'm weally hung-wee"—must be doltish and plain, and most likely savage. Esmeralda had felt the same way about Austin Ibsen, who also pronounced his *R*s like *W*s.

Another one of Esmeralda's opinions, which she espoused to Emma Greene, who changed her sheets every Sunday, went something like this: "That baby, the one that doesn't cry—something must be wrong with him. He most likely suffers from a birth defect. He will only grow up to be a burden to us all. There is something wrong with his face, too—his eyes are too large in his head. He is disfigured, surely, and uglier than any baby I ever saw."

In fact, John Galt Ibsen was a very handsome baby and would turn out to be a very handsome man.

And Esmeralda always thought she smelled gas. It upset her that nobody else smelled it, too. She was always telling everybody that if anybody lit a match the whole ship would go up in a puff of smoke. This was purely psychosomatic. All the ship's appliances, even the ovens and stoves, were electric. There was no natural gas on the ship. In fact, there was hardly any natural gas left back on Earth. The humans had used it all up. So she couldn't have smelled natural gas—at least not gas that was really there.[13]

Meanwhile, little John Galt Ibsen, whose eyes were too

---

[13] Esmeralda was suffering from an olfactory disorder known as phantosmia, a condition in which a person experiences phantom smells and olfactory hallucinations.

big for his head, was getting along fabulously with the English language. He could compose full sentences and was able to ask for things like food and water. But he confused Amanda Sphinx and everybody else when he asked for things in his other native tongue, Gzorazkian. They couldn't understand how he had picked up the alien language so quickly, and because they were still relatively new to decoding the garbled sounds, they could hardly keep up with what little John Galt was saying.

Esmeralda didn't like this either. "It's one more sign of his obvious deformity," she declared to Emma Greene.

Maurice Yanne was fascinated with John Galt Ibsen. How could this child learn the nuances of an alien language and pronounce the strange words with so little effort and speak it as if everyone around him could understand? It was a lingual anomaly, one Maurice would never be able to explain.

Maurice Yanne couldn't be more thankful for a Gzorazkian-speaking child—he suggested that John Galt Ibsen might serve as the primary link between the passengers on the *Destiny Unknown* and the Gzorazkian peoples when it came time to communicate with the aliens one-on-one. And there would come such a time.

Amanda Sphinx did not like the idea of her young child playing translator to Captain Marcus Fincus. Nor did she appreciate the way Maurice Yanne encouraged John Galt Ibsen's use of the alien tongue. It meant that she could not understand what her son was saying half the time. It made her feel inadequate as a mother. John Galt Ibsen would chatter on and on about God knows what, and Amanda Sphinx could only nod and smile.

It only took a few months for John Galt Ibsen to realize that his mother—and everyone else on the ship—didn't understand a lick of Gzorazkian. So he learned to use English when he wanted something or when he had a question. But he still muttered quietly to himself in Gzorazkian. He dreamed in Gzorazkian, too.

When John Galt was eighteen months old and the ship was once again hurtling through the emptiness of deep space, Maurice Yanne requested special permission to conduct private language lessons with John Galt Ibsen. The captain granted his request despite the objections of Amanda Sphinx. The language lessons were less for the benefit of John Galt Ibsen than they were for Maurice Yanne, who wanted so badly to be able to speak the alien tongue. Maurice would sit for long hours listening to John Galt ramble away, catching only a snippet of sense here or there, working daily to make heads and tails of the garbled sounds. Maurice made progress with the language, thanks to John Galt Ibsen, but he never fully mastered it. The words, the technique, the very creation of the sounds were far too complex for Maurice's inferior *pars opercularis*.[14]

So in the case of the Gzorazkian language, the old human

---

[14] Pars opercularis: the part of the human brain responsible for waving the tongue around and creating speech.

saying proved to be true: you can't teach an old dog new tricks.

CHAPTER 16

WHEN JOHN GALT IBSEN was three years old, he began to understand a little of what was going on. He realized that the language imbedded in his frontal lobe, the language nobody else spoke, was not like French, which Barbary Montclair and Maurice Yanne sometimes used to communicate, or like Spanish, which Bartholomew Barbate uttered in his sleep. It was something from another place—a place where there was more than black sky and white stars and gray walls.

Oddly, he remembered just such a place. It had vast craggy plains and blue oceans of water and shooting stars overhead and giant mushroom clouds of dust. Wherever it was that they were going, it must be like the place he remembered.

John Galt Ibsen wondered if the people there would speak to him in this other language that he knew so well. He liked

144

Gzorazkian so much that he carried on private conversations with himself in it. Sometimes he pretended to be as many as five different people at once. He discussed all sorts of things with his imaginary companions—things only a three-year-old with a sizable brain could understand.

"The stars are yellow and white," he would say in Gzorazkian.

"That is because some are sleeping and some are awake," he would reply.

"When we finally get to a star I will put it in a jar so I can have light all the time."

"But you will need to poke holes in the jar so it can breathe."

"And you need to let it out sometimes so it can run around."

"And Bill might peck at the star—you have to protect it from Bill."

"And from the others, too. They always eat so much, and there is not enough food to go around. Mother always says so. The others will eat the star when you are not looking."

"Maybe they will eat me, too, when they get really hungry. I am the smallest, after all, and I fit easily into the oven."

John Galt Ibsen was referring, of course, to the food shortage, which had finally caught up to the passengers of the *Destiny Unknown*. Just as Amanda Sphinx had predicted, they were nearly out of solid food fifteen years into their journey. A few vegetables were pushing up through the soil in Ginger Martin's garden. But as they supplemented their daily diets with more and more astronaut food, their feces became less and less fertile, and even the vegetable garden withered from lack of nutrients.

Had they planned better, they could have made the their natural food stores last them fifty years or more. But they consumed and consumed until nothing was left to hold their feces together.

That's the problem with humans everywhere in the universe: they consume and consume until there's nothing left to hold their shit together.

***

What was Head Chef Barbary Montclair, the man responsible for the famine, to do now? His knives had nothing to chop. His ovens had nothing to bake.

It wouldn't be long before Barbary took a knife to his wrists and an oven to his head. It would take four attempts and five chimpanzee tranquilizers, but he would eventually succeed in killing himself.

Esmeralda would be the first to realize Barbary was cooking himself in an oven. Her room was right above the kitchen and sometimes the smells of cooking wafted up through the vents. Four years after they left Nissan Sentra, and about two months after the kitchen was retired for lack of food, Esmeralda complained of a new smell—that of burning flesh.[15] She had smelled all sorts of things recently, so nobody took her seriously. It wasn't until an hour later—after Elijah Perkins-Borges had sufficiently medicated Esmeralda and tucked her into bed—that he smelled the burning flesh, too.

By the time Elijah got to the kitchen and pulled the chef's head out of the oven, Barbary Montclair, at age sixty-four, was as dead and well done as a Christmas turkey. *He* was the only thing he had ever overcooked in his life.

Esmeralda Fincus declared it a "senseless act." But to Barbary Montclair, it made all the sense in the world: with no food left to cook, he had no reason left to live. It would have been the same as if somebody had taken away Arthur Stanton's piano or Earl Updike's pen or the captain's indomitable sex drive.

***

The captain's sex drive was in no danger of extinction. He had found greener pastures in the form of a woman named Hannah Montgomery. Hannah had been eight years old when she first boarded the *Destiny Unknown* to the salute of a much younger Captain Marcus Fincus. Now,

---

[15] It is not at all uncommon for any *Homo sapiens* suffering from phantosmia to complain of the smell of burning flesh, or so it says in human medical texts.

more than sixteen years later, she was answering to a different sort of salute from Marcus Fincus. Her eight-year-old self would never have conceived of such an arrangement. Hannah and a man thirty-four years her senior?

Yet her twenty-four-year-old self didn't even bat an eye at the notion.

The reason her twenty-four-year-old self didn't bat an eye was this: Hannah Montgomery was *in love* with Captain Marcus Fincus. And it wasn't the kind of fleeting love Emma Greene had felt only in moments of midcoital ecstasy. It wasn't the old, tired love Esmeralda may have felt for Marcus Fincus in moments of reflection and loneliness. Hannah Montgomery had come into possession of a different kind of love, a real head-over-heels kind of love—the kind of love that makes humans extraordinarily stupid.

She had tried to quash her love for Marcus Fincus a million times. The captain was married, she reminded herself. He was old. He had a son somewhere. And if everybody's suspicions proved correct, Marcus Fincus had a daughter somewhere, too.

Hannah Montgomery was a pretty girl. She could easily find a man her own age. So why was a bright twenty-four-year-old girl like Hannah Montgomery throwing herself at a beat-up old man like Marcus Fincus?

One answer: pheromones.

Pheromones account for 95 percent of the stupid things a *Homo Sapiens* does.

***

After she'd graduated from Martha Marigold's class, Hannah Montgomery had studied under Ginger Martin in the seed lab for four years. Following her training in plant and cell biology, Hannah had interned with Elijah Perkins-Borges in the infirmary for another three years, simultaneously memorizing every medical text she could get her hands on. Her specialty was pediatrics. Hannah began treating the children aboard the ship whenever any of them got sick. It was a very active business, what with Elijah's four girls, and Lydia Anne Greene, and now John Galt Ibsen, whom she had helped deliver.

Whenever she had time to spare, and whenever the captain didn't need a quick romp in the sack, Hannah studied to be a surgeon. Elijah didn't really see the point because there was no way to practice surgery without surgical patients. The only surgeries these days were root canals or tooth extractions, and those fell under the jurisdiction of Maisey Perkins-Borges. The last time somebody had tried any sort of nondental surgery on the ship, that somebody had impaled himself on his own scalpel.

Hannah did not want to become a dental surgeon. She dreamed of opening chests and removing hearts and livers and kidneys. Because no hearts or livers or kidneys needed removing, Hannah practiced these operations in her head.

She began by watching old films of surgeries on the giant projector in the media center. Then Hannah would lock herself in a bathroom, put on classical music, and close her eyes and imagine she was doing the surgery in her head, and her hands would move gracefully over the sink as if they were sifting through intestines or sinew or brains.

Her fellow classmate, Robert Stowe, went on to specialize in epidemiology, pathology, and infectious diseases. He worked very closely with Richard Park, the expert immunization specialist, and came to understand the function of every vaccine, as well as the various stages of infection. Another fellow graduate, Raquel Muniz, studied otolaryngology and geriatrics. She worked closely with Elijah Perkins-Borges and saw the passengers whenever they complained of a stiff neck, a sore throat, an olfactory hallucination, and so on. And Harvey England, the fourth medical student to come out of Martha Marigold's class, became an anesthesiologist and radiologist. He studied anesthesiology with Maisey Perkins-Borges, practicing on dental patients. When there were no teeth to pull or cavities to fill, he fiddled around with the radiology equipment in the infirmary; he liked seeing the insides of people.

Harvey England would have really liked the super-spectrum x-ray telescope. Then he could have seen inside every person in the universe.

***

I have observed humans a long time through my super-spectrum x-ray telescope, seeing into their homes, into their bodies, and into their lives. I have written numerous reports documenting their behavior, and I have come to be something of an expert on the human species on my own planet. And there is one thing I have learned about humans that in all my studies I find to be true: human beings are rarely ever happy.

I am convinced it is psychobiological. They have no control over their happiness. They are in that subclass of sentient beings that is capable of comprehending the universe but unable to accept what they comprehend. Their experience is similar to that of a child who has just squashed a bug for the first time—the child understands she has killed the poor bug, but she still thinks she can undo it somehow. That's how humans experience the universe.

I feel sorry for them—human beings, not bugs. If their brains were just a tad bigger, they might make an admirable species—they might even be happy. But as it is, humans are always fighting endless battles to change the things over which they have little or no control.

What makes human beings so interesting, at least for me, is that they have managed to survive for so long in this universe with so little intelligence. I suppose miracles *do* happen.

That is something only humans have: miracles. Our species do not have miracles. Everything is a result of something that came before it and, with proper reasoning, the chain of cause and effect can be traced backward and forward with great precision. These chains of cause and effect are easy enough to comprehend. Their shapes and progressions are based purely on hard, cold scientific probabilities. And in our world, everything happens exactly as expected.

But humans live in a world of miracles. They wonder if a loved one will live or die, and when he or she lives, it is a miracle. They do not know if they will pass an exam, and when they pass, it is a miracle. And when they can't make a decision because they don't know all the probabilities, and they follow a course based on random judgment and succeed, it is a miracle.

The funny thing about all this is that sometimes, because they do not know the probabilities and because they believe in miracles, the thing that is certain to happen based on all my species' calculations does not happen at all for the humans. In fact, the complete opposite happens, defying everything we know about the universe.

Such a phenomenon is only observable in humans. It has come to be known as the Miracle Effect, and it is an object of great study among many of the most advanced scientific communities in the universe.

We think it only happens because humans are incapable of knowing the probabilities. It's like light: sometimes light acts as a wave, and sometimes it acts like a particle, all depending on the way you look at it. I have written many papers describing my theories about the human "miracle." I can only conclude that the miracle is a product of the way humans look at the universe.

And the humans have a name for this thing that makes their universe act as a wave while for the rest of us it acts as a particle. That name is *hope*.

Humans have hope. Hope is what kept the passengers of the *Destiny Unknown* going for all those years in space, after Austin Ibsen blew himself to pieces, after Nissan Sentra was destroyed by meteors, and even after they ran out of solid food to eat.

They had hope. If it hadn't been for hope, they would have all stuck their heads in the oven like Barbary Montclair.

That's the other funny thing about humans: they are not only capable of hope, but they also *need* it to survive. When a human loses hope, as Barbary Montclair did, he or she will usually do any number of irrational things to end his or her life. Most other creatures in the universe have no concept of hope and can go on living without it. But humans need hope as much as they need air or water or food.

And somehow hope changes the course of the universe. The humans don't know it, but whenever they hope, they alter the mathematical probabilities in their favor. And that is something even beings of higher intelligence cannot do.

Throughout my studies, I have come to care greatly for this subintelligent species composed completely of carbon proteins. Human beings can do wondrous things, even without superintelligence, even without superspectrum x-ray tel-escopes, even without anamorphic bodies composed entirely of light.

CHAPTER 17

YEAR 18

THE FIRST MESSAGE the passengers aboard the *Destiny Unknown* got back from the Gzorazkians went something like this:

> Glad to hear from you, neighbor. Sorry you are lost. The universe is so confusing. That is why we hardly go out anymore. We are expecting your ship at the afore-mentioned time. When our extraterrestrial signals team first received your message, we rolled on our backs for hours and hours. Your existence is the most important scientific advancement on Gzorazki since the invention of xeenolux. We anxiously await your arrival. We have plenty of fzexfza to go around, so you won't be hungry anymore.

The passengers aboard the *Destiny Unknown* speculated

that fzexfza[16] must be a common Gzorazkian dish. It sounded delicious, whatever it was, because it wasn't freeze-dried. They were already well into the third year of their freeze-dried food diet. John Galt Ibsen was six years old and could hardly recall the taste of real food. This was also about the time that everybody began to suffer from diverticulitis. The lack of fiber in their diets made them constipated, so much so that they began to bleed from their anuses anytime they tried to shit.

By this time, they were just over two trillion miles from the planet Gzorazki. So they sent another message to the aliens: "Looking forward to seeing you. Where do you recommend we land?" Rather than putting it into music, they made six-year-old John Galt Ibsen say it into a radio because they hoped to impress the Gzorazkians with how quickly they—meaning John Galt Ibsen—had mastered the Gzorazkian tongue.

The message, spoken in John Galt's soprano voice, had to travel across space at a finite speed, and the Gzorazkians had to form a response and then send a message back across space at a finite speed. So it wasn't until the ship was nearly in orbit with the planet before they got an answer: "Just about anywhere is fine."

Land anywhere? Marcus Fincus thought. What a strange thing to say. That kind of answer would not cut it back at NASA. Had it been the other way around, had the Gzora-

---

[16] Pronounced "vex-vah."

zkians been gearing up to land somewhere on Earth, all sorts of wars would have broken out between nations to see whose country would play host to the aliens.

But the Gzorazkians were a nationless people. The whole planet was one big commune of long-faced, round-shouldered creatures that rolled on their backs to express joy and gyrated the folds around their waists to attract mates. There was no division among their peoples, even on a planet almost twice the size of Earth.

How did they manage that?

In the big, wide universe, the real question is this: How did *Homo sapiens sapiens*, a relatively small subclass of sentient beings, manage to become so enormously divided?

***

From space, the planet Gzorazki was a milky-white bulb of quick-moving clouds. Beyond the clouds were hints of red and blue: land and ocean. From the relatively short distance at which they orbited, the passengers of the *Destiny Unknown* and the Gzorazkians could now communicate without any noticeable delay in the radio transmissions. Using John Galt Ibsen as a translator, they agreed to land the spacecraft a few miles above the equator on the continent Yzendorf[17] where the land was flat and level, and where, the Gzorazkians told them, they would be isolated from the busy

---

[17] Pronounced "Hus-sen-dorf."

cities of their people.

The last thing Marcus Fincus wanted was to land a space-ship on somebody's head—unless, he joked privately with Howard Oppenheimer, that somebody was his wife.

The planet Gzorazki had a rotational period of eighteen hours, meaning that every Gzorazkian day was three-quarters of an Earth day. The Gzorazkian year, as they would come to learn, lasted seventeen Earth months. And because of its highly elliptical orbit, Gzorazkians had two months of summer, three months of fall, three months of spring, and nine long months of winter.

And yet, all of this was preferable to no days or nights, no years or months, no seasons whatsoever in the wasteland of deep space.

They set down on Gzorazki on day 6,789 of their journey. Captain Marcus Fincus took charge of the wheel as they made their descent. The landing was beautiful, very well executed, everyone said, especially since Marcus Fincus was still a bit drunk from the celebration the night before. The captain had downed four glasses of champagne, three scotches, two martinis, and a screwdriver in observance of their safe arrival. And then Johannes Levi had handed him the controls of the ship like it was nothing.

Some humans can manage quite a lot on four glasses of champagne, three scotches, two martinis, and a screwdriver.

***

They landed during the early morning when the sky was still dark. But the sun was quick to rise, and when it came over the horizon, it shone dimmer and farther away than any sun the humans had known, casting an ethereal glow over the planet.

The *Destiny Unknown* had plopped down right in the middle of a meadow flanked on all sides by squat trees with broad trunks and wide-reaching branches. All the leaves on the trees and the grass in the meadow—which the ship had squashed flat—and the bushes and the weeds were various shades of pink and red. Not a speck of green was among them.

That should have been their first warning. But the humans did not know much about phosphorus-based life-forms. They did not realize that phosphorus-based plant life produces an agent similar to chlorophyll that makes leaves red the way carbon-based chlorophyll makes leaves on Earth green. No one belonging to the *Homo sapiens* species had never conceived of an entire planet of phosphorus-based organisms— of creatures totally unlike themselves. So they did not think anything of the crimson leaves and the scarlet grass and the rosy bushes and the amber weeds. They were far more interested in catching a glimpse of their alien hosts.

A thin veil of fog lay over the valley, shifting uncertainly from side to side as gusts of wind blew down off the distant mountains. The children—the Perkins-Borges girls and Lydia Anne Greene and six-year-old John Galt Ibsen—were all awake and staring out the portholes on the starboard side of the ship, watching strange white birds flit here and there and peck at fat grubs on the ground. The birds fluttering in the red grass looked like the white sails of ships on the bloody Nile. They, and the wriggling grubs, were the first and only signs of complex life in the early-morning light.

On the main deck, the half-drunk crew peered blearily out into the rising dawn. The dim red sun and the crimson forest looked like a fiery hell. But the white birds, which they would later learn were called cocoyucan, and which were something of a delicacy on the planet Gzorazki, gave the passengers the illusion of safety.

Presently, the ground began to shake, and the little white cocoyucan birds flew away. The crew stared out the front of the ship in silence and watched as four great bulldozers rumbled out of the trees, followed by maybe a dozen walrus-sized, mucous-colored creatures with long faces and round backs and thick, gelatinous bellies.

When John Galt Ibsen saw the Gzorazkians for the first time through the tiny porthole on the starboard side of the ship, he knew that these creatures were the ones whose language he knew so well and liked so much. He felt a strange sense of coming home, even though neither he nor any other human in the history of the universe had ever set foot on Gzorazkian soil before.

The four bulldozers surrounded the ship. Had anybody in CC been lucid enough to form anything more than monosyllabic sentences consisting of *ooh*, *wow*, and *shit*, they might have taken the Gzorazkians' behavior—surrounding them with large bulldozer-like trucks—as a sign of aggression.

Humans are apt to see aggression in almost anything.

As it was, the crew of the *Destiny Unknown* was too hungover to draw any reasonable conclusions.

The bulldozers came to a stop and waved their big, heavy plows at the ship. There was a low, steady rumble, like the sound of a thunderstorm, and suddenly the *Destiny Unknown* jumped six feet into the air. The ship jerked north, then south, then west, and finally east, where the red sun was rising. Everybody on the deck stumbled to the ground. The children fell back from the windows. Esmeralda, who had refused to leave her stateroom, even on this remarkable occasion, rolled right out of bed and sprained her thumb.

The passengers slowly rose to their feet and peeked out at the red landscape. Everything in the meadow stood perfectly still except for the four pulsating bulldozers.

For the rest of their internment on the planet Gzorazki, the *Destiny Unknown* would remain rooted to that spot, bound on all sides by an invisible force. The bulldozers weren't bulldozers at all. Instead of plowing things out of the way, these great big machines kept things in one place using a potent combination of gravitational, electromagnetic, and nuclear forces. On our planet, we have a word for this incredible force. We call it the *everything force*.

We also have a name for the bulldozers that held them there. We call them *natural-force simulators*.[18]

It was this everything force, which humans had long been trying to piece together in labs on Earth, that leashed the *Destiny Unknown* to the planet Gzorazki, and that might have been interpreted as a sign of aggression had the Gzorazkians not uttered in garbled language over a blaring megaphone, "We welcome you in peace."

John Galt Ibsen understood it perfectly. Maurice Yanne had to flip through his notes to get the gist of it, and this is how he understood it: "We offer you melons."

Either interpretation suggested that the humans were welcome on Gzorazki.

And they were.

What neither side knew at that moment was that the humans were carbon-based life-forms and the Gzorazkians

---

[18] Natural-force simulators are not rare in the universe. Like gravity simulators and moleculators, natural-force simulators play an important role in all advanced civilizations. Depending on the planet, natural-force simulators come in all shapes and sizes. Ours tend to come in the shape of sodium chloride molecules—that way they fit neatly into our cochleae. Natural-force simulators combine all four of the universe's natural forces into one single everything force. Most intelligent life-forms have mastered this trick, even if their natural-force simulators are big and clunky like the Gzorazkians' bulldozers. Human beings still struggle with the concept of the everything force—I dare say it is because of their second-rate brains. Human physicists have a name for this phenomenon, even though they are no closer to figuring it out than a chimpanzee is to figuring out thermodynamics. Human physicists call it string theory or, more aptly, the theory of everything.

were phosphorus-based life-forms, and neither could survive in the other's environment.

But the white birds and the grubs and the red plants and the walrus-size Gzorazkians deceived the passengers aboard the *Destiny Unknown*, and because the planet looked relatively safe, and because he was a little tipsy, and because he wanted to show off, Maurice Yanne volunteered to be the first to set foot on the alien soil.

He had been practicing the Gzorazkian language for many years now, and he could just manage to get out this much in the garbled tongue that only John Galt Ibsen could speak with ease: "On this day our two worlds meet for the first time under the same sun. We come in peace."

But when Maurice Yanne stepped out of the ship and onto the red grass, he only got as far as "On this day" before he fell to the ground, dead.

That's what you get for being a cocky son of a bitch.

How Maurice Yanne died will always remain a mystery. Whether it was the freezing cold temperatures of minus 291 degrees Fahrenheit that killed him first or the oxygen-deficient atmosphere, composed entirely of nitrogen and trace amounts of methane, nobody knows. The humans never had a chance to perform an autopsy. As soon as he collapsed, the Gzorazkians descended on his body like flies on manure—they realized right away that this human had died because he was not a phosphorus-based life-form like them. And they were curious to know what kind of life-form he was. So they picked up his frozen body and carried it away to be examined.

They did this so quickly that the humans watching from the portholes and the deck of the ship had little time to digest what had just happened. And when they realized the Gzorazkians had just carried away the body of their signals specialist as if he were a brick or a log, which he essentially *was* in those freezing temperatures, they began to worry.

What the humans didn't realize about the Gzorazkians, and what anyone with a superspectrum x-ray telescope could have told them years ago, is that the Gzorazkians are a race of beings with no regard for life of any kind, phosphorus or carbon based. They are not a violent race. In the scheme of things, Gzorazkians are really quite docile. However, to them, the miracle of life is about as miraculous as an igneous rock or a chewed-up fingernail. It does not occur to Gzorazkians that life in the universe may be something quite special.

Perhaps it isn't.

CHAPTER 18

YEAR 18

THE *DESTINY UNKNOWN* was stuck. It was tethered to the planet by the everything force, which tugged tirelessly at all four corners of the vessel. If Marcus Fincus even so much as tried to wriggle it free, the ship would shred into a hundred pieces. Now that Maurice Yanne was dead, the humans had no one to act as liaison between the Gzorazkians and themselves. A lethal environment—cold enough to freeze the heart in a single beat and deficient enough in oxygen to collapse the lungs in a single breath—surrounded them. Everything was so red, it could have been hell—except for the Gzorazkians, which were a murky booger green, and the little white cocoyucan birds, which on this Hades of a planet looked like merciful angels.

It is a well-known fact that Gzorazkians, despite their complete and total disregard for life, are some of the most harmless creatures in the entire universe. They are slow and gentle. They have no claws or teeth, and no motivation to be anything but docile and friendly, unless there is a famine of some sort, in which case they will eat one another.

So even though it was clear that the Gzorazkians had taken possession of Maurice Yanne's frozen body and of the ship, it wasn't entirely obvious that they were going to turn the humans and their ship into an entertainment attraction at an amusement park. It wasn't entirely obvious to the Gzorazkians yet, either.

The first thing Captain Marcus Fincus did when the Gzorazkians took away Maurice Yanne's body was summon six-year-old John Galt Ibsen to the deck to act as interpreter.

Here is the first question John Galt was asked to put to the long-faced Gzorazkians: What exactly do you breathe on your planet?

"Nitrogen, of course," the Gzorazkians replied over the ultra-high-frequency radio. "What do your people breathe?"

Because John Galt already knew the answer to this, he did not need the captain to tell him what to say. He replied in Gzorazkian, "Oxygen."

The long-faced Gzorazkians could be seen to murmur among themselves, and then one of them asked, "And what is your general composition?"

John Galt Ibsen was instructed to tell the Gzorazkians that they were carbon-based life-forms that breathed oxygen, drank water, and required other carbon-based life-forms to survive on.

The Gzorazkians turned out to breathe nitrogen. They drank liquid ethanol and required other phosphorus-based life-forms to survive on.

When the sun went down that first night on the planet Gzorazki, the passengers aboard the ship learned something else about the Gzorazkians, too: the Gzorazkians glowed in the dark, bright fluorescent pink, like glowworms in a cave. And they could be seen moving about the perimeter of the ship in slow, lazy circles, like neon lamps, taking measurements and notes. After their first conversation with the humans via radio, the aliens had switched off whatever signal it was that had made it possible for John Galt Ibsen to talk to them and were studying the ship carefully, discussing things that none of the humans could hear or understand.

When they found out the humans were carbon-based life variants and not phosphorus-based ones like themselves, the Gzorazkians became very curious. Gzorazkians are curious by nature. Just about as curious as human beings, one might argue. And curiosity can be dangerous. Throughout the history of humankind, many humans were known to do atrocious things to satisfy their curiosity. The only thing stopping most humans from growing human ears on rats and pulling the wings off flies is their basic regard for life—big and small.

Gzorazkians were just as curious as humans are. But they had no regard for life—big or small—and so curiosity had overcome any sort of compassion they might have felt for the humans. Instead of treating the humans as equals, as they might have done with any ordinary *phosphorus*-based life-form, and instead of discussing things with them to see if maybe they didn't want to be held down by the everything force, or if perhaps they'd prefer to have the body of Maurice Yanne returned to them, the Gzorazkians treated the humans just as humans treat lab rats and offered no explanation whatsoever for anything they did.

And they did all sorts of things. After about a week or so of hovering about the ship, a party of phosphorus-based engineers and physicists and astronomers and biologists from the farthest reaches of Gzorazki did the one thing the humans did not expect: they figured out a way to hack the supercomputer of the ship, and they opened the front door and walked right in. They wore white, protective jumpsuits with nitrogen-filled helmets and little air conditioners that kept them a comfortable minus 291 degrees Fahrenheit.

Even though he was only six years old, John Galt Ibsen was the first person to greet the Gzorazkians. The captain stood close behind with Johannes Levi and Melanie Lorne and Deidre Hundt and George McGraw and a slew of midshipmen and midshipwomen.

John Galt Ibsen asked in the alien tongue, "What do you want?"

The Gzorazkians just pushed right past him, and when the captain tried to bar their way, the Gzorazkians pulled out a long silver rod and zapped him. The rod was harmless; it simply sent a signal to the brain that told the little neurons and receptors there that it was time for beddy-bye. When the rod made contact with the captain's shoulder, he let out a sleepy yawn and fell to the floor. Johannes Levi, thinking the captain dead, threw up his hands and surrendered immediately.

There were four space suits on the ship, each with enough oxygen to last the humans three days outside the ship. The space suits came equipped with heaters that kept their wearers a comfortable seventy-two degrees Fahrenheit. The Gzorazkians, with gentle prodding, made Deidre Hundt, Melanie Lorne, Johannes Levi, and a trembling George McGraw climb into the space suits and follow them out onto the grassy meadow and into a waiting vehicle.

All four humans were returned three days later, with empty oxygen tanks and no recollection of what had happened to them and scarred bodies, bruised and cut and stitched back up.

Three days later, the Gzorazkians returned and made the same four crew members get into the same four space suits with four brand-new oxygen tanks, and they took them away again.

This time only three humans returned. While in the custody of the aliens, Deidre Hundt had woken from whatever anesthetic the Gzorazkian doctors had administered. She had seen her guts scooped out and sitting beside her. And she had seen poor Johannes Levi on an examination table, his head completely severed from his body and his brains being vacuumed out through his neck. When she related her story to the rest of the passengers on the ship, they cried out in terror. Here was their worst nightmare: they were being dissected like lab rats.

John Galt was put on the radio to demand exactly what the Gzorazkians thought they were doing. The demand was met with static.

What they were doing, however, was this: the Gzorazkians were studying the humans to see what made them tick. If they could understand the correlation between carbon-based life and phosphorus-based life, the Gzorazkians might be able to solve the one big mystery of the universe: how does life begin? The humans were specks in a petri dish as far as the Gzorazkians were concerned. If one human being died on the operating table, there were forty-nine others to choose from.

The Gzorazkians also figured they could breed the humans to augment their supply.

And after about three weeks, that's exactly what they began to do.

CHAPTER 19

YEAR 18

THE GZORAZKIANS came onto the ship with their tran-quilizer probes, and they zapped everybody in their path. They swept past Deidre Hundt, Melanie Lorne, and George McGraw and went straight for four new victims: Albert Morris, Anita Lund, Emma Greene, and Hannah Montgomery. The hostages climbed unwillingly into space suits, and off they went into the waiting vehicles.

When they returned, they had no memory of what had befallen them. Not one of them had any cuts or bruises, or any hint of injury whatsoever. However, a week later, Anita Lund, Emma Greene, and Hannah Montgomery began to sense something strange stirring in their bellies. A quick examination by Elijah Perkins-Borges revealed that all three women were pregnant.

Every few days, the Gzorazkians whisked the pregnant women away to their laboratories, where they were given routine shots and checkups and ultrasounds. Before returning to the ship, the women were forced to swallow thick green pills that smelled of manure.

The fetuses developed quickly, much more quickly than was normal. When Elijah and his medical staff examined the women a fortnight later, they could see little heads and noses and fingers and could easily identify the sexes of the babies. When Emma Greene had a miscarriage in her third week, the infant was almost fully developed, with little glassy eyes and a mop of brown hair on his head.

In the fourth week, Anita Lund gave birth to a healthy baby boy, eight pounds, four ounces. She named him Ryan Hollander after the boy she had kissed at Craighead Caverns in her youth.

A few days later Hannah Montgomery gave birth to Mitchell Xavier Montgomery, nine pounds, seven ounces.

Both Ryan Hollander and Mitchell Xavier Montgomery would inherit the stout frame and droopy eyes of their biological father, Albert Morris, manager of Clean Space Janitorial Services.

How, Elijah wondered, could the fetuses develop so quickly? What were the Gzorazkians doing to these women?

The answer: somewhere in the green pills that smelled like horseshit was something that caused the women's reproductive processes to speed up. That something was a chemical compound called xeenolux.

Shortly after the birth of Ryan Hollander and Mitchell

Xavier Montgomery, the Gzorazkians took Albert Morris, Emma Greene, Anita Lund, and Hannah Montgomery away again, and when they came back, Albert's testes were drained and the women's fallopian tubes were swimming with his spermatozoa yet again.

***

Meanwhile, Marcus Fincus was hatching a plan to get them the hell out of there. Maurice Yanne was dead, his lungs collapsed and his heart frozen. Johannes Levi was gone, his head lopped off and his brains vacuumed out. Three of the passengers had been violated by a turkey baster filled with Albert Morris's sperm—not once but twice now. And because the planet was dominated by phosphorus-based life-forms, there was nothing anywhere on the planet for them to eat—they were still surviving off the emergency stores—the freeze-dried astronaut food.

The Gzorazkians had plenty to eat. They survived on a diet of raw fruit from the fzexfza trees and the roasted bodies of the cocoyucan birds. Both proved toxic to the humans, possessing poisonous levels of hydrazoic acid, which is highly explosive at room temperature.

They learned of this on an occasion when the Gzorazkians arrived to take Emma, Anita, and Hannah away for their routine examinations. As the Gzorazkians entered the ship, a stray cocoyucan bird flew in though the open hatch.

173

As soon as its little feathered body hit the warm air in the ship, it swelled up like a balloon and burst like a bomb. The levels of hydrazoic acid in its blood created an explosion powerful enough to blow the head off the nearest Gzorazkian.

That's when Marcus Fincus got it into his head that they might be able to collect enough hydrazoic acid to blow the Gzorazkians to smithereens.

It seemed plausible, but bringing hydrazoic acid onto the ship was like inviting a hand grenade in for tea. So they went about collecting hydrazoic acid very slowly over a period of many months. Every time the Gzorazkians entered the ship, they tracked in mud and grass and little bits of dried leaves on their big boots. When the Gzorazkians were gone, Ginger Martin and Richard Park gathered the little bits of grass and leaves with tweezers and stored them away in freezers in the lab. At night, when the Gzorazkians were less likely to peer through the portholes, Ginger Martin and Richard Park went to work extracting trace amounts of hydrazoic acid from the scraps of leaves and grass.

It was hardly anything at all—dewdrops. But collected over many months it could, just maybe, amount to something. So they collected and extracted and stored the hydrazoic acid away in an icebox, one drop at a time.

***

In the meantime, the Gzorazkians had taken a special interest in John Galt Ibsen. They were curious to know how this Earthling had come to understand their language so well. They built him a child-size space suit, and they let him out of the ship to roam among them. He was just a child, and because he understood the Gzorazkians so well, he did not fear them as the others did. He was allowed to wander the grassy valley where the ship lay stranded, guarded on all sides by small armies of long-faced, round-backed Gzorazkians who treated John Galt like a pet poodle.

Amanda Sphinx could hardly bear to watch her little boy being paraded about thus. The sight of John Galt cavorting with these monsters was so unbearable to her that she resolved to spend her days in the library reading up on how to transform trace amounts of hydrazoic acid into a weapon of mass destruction.

Meanwhile, John Galt Ibsen was getting to know the Gzorazkians better. Yes, they could be ruthless and cold. But when they weren't cutting off human heads or impregnating innocent women, they were remarkably similar to humans. The Gzorazkians were gentle and loving with their young ones. They told jokes and made up stories to entertain one another. The Gzorazkian children often played in the meadow with a bouncy kickball. They always invited John Galt to join them and, whenever he did, the children fought over whose team he would be on.

So John Galt Ibsen became a dual citizen of sorts. Every

day after lunch, he put on his space suit and went out to play with the Gzorazkian children. He was always back in time for dinner. Amanda Sphinx would emerge from the library and ask him if he had enjoyed himself. And John Galt would nod and slip out of his space suit. After dinner, Amanda would tuck him into bed, and then she would descend to the laboratories to share with Ginger Martin and Richard Park what she had learned that day about bomb making.

Amanda Sphinx had mixed feelings about John Galt playing with Gzorazkian children. She did not want him to stay forever cooped up on the ship, and she figured so long as John Galt was friends with the long-faced creatures, they were less likely to vacuum his brains out of his head. She did not yet know that the Gzorazkians would just as happily vacuum the brains out of their own children's heads if they had a good reason to do so.

CHAPTER 20

YEAR 18

PRETTY SOON A SMALL CITY sprang up around the ship. There were little huts and labs and mess halls squirming with Gzorazkian scientists from all over the planet. The children of the scientists played games around the ship, sometimes bouncing a ball against its walls.

Esmeralda complained of a pounding in her head. Whenever the drumming of the ball on the side of the ship began, Esmeralda clambered out of bed and screamed at the Gzorazkian children through the stateroom porthole. The Gzorazkian children seemed to like this, so they went on bouncing the ball against the ship, pointing and laughing whenever Esmeralda showed up with her hair in curlers.

John Galt Ibsen was their only contact with the outside world. He came back with tidbits of gossip he learned from the other kids. This is how they learned that the Gzorazkian government had fenced off a section of land ten miles in diameter around the ship. Just beyond this perimeter were hordes of Gzorazkian civilians hoping to get a peek at the visitors from outer space. John Galt Ibsen brought back a magazine he had scavenged out of a waste bin. In it was a series of photographs of Johannes Levi, his body sliced into cross-sections, and the pieces labeled in Gzorazkian lettering that not even John Galt Ibsen could read. The centerfold was a picture of Johannes Levi's head in a jar, his eyes wide open, with an abnormally wide grin on his face.

These photographs prompted Ginger Martin and Richard Park to work faster to extract hydrazoic acid from little bits of leaves and grass tracked onto the ship. Nobody wanted to be the next Johannes Levi and have a smile stretched clear across his or her face like a Cheshire cat.

And nobody wanted to be one of the artificially insemi-nated women growing fetuses in their wombs at an unnatural rate. Emma Greene suffered the most of the three. She was thirty-eight years old, and her body had just begun to settle down for the long sleep of menopause when she found her-self unexpectedly violated by a turkey baster full of Albert Morris's sperm. She was pretty much on her last leg as far as reproduction went. She only had about three or four dozen viable eggs left in her ovaries, and her aging body was no longer equipped to deal with the pressures of pregnancy.[19]

---

[19] Emma lost the first six children she carried, much to the curiosity of the Gzorazkians, who had no idea why a woman of Emma's age would expe-rience difficulty giving birth. It was only on the seventh attempt, just

***

After the second month marooned on Gzorazki, and after Emma Greene's second miscarriage, the landscape around the ship began to change. The compound had grown in size. The adobe huts were replaced with brick-and-mortar buildings. The roads were paved with sticky tar, and a fleet of construction vehicles rolled in from the outside world: bulldozers, cranes, forklifts, and an assortment of vehicles unknown to man. The passengers of the *Destiny Unknown* looked on from the portholes of the ship and watched as ditches were dug and tracks were laid for the first-ever human zoo.

The Gzorazkians were building an amusement park with rides and shops and games and a dunk tank and swings and a carousel, with the *Destiny Unknown* at the center of it all— the main attraction. A winding trail of scaffolding was erected around the ship, directing foot traffic past the windows on every level—past the commissary and the laboratories, past the bedrooms and the storage facilities, past CC— so the Gzorazkians could see into many of the rooms and

---

before the passengers of the *Destiny Unknown* escaped, that Emma gave birth to a healthy baby boy. The other two women were more successful. Hannah Montgomery managed to pump out six boys, each four or five weeks apart. Anita Lund carried seven babies to full term, delivering every single one on the twenty-first of the month like clockwork.

observe whatever the humans happened to be doing.

When the park first opened, ten thousand Gzorazkians came to see the humans in their oxygen tank, crowding around the portholes, banging on the glass, making all sorts of noises and faces, slobbering over fried cocoyucan on a stick, and waiting for the humans to do something interesting.

The only passenger comfortable with all this attention was Bobo the chimp. Bobo was born in a subterranean zoo where every crap he took was caught on somebody's video camera and splashed all over the Internet. So Bobo didn't seem to mind when all the Gzorazkians started crowding around portholes and banging on the glass and making all sorts of faces. He ate, slept, and defecated as he always had.

The rest of the passengers were not quite as comfortable eating, sleeping, and defecating in front of the Gzorazkian tourists. Many passengers took to hiding down below during the day and waiting until dark, when the park was closed, to surface for food and water.

***

John Galt Ibsen was no longer allowed to mix freely with the Gzorazkian children. He was taken out every day and made to walk up and down in front of Gzorazkian crowds. The ringmaster, a tawny-gray Gzorazkian female, taught him to perform all sorts of tricks—like touching his toes and blinking his eyes and crawling on his hands and knees—on command. Being only six years old, he did not resent this treatment; he was always rewarded with uproarious applause. And he was just as curious to know about the Gzorazkians as they were to know about him. So he observed the Gzorazkians closely from his little podium. He watched them run around and play carnival games and spin upside down on roller coasters, and he listened carefully to all their talk. While eavesdropping on a conversation between the ringmaster and one of the stagehands, John Galt Ibsen learned something else: Gzorazkians eat their young.

Due to the planet's highly elliptical orbit, winter on Gzorazki was so long and cold that the planet would descend into darkness and famine for seven months out of the Gzorazkian year. So every year when winter set in, the Gzorazkians would slaughter, skin, and roast their own children to feed the rest of the family.

This practice of feasting on their young led to the invention of xeenolux, which they had been administering to Emma Greene, Anita Lund, and Hannah Montgomery. It accelerated the speed of pregnancy so that the Gzorazkian females could give birth to as many as seven children each winter to be harvested for food.

When six-year-old John Galt Ibsen learned what was being done to the Gzorazkian children each winter, he got it into his little head that he would be next on the menu. And this very well may have been true if John Galt Ibsen had been a phosphorus-based life-form. As it was, John Galt's flesh and blood was just as poisonous to the Gzorazkians as theirs was to John Galt.

As the months progressed, the weather became bleaker. The cocoyucan grew fewer, and the fzexfza turned brown and fell from the trees, and the prices of fried cocoyucan continued to rise until at last the park restaurant closed for the winter.

Then John Galt Ibsen noticed something else: each day, as he performed in front of the crowds, there seemed to be fewer and fewer children, while the adults seemed to be getting fatter and fatter. Eventually many of the children belonging to Gzorazkians in the compound, the ones John Galt had played with over the autumn months, began to disappear. And only the strongest, healthiest children were spared. They would grow into strong, healthy adult Gzorazkians who would, in turn, skin, roast, and eat their own children in winters to come.

CHAPTER 21
YEARS 18-19

AS METHANE SNOW began to fall in the valley, the Gzo-razkians closed the amusement park for the long winter, and John Galt Ibsen began to spend more time back on the ship. The Gzorazkian ringmaster took John Galt out from time to time for the amusement of private guests and dignitaries. But mostly, due to heavy snowfall and torrential methane rains, the humans were left alone for the winter. That is, excepting Emma Greene, Anita Lund, and Hannah Montgomery who, five months after their initial abductions, remained under the close observation of Gzorazkian obstetricians; all three were pregnant for the fifth time.

Emma Greene had been unable to bring a pregnancy to term under the Gzorazkians' care; she had suffered four mis-carriages and was severely depressed from the psychological toll. Her skin and muscles began to sag and droop from the physical strain, and every inch of her body felt decades older than when she first set foot on Gzorazki. She celebrated her thirty-ninth birthday in the infirmary under the watchful eye of Elijah Perkins-Borges. Emma was just about to blow out her birthday candles, which burned feebly in a round mold of astronaut paste, when she began to bleed. Elijah ushered Lydia Anne Greene and the other visitors out of the room. They returned several hours later to find Emma staring vacantly into a bloody pile of washrags. The baby would have been a boy.

That night Emma Greene tried to kill herself. Raquel Muniz found Emma the next morning on the infirmary floor in a pool of blood with a suicide note crumpled in her hand. But before Raquel could call for the doctor, the Gzorazkians burst into the infirmary. They scooped Emma up and slipped her pale body into a space suit. And off they went.

For weeks, there was no sign of Emma Greene. Lydia Anne, her only daughter, grieved for her mother under the care of Elijah and Maisey Perkins-Borges, while the other passengers redoubled their efforts to collect enough hydrazoic acid to assemble a bomb.

Emma Greene reappeared one morning in the air-lock chamber. The Gzorazkians had brought her aboard the ship in the middle of the night and left her sitting alone in a roughly soldered wheelchair. She was as bald as a peach; not a single hair was left anywhere on her body.

After a thorough examination, Elijah Perkins-Borges found evidence that a small drill had been inserted into the back of Emma's head—bits of her brain had been removed, making Emma as docile as a kitten and as dumb as a doornail. She sat for hours on end staring into space.

And she was pregnant for the sixth time.

When Marcus Fincus first set eyes on Emma Greene in her feeble condition, he retched. Marcus Fincus could not reconcile the rich memories of his former mistress with this hairless, sexless lump of flesh. And it troubled him deeply.

But Marcus Fincus would soon forget his affair with Emma Greene completely. He would forget a lot of things. For some time now, Marcus Fincus had been exhibiting symptoms of dementia: He sometimes inquired about Johannes Levi or Maurice Yanne, both of whom were long gone. He grew angry and confused when he encountered John Galt Ibsen in the corridors and mistook him for the long-lost Jason Fincus. And on occasion he awoke in the middle of the night and sat at the controls of the *Destiny Unknown*, thinking he was still adrift in space, only to jump out of his skin whenever a Gzorazkian sentry strode by on the other side of the viewport.

Some things, however, the captain did not forget. Now that his most recent mistress, Hannah Montgomery, had become a baby-making machine, the captain had to find another outlet for his libido, which, at the age of sixty-one, proved no less potent than it had been at the age of twenty-one.

Much to her dismay, the captain abandoned Hannah

Montgomery for a new liaison: Margaret Frost, the arts and literature teacher. Margaret had started out as Martha Marigold's pupil, had risen to become Martha Marigold's apprentice, and was now in the process of annexing most of Martha Marigold's duties as schoolteacher. Margaret Frost, like Hannah Montgomery, was twenty-seven years old and remembered meeting the captain as a young girl boarding the ship. But unlike Hannah Montgomery, Margaret wasn't sleeping with the captain out of some foolish quest for love. No. Margaret Frost simply wanted a good romp in the sack.

Before catching the eye of the captain, Margaret had aspired to bedding all of the men on the ship her own age, the boys she had gone to school with. In this endeavor, however, she had enjoyed only mild success. It wasn't that she wasn't pretty. She was a very beautiful girl. But Margaret had one trait, one annoying quality that made it virtually impossible for any person to bear her company for more than fifteen minutes—Margaret was an incessant talker.

Many of the men who had tried had given up just before the finish line. Margaret kept talking, all through the kissing and the petting and the stroking. Try as they might, her suitors could never bring themselves to commit the final act of passion in the face of such unassailable odds.

But when Captain Marcus Fincus went on the prowl for a new mistress, Margaret Frost saw her chance. She caught him one evening when he was alone on the bridge. The captain had wandered in after curfew in one of his demented states, thinking they were still trillions of miles from solid ground. He sat in his chair and gazed out the viewport at a handful of long-faced, round-backed elephant seals in lab coats. He was wondering what in the world elephant seals were doing out in space when Margaret Frost crept quietly through the door to CC, which Marcus Fincus had left ajar, and surprised the captain by jumping onto his lap.

She felt his erection spring up almost instantly. And even though she talked nonstop, she managed to get him undressed without any noticeable change in the stiffness of his member.

The truth was this: he wasn't listening to her at all. The captain had the uncanny ability to tune out any sort of unpleasant chatter. After all, he had been cooped up with Esmeralda Fincus for nineteen years.

Once Margaret had stripped him down and taken off her own clothes, to the elation of the Gzorazkian onlookers, she climbed aboard. The captain's skin was raw and leathery like sandpaper. Margaret Frost didn't mind. He surrendered to her every whim. So she satisfied herself in all the ways she imagined a woman could be satisfied until he erupted on her thigh.

The Gzorazkians rolled on their backs in elation.

***

When the Gzorazkians brought Emma Greene back to the

ship with parts of her brain missing, she no longer recognized her thirteen-year-old daughter, Lydia Anne Greene. Lydia Anne was grief stricken. She had grown up not knowing her father, and now she had lost her mother. Lydia Anne was at that impressionable age when she desperately needed somebody to scream and throw things at, somebody to hate when the hormones raged, somebody who would love her no matter what she said or did in the volatile years of her adolescence.

Because she had no such person in her life, Lydia Anne Greene was forced to grow up much too fast. She began taking care of her mother, who could no longer do anything very useful except carry a baby in her stomach. With the help of Anita Lund, they changed her bedsheets and fed her astronaut food and got her in and out of her pajamas. Lydia Anne Greene mastered the art of finding a vein for an intravenous needle and learned how to take Emma's blood pressure and how to check her temperature, and she even kept a chart marking her progress.

Emma Greene had her sixth miscarriage a few weeks later, and this time she didn't cry or curse or even flinch. When Elijah Perkins-Borges offered to dispose of the embryo, Emma Greene dropped six silver nickels into his hand and said, "Bury it with these." Nobody knew how long she had held on to those nickels or why she wished them buried with the fetus, and nobody asked. Elijah Perkins-Borges flushed them down the trash chute with the bloody remains of Emma's child.

Amanda Sphinx pitied poor motherless Lydia Anne Greene. So she invited Lydia Anne to join her in her cabin. John Galt Ibsen slept in a child-size bed at one end of the room, and Amanda Sphinx slept next to Lydia Anne on the queen-size bed Amanda had once shared with Austin Ibsen.

Every morning, Lydia Anne checked on Emma Greene to see if her condition had improved overnight. And every morning, Emma Greene looked at Lydia Anne and asked, "Who the hell are you?"

Lydia Anne would reply, "I've come to change your bed-pan," and she would help Emma Greene sit up and eat her breakfast and would take her blood pressure and then leave without a hug or a kiss or any other sort of friendly reassurance that the woman inhabiting Emma Greene's body was still, in fact, her mother.

Then Lydia Anne would return to Amanda Sphinx's cabin to dress for school. She helped John Galt Ibsen into his clothes, and together they would walk down the long corridor holding hands until they reached Ms. Marigold's schoolhouse, a small, warmly lit room on the second level of the living quarters, where for two hours every day they would study arts and literature with the disheveled mistress of Marcus Fincus, Margaret Frost.

During those dark days on Gzorazki, going to school was just something for the kids to do to occupy their time. Nobody thought the children were going to grow up to have meaningful lives. They imagined that they would forever be trapped on the planet Gzorazki in a human zoo, their every movement being watched by a thousand prying eyes. They also knew the children would live short lives; at the rate they were going, they would run out of astronaut food before any of the children reached forty.

The Gzorazkians were doing a poor job coming up with an alternative source of food for the humans. They had tried and failed to produce a carbon-based compound that would supplement the diets of the passengers on the ship. The first time the Gzorazkians brought them what they hoped would pass for sustainable food, it came in the form of a pale rubbery cube. Because the passengers of the *Destiny Unknown* were so tired of astronaut food, and because their bodies craved any other form of sustenance, they were quick to converge on the rubbery cube. Not only did the rubbery cube cause severe diarrhea, but it also caused severe hallucinations. For nearly six hours, the passengers of the *Destiny Unknown* were running about the ship, scratching madly at what appeared to be small spiders crawling up and down their arms and legs.

The passengers on the *Destiny Unknown* were more cautious the next time the Gzorazkians served up a rubbery cube. But since the humans were just as invested as their captors in finding an effective substitute for food, the bridge crew drew straws to determine who would be the first to sample whatever the Gzorazkians had cooked up.

Nothing the Gzorazkians invented ever stayed down for long. The unlucky men and women who swallowed the stuff suffered an assortment of ailments: hives, rashes, headaches, fevers, diarrhea, and dizzy spells. And nobody was ever any more nourished for it.

***

Hannah Montgomery was pregnant with her sixth child when she learned that the captain, with whom she was so very much in love, was sleeping with Margaret Frost. Although she pleaded desperately with him, Hannah could not convince Marcus Fincus to give her another chance. Thanks to that mysterious compound xeenolux, Hannah was the mother to five small children with a sixth on the way, and the captain had never been fond of children. He had barely tolerated Jason Fincus.

The sorry truth of the matter was that neither Esmeralda nor Marcus Fincus were suited to raise children; Esmeralda possessed no detectable trace of motherliness, and the captain was far too much of a Casanova. Except for the rare moments of familial affection captured on daytime talk shows and splashed across the covers of pop magazines in the days leading up to the *Destiny Unknown*'s departure, Jason Fincus had never known parental affection.

Nevertheless, Hannah Montgomery went to the captain one night while he was sitting at the controls of the ship watching the methane snow come down outside. The door was ajar, as it was most nights when the captain was in. Hannah dropped to her knees before the captain and begged to be taken back. Marcus Fincus waved her away.

"Can't a man have any privacy around here?" he barked.

He was, in fact, waiting for Margaret Frost to appear at any minute to sit on his lap.

Hannah Montgomery left without a word. She was just turning a corner when she bumped into Margaret Frost. Hannah's fury was so great that she launched herself and her swollen belly onto Margaret and tore at her hair, clawed at her eyes, and punched at her face, knocking out several teeth and breaking Margaret's pretty little nose.

Then Hannah ran off, leaving Margaret and her teeth on the floor of the corridor.

Margaret went to Elijah and Maisey Perkins-Borges straightaway to have her missing teeth replaced and her broken nose reset. The captain was never made aware of any of this—neither Margaret nor Hannah wanted word to get around that there had been a squabble between two of the captain's mistresses.

The captain waited for Margaret to join him on the empty bridge, growing more impatient with each passing minute. When he finally concluded that he had been stood up, he relieved himself in front of a single Gzorazkian zookeeper that happened to be making the rounds.

After Margaret Frost failed to appear that night on the

bridge, Marcus Fincus lusted after her more than ever. That is the way it works for 87 percent of all humans: they want only what they can't have.

***

Hannah went into labor the next morning. She sweated and panted and screamed, and Maisey held her hand just as she had held Margaret's hand the night before when Elijah snapped her broken nose into place.

Hannah's baby weighed a whopping sixteen pounds five ounces, the biggest baby ever born on the *Destiny Unknown*. He was as pink as a piglet, with a fierce cry that alerted everyone on the ship to his sudden arrival. Hannah held the newborn boy for about five minutes before the Gzorazkians appeared to take him away. Just before he was wrenched from Hannah's arms, she gave him a name: Reginald Montgomery, after her great-great-grandfather, who had been the largest baby born in human history at twenty-three pounds two ounces.

When the passengers sat down to supper that night, the crew drew straws to see who would be the first to sample the rubbery cube that had just arrived from the Gzorazkian food lab. Deidre Hundt drew the unlucky straw. She hesitantly sliced into the pink cube, took a bite, and braced herself for the usual side effects. But none came. The cube was edible! The passengers rejoiced. At last the Gzorazkians had come up with an adequate substitute for food.

The cube was passed around the cafeteria until only a sliver was left, which Maisey Perkins-Borges brought to Hannah in the infirmary.

Hannah bit into the rubbery morsel and felt a tiny crunch. She spat it out and examined the chewed-up goo. Then she found what had made the crunch: a tiny human fingernail.

The rest of the passengers, still enjoying their portions of cube in the cafeteria, heard Hannah's scream all the way from the first level. And they dropped their forks in sudden realization. They had just eaten Reginald Montgomery.

CHAPTER 22
YEAR 19

THE GZORAZKIANS, unable to come up with a solution to the humans' food shortage, had decided to deal with the problem the way they dealt with the winter famines on their own planet: the humans would have to eat their young.

And when the Gzorazkian nutritionists saw how much the humans were enjoying Reginald Montgomery, they patted themselves on the backs and immediately sent a letter off to the Gzorazkian press with the tagline "Humans eat their own young. More like us than we thought."

But when the humans unexpectedly threw down their forks and stuck their fingers down their throats to induce vomiting, the Gzorazkian nutritionists were baffled—here the humans were perfectly capable of digesting Reginald Montgomery, but instead they were voluntarily throwing him up all over the floor.

"What a waste of perfectly good protein," the Gzorazkians murmured to one another.

Another press release went out correcting the first: "Humans would rather starve to death than eat their own young. Further proof of inferior intelligence."

***

It was high time they got out of there. The passengers had collected several kilos of red roughage tracked in on the boots of Gzorazkian technicians. Ginger Martin and Richard Park spent many late nights in the lab with little syringes and compressors and steamers and tweezers and, as carefully as possible, squeezed every ounce of hydrazoic acid out of every specimen of phosphorus-based flora that had come their way. The result was a pickle jar full of hydrazoic acid.

When the pickle jar was brimming with the explosive compound, it was time to set the trap. Now it was up to Amanda Sphinx, who had found everything she needed to know about explosives in the supercomputer's vast digital database, to design four powerful bombs to be used to blow up the four menacing bulldozers that held them fast to Gzorazki.

Worried that the Gzorazkians could understand English, the passengers invented a code name for the bombs. They called them "the biscuits." "How are the biscuits coming along?" they would ask Amanda Sphinx. "Is the dough rising on schedule?"

For many weeks, all anyone could talk about were biscuits, except for Emma Greene, that is. She had no room in her scrambled brain for talk of biscuits. Most of her time was spent staring out at the methane snow from the starboard cabin she shared with Anita Lund.

Lydia Anne Greene stayed by her side, feeding her, changing her linens, and checking her vitals. In the fourth week of Emma's seventh pregnancy, Harvey England performed an ultrasound and confirmed the baby was alive and kicking. It was a boy, Harvey confided to Lydia Anne; he had ten fingers and ten toes, and he would probably grow up to look just like Albert Morris.

Lydia Anne Greene gaped at the squirming figure on the pulsating ultrasound and started to cry.

Emma Greene had no such reaction to the blob of black-and-white static. She grimaced at it as though it were a bug.

"Nurse," Emma barked at Lydia Anne Greene, "whatever that is, I don't want it."

Lydia Anne Greene named him Emmett, after Emma.

"What's an Emmett?" Emma Greene demanded.

***

On the other end of the ship, Esmeralda Fincus was cooped up in her cabin arranging and rearranging pillows. She was like a caged bird, guarding her stateroom with fierce attachment. She never went out, and she didn't welcome visitors. And nobody bothered to keep her informed—especially not the captain, who nine nights out of ten slept in his big comfy chair on the bridge. So when Anita Lund came in to vacuum the floor and started talking about the biscuits in the oven, Esmeralda thought she actually meant real biscuits.

"That's what I smell burning," Esmeralda announced.

Then after a pause she added, "If anyone deserves a biscuit, it's me. I think I am owed a biscuit, being the captain's wife and all."

Anita Lund nodded and said, a little more forcefully than either of them expected, "Yes, if only I could give you a biscuit right now."

***

The bombs, when finally constructed, were crude things. They looked like something out of an elementary school science fair: long cylindrical canisters with screws and wires and knobs, a pressure gauge, and a digital thermometer. And somewhere deep inside the canisters was the hydrazoic acid, which, via remote control, could be made to ignite at any time.

Each bomb had a safety latch, which had to be unhinged manually to prevent the bombs from detonating inside the ship. But even with the safety latch, the passengers were wary of going anywhere near the things.

Emma Greene was due to give birth any day now, which

gave the passengers added incentive to make their escape, lest the Gzorazkians try to cook little Emmett Greene, too. The plan was made, and the date was set. There was no turning back now.

It was a Tuesday by the Earth calendar. Because it was the dead of winter on Gzorazki, the park was closed, and the only living things out in the valley were the zookeepers and a few stray scientists who lived year-round on the compound. As the sun set lower and lower in the sky, most of the Gzorazkians who had ventured out into the snow returned to the comfort of the bungalows at the edge of the park. Those who remained did so begrudgingly—they were the nighttime security, and they prowled the perimeter of the park, circling ever inward toward the ship and then circling outward again until they reached the edges of the valley. It was a cold night, even by Gzorazkian standards, and as the sun set, the passengers on the ship, pretending to go about their everyday business, could see the fluorescent glow of the security guards shimmering pink in the deepening twilight.

One thing John Galt Ibsen had learned parading among his captors was that Gzorazkians have terrible night vision. Their bodies had evolved to glow in the dark so that they could make out one another in the darkness.

When the sun had set and the whole of the valley lay in shadow, it was time to unleash the attack. For many weeks, the humans had studied the nighttime trajectories of the glowing pink gourds, and they knew exactly how to maneuver around the ship without ever being seen or heard.

Four deckhands were ordered to plant the bombs at the bases of the bulldozers: George McGraw, who was eager to "blast them all to hell"; Edith Young, a midshipwoman who had assisted Maurice Yanne before he died and who was now, for lack of a better word, unemployed; Percival McQueen, a midshipman with the dirtiest mouth anybody had ever heard; and James Nguyen, another midshipman.

They were told that they had very important jobs, that they had been selected for a mission of great honor, and that they stood the best chances of eluding the Gzorazkian scum.

The real reason they were chosen was this: they were expendable.

So these four neophytes suited up in the service closet where their Gzorazkian keepers could not see them. They adjusted the pressure gauges and the thermostats on their space suits to withstand the icy, hostile conditions that awaited them. And when all the glowing pink security guards had disappeared around the quarterdeck, they engaged the starboard air lock and, bombs in tow, dropped noiselessly into the methane snow.

The passengers watched with bated breath from their cabin portholes. They could just make out the outlines of the four mercenaries against the crystal-white snow. The bulldozers loomed one hundred yards away, and the snow measured three feet deep, so it was with great effort that they made their ways to the respective targets.

The Gzorazkian guards executed their rounds like clock-work. The four crew members knew exactly what evasive maneuvers would prevent them from being found out. They sidestepped and sashayed and ducked and trotted, zigzagging through the snow like a troupe of dancers. Never once did the Gzorazkians suspect that the humans, at times merely inches away, were among them so abysmal was their night vision.

A quarter hour of this manic game of hide-and-seek, and the four mercenaries at last arrived at their respective posts. They got down on their bellies like dogs and dug little pits underneath the bulldozers for the bombs. Keeping the Gzorazkian guards in sight, they camouflaged the bombs with snow and quickly began the involved dance that would carry them back safely.

All seemed to be going according to plan, and it looked as if the captain wouldn't have to expend any of his expendable crew members after all, when suddenly a Gzorazkian guard, in the course of his rounds, stumbled on human footprints in the snow, footprints belonging to Edith Young. The Gzorazkian guard stopped dead in his tracks, and the whole dance was thrown into chaos. The four crew members froze and waited to see what the perplexed guard would do next.

The guard, squinting in the dark, began to follow the footsteps closer and closer to where Edith Young lay hunched in the snow. She was paralyzed with fright. Nothing—not the roaring scream within her psyche nor the silent wills of those watching from the portholes—could get her to move another inch.

Edith remained rooted to the spot as the glowing ember that was the Gzorazkian guard edged ever closer, straining to see past the tip of his snout.

The guard was almost on top of Edith when a long beam of white light shot across the valley, illuminating a patch of snow a few feet from where the guard stood. The guard turned and, with his beady eyes, followed the beam of light to its source, as did the eyes of every passenger aboard the *Destiny Unknown*.

What they saw was this: John Galt Ibsen stood in the snow in his child-size space suit, a high-voltage flashlight in hand. He waved the light back and forth across the snow so the guard would see him. The guard turned around and made for the child, thinking it was John Galt's footprints he had been following all along.

When he finally caught up with John Galt, a few words were exchanged, and then the Gzorazkian gripped the boy by the arm and led him back to the ship. The guard triggered the air lock with something that looked like a garage door opener, patted John Galt on the shoulder, and nudged him inside.

When the hatch closed, the guard continued on his usual route, and the dance began again. Edith Young unglued herself from the snow and inched back to the ship in a stupor. She could not feel anything in her fingers and toes.

Amanda Sphinx retrieved John Galt Ibsen, showered him with kisses, and scolded him for being so foolish. John Galt Ibsen was perplexed—it seemed his mother could not decide whether to be angry or proud.

The four others returned some minutes later, caked in methane snow and shivering all over—not because they were cold, but because they had come so close to being caught. Edith Young didn't know how to thank a six-year-old boy for saving her life, so she went to her trunk and dug up an old Hershey's chocolate bar she had been saving, one of the last traces of real food on the ship, and handed it to John Galt. He devoured it hastily. It was the first time John Galt Ibsen had ever tasted real chocolate.

Marcus Fincus invited John Galt Ibsen and his mother to stay on the bridge and watch the rest of the spectacle unfold from the main deck.

The bombs had very patriotic names: Justice, Freedom, Felicity, and Chance. Howard Oppenheimer typed his ID into the control panel, and for the first time in seven months, the engines of the *Destiny Unknown* hummed to life. A great flurry of snow and ice spewed out from beneath the ship, throwing the guards into a frenzy. Within moments, an alarm sounded, and the compound came to life. Every bungalow lit up in the darkness, and a mass of pink fluorescent blobs surged toward the ship.

Then the captain gave the command. "Justice—*go!*" and James Nguyen flipped a switch. For a fraction of second, nothing happened. Then, in the northeast corner of the valley, there was a mighty roar as one of the bulldozers disappeared in a flash of light.

The Gzorazkians scattered. Some took refuge in the bungalows, others sprinted for the edges of the compound, and still others dove toward the ship, hoping the humans were not stupid enough to blow themselves up.

The captain cried, "Freedom—go!" and Percival McQueen threw his switch. There was a second explosion as the northwestern bulldozer crumbled to the ground.

Before the captain could give the command, Edith Young detonated Felicity, and the crew cheered as the third bulldozer fell.

The ship was off the ground, hovering twenty feet in the air, tethered only by a single thread of everything force. The Gzorazkians who'd had the sense to rush the ship were gathered below, aiming harpoons at the craft's underbelly. But they couldn't find a mark—the *Destiny Unknown* bucked and hitched, making broad arching sweeps across the valley and tugging tirelessly at the final bulldozer.

Then the captain gave the last order, "Chance—go!"

George McGraw flipped his switch and...nothing.

George McGraw tried again and again, yet the bomb would not detonate. The remote was passed to the captain, who had his hand at it to no avail. Then it was passed to the engineers, who popped open the back and peered inside to see if they had gotten all the wiring right.

And then George McGraw, who was staring out the window at the chaos below, said, "I forgot to remove the safety latch, sir."

Everybody on the deck froze. Then the captain launched himself onto George McGraw. A bloody brawl left George McGraw with a dislocated jaw before the captain was dragged to the other side of the deck and was restrained by his loyal deckhands.

Meanwhile, the ship swept about the valley like a fish caught at the end of a line, tugging so hard at the everything force that the joints and crossbeams in the hull were beginning to buckle. It was John Galt Ibsen, that marvelous child, who had the sense to take the wheel and keep the ship from shredding itself to pieces.

There was no escaping even one bulldozer of everything force. While George McGraw lay bleeding on the floor and Marcus Fincus struggled against the hold of Howard Oppenheimer, John Galt Ibsen guided the ship back into place and held it high enough above the ground to keep the Gzorazkians with their harpoons and tranquilizer probes from boarding. And then there was nothing left to do but wait.

CHAPTER 23

YEAR 19

BY MORNING, the Gzorazkians had uncovered the fourth bomb and disposed of it, but only after they had determined that hydrazoic acid was the primary explosive agent. Then three more bulldozers trundled into the meadow, and together with the remaining fourth, they lowered the *Destiny Unknown* to the ground, where it was anchored and secured.

There were no weapons on the ship save two handguns, a few butcher knives, and four flare guns that could at the very least render an average-size Gzorazkian unconscious. Other than that, the humans were defenseless. They had not anticipated waging war with an alien species, which is ironic since humans are almost always anticipating waging war with someone.

The passengers armed themselves the best they could— Marcus Fincus and Howard Oppenheimer with the pistols; Deidre Hundt, Melanie Lorne, Percival McQueen, and James

Nguyen with the flare guns; and the rest of the crew with knives and forks and rolling pins. On the captain's orders, George McGraw brandished only a basting brush.

The bridge crew manned the air locks while the rest of the passengers retreated to their cabins. Amanda Sphinx and John Galt Ibsen sequestered themselves in the downstairs service closet.

An army of Gzorazkians with tranquilizer probes had amassed outside. The captain was determined to keep the aliens from boarding; he was sure they had come to remove bits of their brains to make them placid and taciturn like Emma Greene, who remained staring out of her cabin window while Anita Lund and Lydia Anne Greene barricaded the bedroom door.

The captain led the vanguard, pistol loaded and his finger on the trigger. When the air lock hummed open and the first Gzorazkian stepped aboard, the captain wasted no time. With incredible precision, Marcus Fincus fired a single bullet into the intruder's head. The bullet didn't kill the intruder—Gzorazkians have extremely tough skulls. Rather, the rush of heat and oxygen that flooded his helmet asphyxiated him within seconds.

The Gzorazkians retreated at once. None of them was fazed by the death of their fellow Gzorazkian, of course. Death does not faze a Gzorazkian. But they hadn't expected a proper resistance from the humans, who, up until then, had done so little to fight back.

The gunshot resounded throughout the ship like a rocket blast. For those stowed away in the hull, it came to them only in vibrations. Then there was silence.

The silence dragged on for hours. John Galt Ibsen fell asleep in his mother's lap. Some of the other children started up games of cards in the rooms where they were waiting. Even the deckhands became distracted and took turns watching the air locks so the others could eat and sleep.

After what seemed like an eternity, a large truck rolled into the valley and circled the *Destiny Unknown*. The ship's crew regrouped and took up their stations while Deidre Hundt followed the truck's progress around the perimeter of the ship. The truck braked near the northeasternmost corner of the ship. Then the Gzorazkians unraveled a large hose from the truck, and the nozzle disappeared somewhere out of sight beneath the vessel.

When the truck hummed into action, it took Deidre Hundt only a moment to recognize what they were doing: they were piping some sort of chemical into the air supply of the ship. But before she could warn the others, the gas hit her and she toppled over.

The gas was hazy and pungent, and it poured out of the vents and heating shafts and crept along the ground, slipping under doors and through keyholes. The crew members guarding the air locks fell flat within seconds, their weapons clattering like a drawer of utensils.

When Lydia Anne Greene saw the hazy gas pour in

through the ventilation shaft, she rummaged through her emergency kit, which she had shrewdly assembled as the others were arming themselves with blunt objects, and pulled out the portable gas masks she had swiped from the infirmary. Before the gas could creep into their lungs, she and Anita fitted themselves with the masks. Then they fitted one over Emma Greene's blank face.

Within minutes, Lydia Anne, Anita Lund, and Emma Greene were the only people aboard the ship still fully conscious. It was a good thing, too, because, at that very moment, Emma Greene's water broke. Anita and Lydia Anne laid Emma down on the bed, stripped off her clothes, and began timing her contractions.

Meanwhile, the Gzorazkians roamed the ship, gathering the unconscious bodies of the passengers and dragging them into the library and piling them in the middle of the floor like sacks of bricks. It took them a good hour before they reached the barricaded room where Anita Lund and Lydia Anne Greene were working to pry a baby from the cervix of Emma Greene.

The barricade held long enough for the women to successfully deliver Emmett Greene from Emma's womb. Anita Lund, being a sensible woman, removed her gas mask and placed it over the head of the screaming newborn. Then she collapsed in a heap on the floor.

The placenta and the rest of the bloody afterbirth came next, splashing onto the bed. Lydia Anne toweled the baby off and wrapped him in a pillowcase. Emmett cried loudly as the Gzorazkians hammered away at the barricaded door. Only then did Lydia Anne notice that Emma lay pale and still upon the bed, her eyes wide open and staring blankly at the ceiling. When Lydia Anne checked Emma's pulse, she found that Emma's neck was already cold and stiff.

The Gzorazkians swooped in and carried off the body of Emma Greene. Then they apprehended Lydia Anne, baby Emmett, and the unconscious Anita Lund and hauled them into the library where the rest of the passengers were piled haphazardly on the floor. Lydia Anne's first thought was that everybody she had ever known was dead. But when she checked the pulses of the still bodies, she found them alive and breathing.

The Gzorazkians, having hacked into the mainframe of the ship, jammed the doors of the library and music room and shut off the flow of toxic gas.

The passengers awoke in a tangle of limbs. Deidre Hundt found herself at the bottom of the heap with three cracked ribs; she cried desperately for help as everyone pushed and shoved to unravel from the writhing mess that had accumulated on the floor. Another voice rang out from the bottom of the dogpile—it was Esmeralda Fincus. She could be heard screaming shrilly, "Rape! Rape!" although no such thing was occurring.

Once everybody was sorted out and Deidre Hundt was tended to, the passengers of the *Destiny Unknown* hunkered down and watched the Gzorazkian sun arch across the sky through the great glass dome. They were mostly thankful that none of them, save Emma Greene, was dead. After some time, Amanda Sphinx decided to lighten the mood by playing a waltz on the piano in the music room below. Arthur Stanton joined her sometime later on the fiddle, and their lyrical duet drifted up the spiral staircase and into the library, lending some peace of mind to the passengers huddled around the musty old bookshelves and antiquated furniture.

Finally the Gzorazkians arrived with a coffer full of astronaut food and four jugs of water. They kept watch over the humans as they ate, and when all the food and water were gone, they took Richard Park and Ginger Martin and little John Galt Ibsen with them into the hallway outside.

This is what they said, and little John Galt translated: "Where did you get the hydrazoic acid?"

Richard Park told them.

"Do you have any left on the ship?"

Richard Park and Ginger Martin both answered no.

Then the Gzorazkians took Ginger Martin and Richard Park and John Galt Ibsen into the laboratory where they had already found the pickle jar with four remaining tablespoons of hydrazoic acid.

Richard Park shrugged.

Until that time, the Gzorazkians hadn't been sure if human beings were capable of lying, as it is a rather uncommon talent in the universe.

Once the Gzorazkians had confiscated the pickle jar, they asked if any other explosives were aboard the ship.

"No," Richard Park said. "That's everything."

The Gzorazkians muttered skeptically. And then they took Richard Park and Ginger Martin and John Galt Ibsen on a walking tour of the entire ship, during which they searched every cabin, closet, and lavatory for any other little surprises the humans might be hiding.

When they got to the hull of the ship, where the humans kept the bags of seed and grain, one of the Gzorazkians stuck an arm into a sack of wheat germ and then jumped back with a scream.

Attached to his gloved finger was a rat the size of a baked potato. The rat's teeth had pierced right through the finger of the space suit, releasing an icy spout of nitrogen. The rat fell to the floor, stunned by the frigid air, and the afflicted Gzorazkian quickly plugged up the leak in his space suit with the thumb of his other hand.

The Gzorazkians searched the remaining sacks, scooped up half a dozen writhing rats, dumped them into a temperature-controlled icebox, and carried the vermin away to be studied.

When the search was completed and no hydrazoic acid was found anywhere else on the ship, Richard Park, Ginger Martin, and John Galt Ibsen joined the others in the library, where the first thing Richard Park said, pointing a finger straight at Esmeralda Fincus, was this: "I told you so!"

There were, in fact, rats on the ship, rats carrying the bacteria *Rickettsia typhi*, which had killed Brandelyn McCormack seventeen years earlier. Rats that Esmeralda Fincus had argued could not possibly exist under the watchful eye of her husband.

The great debate was finally settled.

CHAPTER 24

YEAR 19

WHEN THE GZORAZKIANS were satisfied that the humans possessed no other traces of hydrazoic acid, they disembarked and unbarred the doors to the library.

At last, the passengers were free to roam about as they pleased. Esmeralda returned promptly to her stateroom, only to find everything in disarray. And just like a persnickety bowerbird, she began sorting and arranging and moving things back the way she liked them.

The captain and his crew—except for Deidre Hundt, whose ribs needed examining in the infirmary—returned to the bridge to assess the damage. All their weapons—the pistols and flare guns and knives and rolling pins—were still in their possession. The Gzorazkians had left them exactly where they had fallen. The humans assumed this was a gross oversight on the part of their captors.

The truth of the matter was this: the Gzorazkians were

curious to see if the humans would turn the weapons on one another.

***

The following evening, just as the sun was setting over the valley, Lydia Anne Greene saw her mother for the last time. Lydia Anne was gazing out the porthole at the methane snow, cradling little Emmett Greene in her arms, when a procession of Gzorazkians marched by with shovels and picks and hoes. They came to the edge of the clearing and began digging. Then they brought out the corpse of Emma Greene. Parts of her shaved skull looked like they had been hewn open and then soldered back together, and a series of large, sewn-up scars crisscrossed her abdomen.

They dropped her broken body into the hole and covered it with mud and snow.

***

Little Emmett Greene was an easy baby. He mixed right in with Anita's seven newborns and Hannah's six boys. Most of the other passengers never knew exactly whose kids were whose. They were all about the same age, having been born over the span of seven months.

The mothers would breastfeed until their nipples throbbed, and then they'd fall back on the ship's limited supply of infant formula. And Anita and Hannah were quick to lend a hand in the care of Emmett Greene, even if that meant nursing him from time to time.

The other passengers helped look after Emmett, too. But the real burden fell to thirteen-year-old Lydia Anne. She rocked Emmett to sleep at night, burped him when he was gassy, changed his diapers ten times a day, and carried him with her wherever she went. Everybody was so busy worrying about the Gzorazkians and arguing over what to do now that none of them noticed how much like a mother young Lydia Anne had become.

All the babies born on Gzorazki would grow up to be stubby people, the tallest reaching only five feet three inches. They had stubby hands and feet, and stubby little noses, too. Several factors could have explained this: The xeenolux, which expedited the pregnancies, could have caused deformities in the embryos. The powerful gravity on the planet Gzorazki could have stunted the growth of the infants in the womb. The shortage of milk and infant formula might have led to underdeveloped bones. Then there was the father of all these babies, Albert Morris, who was a stumpy man with stumpy genes.

***

Lydia Anne took to staring out portholes at the methane snow, just as her mother had done, cradling Emmett Greene in her arms and contemplating all the ways she could end her misery. She sometimes wondered where her father was and why he wasn't rushing to her side to spare her this unhappy existence.

Captain Marcus Fincus was wondering the same thing: Where was the father of this poor girl, and why wasn't he doing his duty by her? The dementia had made him forget long ago that *he* was the father of Lydia Anne Greene.

Thinking only of his duty as captain of the ship, he suggested to Esmeralda that they take the Greene children in.

Esmeralda derided him. "Why? So you can lose them, too?"

She was, of course, referring to the loss of Jason Fincus, their one true son. Marcus Fincus had forgotten all about Jason Fincus. Then, a few days later, he forgot all about Lydia Anne and Emmett Greene.

So Lydia Anne and Emmett Greene spent their days with Anita Lund and her seven children, talking of things like colic and diapers and milk temperature, so that Lydia Anne sometimes felt decades older than she really was.

***

Then one night, as Lydia Anne was staring out at the desolate landscape and imagining hanging herself from one of the barren trees, she noticed a commotion in the Gzorazkian compound at the edge of the clearing. A medical vehicle came and went, and then another, and then another. This went on all through the night.

The next morning, the meadow was deserted. The Gzorazkian guards had disappeared. So had the zookeepers and the biologists in their white lab coats.

Lydia Anne alerted the captain, who immediately armed his crew with pistols and flare guns and knives and rolling pins, and posted them at the air locks should the Gzorazkians launch another attack.

But the Gzorazkians never ventured into the meadow. They could be seen at the edge of the clearing, darting from bungalow to bungalow, wearing what appeared to be surgical masks and gloves.

The following morning, the Gzorazkians began erecting large clear domes around some of the buildings—most notably the laboratory where they had taken Johannes Levi to have his head chopped off. By midafternoon, they were dragging dozens of dead bodies into the meadow—Gzorazkian bodies.

For three whole days, the bodies kept coming. They were heaped in a pile midway between the ship and the bungalows. The passengers watched nervously as the Gzorazkians would venture out into the meadow, throw another body onto the pile, and then sprint like mad back to the bungalows.

Eventually, large trucks came to take the dead bodies away. Buses came, too, whisking away families with children. And still more and more dead bodies kept turning up.

Then several armored cars rolled into the compound, and Gzorazkians in hazmat suits poured out and began marking off the boundaries of the compound with flags and red tape. They started with the ship, planting heavy posts in the snow and erecting a tall chain-link fence around the vessel.

A week went by with no further signs of the Gzorazkians whatsoever. The compound was quiet. The bungalows were dark. An eerie silence crept over the valley.

Then something miraculous happened. A single Gzorazkian, dressed head to toe in a hazmat suit, trudged into the empty meadow with a red icebox held at arm's length. He stopped briefly at the tall fence surrounding the ship and then—hesitating only a moment—he lobbed the red cooler over the fence and ran back the way he had come.

Marcus Fincus ordered George McGraw out into the snow to retrieve the icebox.

George McGraw trudged through the snow in his heavy spacesuit. He lifted the red cooler carefully in his hands, thinking maybe this, too, was a bomb, a final retaliation.

He made to return to the ship, but the captain, standing in clear view on the bridge, waved at him to stay where he was. Then the captain motioned for George McGraw to open the cooler right then and there in the methane snow. George McGraw slid back the white lid.

Rats. Six furry, frozen rats. They were the rats that had been taken from the ship weeks ago—dead, yellow teeth bared, piled one on top of the other.

George McGraw angled the icebox so that everyone on the bridge could see.

And then another miracle occurred. The constant humming from the bulldozers—which had accompanied their lives every day since they had landed on that forsaken planet—suddenly stopped. The ship creaked and groaned, releasing pent-up tension in its joints and crossbeams. Then silence.

The *Destiny Unknown* was free.

George McGraw leaped aboard the ship just as the humans received their final transmission from the Gzorazkians, which John Galt Ibsen translated.

"Go away and take the furry things with you."

The captain didn't need an invitation. He revved the engine, and in a matter of seconds, the *Destiny Unknown* was out of sight.

***

Let us stay a little while longer on the planet Gzorazki. Nearly two million Gzorazkians died of typhus fever before the outbreak could be contained. The Gzorazkians never did develop a vaccination. Rather, they euthanized any Gzorazkian they suspected of having the disease and catapulted the dead bodies into space. The outbreak was ranked the third-most devastating epidemic in the history of the planet. And

Gzorazkian children—those who survived the winter feasting—were always taught to avoid humans and their furry companions should they ever make contact again.

BOOK THREE: ADRIFT

CHAPTER 25
YEARS 19-23

WHEN I CAUGHT UP with the *Destiny Unknown*, the captain had steered the ship clear of the Gzorazkian sun toward a cluster of nineteen bright stars that appeared—although the humans had no scientific evidence to support it—to be relatively close. Nobody had any better ideas, and because the cluster was so dense, it seemed reasonable that they might find a life-sustaining planet orbiting one of these bright stars.

They called the cluster the Keith Cluster after the Scottish clan to which Captain Marcus Fincus claimed some distant affiliation, and whose crest he had tattooed on his shoulder. A pulsing Cepheid variable star in the cluster put its distance between four and eight light-years away.

They still had a good twenty-five years' worth of astronaut food left in the hull of the ship, and because nearly as many people had died as had been born on the journey, they were in decent shape for another interstellar adventure.

The six rats that had been responsible for the outbreak of typhus on Gzorazki were hailed as heroes. Elijah Perkins-Borges, a veterinarian at heart, ran several tests on the little rat corpses to be sure none of them was carrying some other disease that could prove fatal to anyone on the ship. The rats tested negative for everything but that menacing bacteria *Rickettsia typhi*.

The six rats that had saved their lives were scrubbed and stuffed and put on a shelf in the library to be admired by the passengers. And despite Esmeralda's objections to living on a ship full of vermin, nobody dared harm any of the remaining rats stowed away down below. So when the humans did at last colonize a new planet, rats and fleas abounded and forever plagued the humans, as they had done on Earth.

Now that the ship was aloft, the passengers of the *Destiny Unknown* found themselves happily employed again and very busy indeed. The ship had been out of service for thirty-two weeks, and it needed a good fixing up. The engineers went into the bowels of the ship to perform routine checkups on all the essential components. Fortunately, they found most everything to be in working order—here a screw needed tightening, there a gear wanted oiling, but otherwise, the ship was in good shape.

At the ripe old age of fifty-seven, Bartholomew Barbate was called on to inspect the wiring of the ship's controls and to replace a few faulty circuits. He was slow and grumpy and tired of being pulled out of retirement to perform what he considered mundane tasks such as screwing in light bulbs and flipping fuses. On top of that, it seemed to him that the serving portions in the commissary were diminishing by the day. What was once a feast had been reduced to a single gel pack, a powdered drink, and a multivitamin for every breakfast, lunch, and dinner. For the first time in his life, Bartholomew Barbate was losing weight.

And for a long time the passengers were, for the most part, happy. Nobody was afraid of having his or her brains vacuumed out. And except for Esmeralda going on and on about the smell of rotting fish and burning hair and sour milk, there were no complaints and no mishaps for four glorious years.

Martha Marigold retired, and Margaret Frost founded the Martha Marigold Preschool for the stubby-nosed children who had been born on Gzorazki.

Lydia Anne Greene turned seventeen, and one day little Emmett Greene called her *mother*.

"No," Lydia Anne replied. "You don't have a mother."

"Do I have a father?" Emmett asked.

"Not that I know of," she said, lying, even though he bore a striking resemblance to Albert Morris.

"Then where did I come from?"

"I picked you off a tree."

"Why?"

"Because I wanted a brother."

"Oh," he said. This seemed like an entirely reasonable explanation to him.

Around the same time, John Galt Ibsen turned eleven. He was easily smarter than the other children, and when he and Emmett Greene were alone in the library thumbing through picture books about knights and dragons, John Galt said to Emmett Greene, "You *did* have a mother. She died when you were born."

"Why?" Emmett Greene asked.

"Because aliens sucked the brains out of her head."

"What about my father?"

"He's the guy who does the laundry," John Galt answered.

"Oh."

Later that evening, Emmett Greene and John Galt Ibsen sneaked downstairs and peeked into the laundry room to get a closer look at Albert Morris. Emmett Greene hadn't ever really paid him much attention before, and he saw right away that Albert Morris was short and fat and hairy and that he had sweat stains under his armpits and was prematurely balding. For a dad he was unimpressive. But he was something. And Emmett Greene loved him instantly.

***

John Galt Ibsen and Emmett Greene were spending a lot of time together. Emmett followed on John Galt's heels wherever he went and sat across from him in the commissary and sometimes spent the night on the floor in his and Amanda Sphinx's cabin. They were like brothers. And since neither of them had a father, they relied heavily on each other for affection.

And so it was that John Galt Ibsen was the first to notice the bluish tint to Emmett Greene's skin. It was most evident in his lips and around his fingernails—skin the color of blueberries. It spread to his cheeks and hands whenever they played a game of tag in the library or raced from one end of the ship to the other.

Lydia Anne had noticed it once or twice, too, when Emmett Greene came back from playing with John Galt. She would touch his forehead with the back of her hand and ask him if he felt ill. He always said he felt fine.

The truth was he didn't feel fine. He was often tired, and his breathing was uneven. Every so often he would feel his heart jump, like a drum missing a beat, and he would stagger a little to one side and rest his head against the wall until the feeling passed.

Then one day, when John Galt Ibsen was conducting a game of "red light, green light" in the corridor, Emmett Greene fainted midsprint and fell face first onto the carpeted floor. Elijah Perkins-Borges was summoned immediately; he managed to rouse little Emmett, whose lips and ears and nose were blue.

They took him to the infirmary, where Hannah Montgomery put a stethoscope to his chest and heard what she described as a *murmur*. She sent him off to Harvey England for chest x-rays, which revealed an enlarged heart in his exceptionally tiny body. To be thorough, and because he had never done it before and didn't want to miss the opportunity, Harvey England conducted an echocardiogram to check for heart defects. He detected a rather severe leak in the right and left atriums of the heart due to a faulty tricuspid valve.

Emmett Greene was diagnosed with Ebstein's anomaly, which explained the blue discoloration of his skin, his trouble breathing, and his fatigue. Because his condition had been overlooked for so long, the leak had grown so severe that little Emmett was in desperate need of surgery, lest he die of heart failure.

The only person who knew anything about heart surgery was Hannah Montgomery, who had been practicing on the empty air above the bathroom sink for years.

Lydia Anne Greene appealed to Hannah to have the surgery done. Hannah protested at first, claiming to know nothing about repairing a tricuspid valve in a four-year-old child. But when she saw little Emmett Greene on the table, his blue lips quivering, she confessed that she had practiced the surgery a dozen or so times—in her head—and knew the procedure well enough. However, she wasn't sure that she was fit to cut open a real, live, beating heart, especially since she had never seen a real, live, beating heart before—except in textbooks and films.

Lydia Anne pleaded, and seeing no other option for Emmett Greene, Hannah agreed to research the surgery further and practice it a few times in her head before making any final decisions. Meanwhile, Emmett Greene remained in the hospital bed, carefully monitored by machines and charts and a beeping electrocardiograph. Only after Emmett Greene went into cardiac arrest two weeks later, and after several electric shocks to his enlarged heart brought him back to life again, did Hannah Montgomery agree to repair the leaky valve.

She performed the surgery with her eyes closed. Every now and then she blinked open a single eye to make sure her scalpel was in the right spot, but otherwise, she worked blindly, visualizing every cut and every stitch as she had done more than a dozen times in the bathroom mirror.

And when it was over, Emmett Greene's heart thumped out a regular beat, and his lips were the color of raspberries.

After her success, there was no doubt in Elijah's mind that Hannah Montgomery belonged in the surgical ward. Passengers who had been coping with heart and liver and kidney ailments for years—because there hadn't been a trained surgeon since the death of Dr. Myles Jamison—thronged to the infirmary to be healed by this new virtuoso. Hannah Montgomery performed every surgery with her eyes closed. And she never once slipped in a pool of blood and fell on her own scalpel like the late Dr. Myles Jamison.

Hannah could not, however, save Bartholomew Barbate.

He had lost so much weight so quickly on the astronaut diet that his body was unable to cope with the stress, and one night in his sleep his heart simply stopped trying.

They carried him out of his room on a stretcher, naked, since he slept in the nude. It took six grown men to lift him. He had been sixty-one years old, and although he had lost a whopping 227 pounds over the past four years, he still weighed as much as a refrigerator.

Bartholomew Barbate was the first and only passenger aboard the *Destiny Unknown* to die of natural causes. He was shot into space in a periwinkle bathrobe, since that was all anyone could manage to fit on his enormous stiff body.

When the power went out on the ship a week later, it took the entire crew twelve hours to figure out what Bartholomew Barbate had been doing all these years to keep them illuminated. It was this: unplugging the battery and then plugging it back in again.

Anything more complicated than that was beyond them. They had lost Austin Ibsen years before, and they had failed to produce an adequate electrical engineering apprentice since, so for the next twenty-one years, as small bits and pieces of the ship malfunctioned—the coffee maker, the PA system, the sliding doors—the passengers would shrug and say, "Well, there goes that." And they would go on living without whatever it was. In that way, the *Destiny Unknown* was getting older, too.

CHAPTER 26

YEAR 24

THE FOLLOWING JANUARY, Martha Marigold celebrated her seventieth birthday with a party. There were balloons and streamers and a jazz band composed of Amanda Sphinx, Arthur Stanton, and the four Perkins-Borges girls. It was meant to be a surprise. However, Martha Marigold caught on to the ruse when Ruth and Olivia Perkins-Borges quizzed her about her favorite jazz musician, her favorite color, and her favorite flavor of astronaut paste.

Incidentally, the only person who was surprised by the surprise party was Captain Marcus Fincus, who had seated himself in the library among the balloons and streamers and gifts and had promptly forgotten why he was there. When Martha Marigold walked in and everybody yelled surprise in unison, he sprang up like a jack-in-the-box, drew the pistol he had been packing since their departure from Gzorazki, and swung it around like a poorly handled fire hose.

Howard Oppenheimer and George McGraw eased the captain back into his chair and wrenched the sweaty pistol from his hands. They hid it in the downstairs service closet inside a box of laundry detergent.

When the captain finally realized he was at a birthday party, he barked, in a voice loud enough to carry to the back of the ship, "Who the hell is Martha Marigold?"

Deidre Hundt escorted the captain back to his cabin and deposited him in bed next to a protesting Esmeralda Fincus.

"I don't want him here!" Esmeralda cried. "He wets the sheets." To which the captain responded by crying like a baby.

Deidre Hundt closed the door on the bickering couple and stood guard until, at last, the captain and his wife fell asleep.

The jazz band played until nine o'clock, after which Martha Marigold thanked everybody with an eloquent speech that she pretended to make up on the spot. Then the guests retired to their cabins.

Much later that night, Elijah Perkins-Borges sat straight up in bed, much to Maisey's bewilderment, and switched on the lamp. He had just remembered that it was Bobo's birthday, too. The chimp was twenty-six.

***

The following morning, the captain had no recollection of the party. He only wondered where his pistol had gone.

Esmeralda drove him out of bed with three hard kicks. Then she rolled over and went back to sleep.

In the mess hall, Deidre Hundt politely ushered the captain to the front of the line, afraid he might have another outburst if he wasn't served immediately. Everybody found some excuse to take breakfast in his or her own room, and the captain found himself sitting alone in the cafeteria with John Galt Ibsen, who regarded him with bold indifference.

John Galt Ibsen, prone to telling the truth, told him what happened the previous evening.

The captain was startled and ashamed. Then, slipping into another fit of forgetfulness and believing John Galt Ibsen to be his very own Jason Fincus, he said, "When I am no longer able to run this ship, I want *you* to be captain."

John Galt Ibsen shrugged and squirted a glob of toast paste onto his spoon. He knew it was just crazy talk. The captain was giving him what the passengers began to refer to as "the foggy eye," which meant the captain's mind had traveled back in time a decade or two. As it was, John Galt Ibsen was already planning to be captain someday. He knew full well that it didn't matter whether Marcus Fincus wanted it or not.

***

In the rare moments that Marcus Fincus was fully lucid, he was thankful to John Galt for his honesty. Nobody else would dare tell him that he was suffering from dementia and was no longer fit to captain a ship. On the days when the captain had the foggy eye, Howard Oppenheimer took it on himself to steer the ship in the right direction. Howard was a passive, quiet man—not much of a leader. He nudged the ship this way and that when the captain wasn't paying attention, wordlessly keeping course as the captain rambled on about his past affairs.

Howard Oppenheimer was not a young man, either. He would turn sixty-one at the end of the year, and although he still had all his wits about him, he was anemic and suffered from chronic fatigue. So when the captain was swiveling around in his chair regaling the crew with stories of his earliest trips to the moon, Howard Oppenheimer dozed at the controls with his face smashed against the keyboard and his arms dangling at his sides.

Surprisingly, the oldest man on the ship, Arthur Stanton, now eighty-five, was doing just fine. He had excellent genes and came from a long line of centenarians, the most recent of whom was his 113-year-old mother, who was still alive and living with Arthur's brother on Earth. Arthur would be the first man ever to set foot on the planet Vesta at the ripe old age of 104. And he would die painlessly of a stroke while tending his vegetable garden on Vesta just four days before his 112th birthday.

***

When John Galt Ibsen turned fourteen, he graduated from high school with excellent marks, having skipped two grades and having demonstrated proficiency in science, math, music, history, and literature. He was granted access to the bridge, where he started out as an assistant to Howard Oppenheimer, taking over the navigational controls whenever the old man fell asleep on the job or whenever the captain stormed off in a demented fit.

Emmett Greene idolized John Galt Ibsen, and told his teacher, Margaret Frost, that when he grew up he was going to be just like John Galt.

Margaret laughed and said, "But John Galt is just a boy." Emmett Greene crossed his arms and snorted like a horse.

But even Margaret Frost was well aware that John Galt Ibsen was no ordinary boy. She hadn't forgotten how he had served as interpreter after Maurice Yanne dropped dead in that hellish meadow on the planet Gzorazki, or how he had saved Edith Young that night in the methane snow.

Emmett Greene wasn't the only passenger who idolized John Galt. Lydia Anne Greene, six years John's senior, caught herself admiring how tall John had grown, how defined his jaw had become, how he seemed to be cracking the mysteries of the universe when he thumbed through Heisenberg's "Über den anschaulichen Inhalt der quantentheoretischen Kinematik und Mechanik"[20] on his lunch breaks.

---

[20] Translated "On the Empirical Content of Quantal-Theoretical Kinematics and Mechanics."

Lydia Anne was studying to be an ob-gyn and was the go-to girl whenever any of the women on the ship had any problems down below. Ever since Emma Greene died giving birth to Emmett Greene, Lydia Anne had been searching for resolution to her mother's death in the study of obstetrics. She preferred to study in the library because she knew John Galt Ibsen would be there, sometimes until two in the morning, reading about circuits and electromagnetism and particle physics.

Late at night, when they were the only people left in the library, Lydia Anne would put on astronaut tea, and they'd talk about whatever they were working on.

John Galt Ibsen was deeply immersed in his studies, and Lydia Anne had to do everything in her power to make herself more noticeable to him. She had the advantage of being an older woman and well developed. Her breasts were full and high, so she wore shirts that hinted at the cleavage beneath. She straightened her hair with a curling iron so that it fell in long, layered sheets around her shoulders. She'd twirl her coiffed hair and gaze at John Galt across the library, and wonder how a fourteen-year-old boy could be so indifferent.

Lydia Anne Greene also had the advantage of looking very much like her mother, Emma. At nineteen, she was considered the most beautiful girl on the ship, surpassing the Perkins-Borges girls in both figure and form. And sometimes when the captain saw Lydia Anne in the hall, he'd make a crude pass at her, mistaking her for Emma Greene, having forgotten long ago that he was, in fact, Lydia Anne's father.

Some of the older men on the ship showed undisguised interest in Lydia Anne Greene, making grand overtures toward her and sending her pretty little gifts. However, unlike her mother, Lydia Anne was not interested in men twice her age. She wasn't even interested in *men*, per se. She was interested in John Galt Ibsen, and she preferred to be left alone to pine for him all by her lonesome.

It was easy to fall in love with John Galt Ibsen. He was handsome, intelligent, and destined to command the *Destiny Unknown*. All the other girls had crushes on him, too. The Perkins-Borges girls drew straws every evening to see who would get to sit next to him at dinner. But John Galt Ibsen paid them little attention. He sat with his nose in a book, concentrating on complex mathematical theories and jotting down indecipherable symbols on his note pad. This or that Perkins-Borges girl would undertake to engage him in conversation about everyday things, like the waning food supply, or the health of Bobo the chimp, or the latest gossip about Margaret Frost and her affair with the moribund captain.

John Galt Ibsen would play the part and nod whenever there was a pause in the conversation, all the while working out some mathematical conundrum in his head.

At the end of it all, one or another Perkins-Borges girl would walk away feeling light as air, certain she had won his heart, and John Galt Ibsen would have solved some unexplained phenomenon of the universe.

The only person John Galt Ibsen regarded with any esteem was his mother, Amanda Sphinx. She nearly equaled him in intelligence, and she had the advantage of years of experience to draw on.

So when Amanda Sphinx informed John Galt that he was unwittingly breaking the hearts of his female companions, he nodded gravely and immediately informed the Perkins-Borges girls that he was not interested in pursuing anything more than friendship. They nodded cheerfully and went off to their separate rooms to cry.

John Galt fed Lydia Anne Greene the same line, but he truly meant it when he said he wanted to stay friends. He continued to meet her in the library at all hours to talk about biology and physics and math. Sometimes they would slip into discussion of other things, like the future of NASA's New World Population Project or what they imagined a perfect world to be like: vast oceans, great sweeping plains, an unlimited supply of fresh oxygen—not the old recycled stuff manufactured by the moleculator. And they talked about what it was like growing up without fathers, and Lydia Anne told John Galt everything she could remember of Austin Ibsen.

Now and then, one of the Perkins-Borges girls would pass through the library, feigning some interest in a book that she couldn't reach on the topmost shelf, and she would interrupt

John Galt Ibsen and Lydia Anne Greene and request assistance.

Lydia Anne Greene would raise her eyebrow at John Galt, speaking a shared language that said, "Silly flirts." And John Galt would retrieve the book and return to Lydia Anne Greene, leaving whichever Perkins-Borges girl it was alone with a book she never wanted in the first place.

After the whole clan of Perkins-Borges girls had repeated the same routine a dozen or more times, Lydia Anne Greene said to Maggie Perkins-Borges as she reached for another book, "Oh, but didn't you read that one last week? If you are still interested in the reproductive processes of muskrats, then I recommend Dr. Irving's brilliant study on muskrat monogamy. It's over there." She pointed to a shelf on the back wall.

Maggie sniffed and said, "Never mind." Then she went away empty-handed.

John Galt Ibsen and Lydia Anne Greene had a good laugh, and they laughed even harder when Lydia Anne admitted she had in fact read both books on muskrats, as had he.

***

Later that year, Bill the African grey parrot caught a cold, and even Elijah's expert care could not save him. Shortly afterward, they found Bill lying dead at the bottom of his cage, wedged between the water dish and a plastic ball with a bell. The last thing Bill said was "Land Ho!"—a trick Maisey Perkins-Borges had taught him for a laugh.

They held a funeral for Bill. Rather than shooting him out to space, they buried him in the barren vegetable garden with his favorite toy: a plush gingerbread man doll whose button eyes had been pecked out years ago.

Bill's final broadcast, "Land Ho!" was timely. They were approaching the first star in the Keith Cluster. The star was a fiery red giant so near the end of its life that it had already swallowed all of its surrounding planets and moons and asteroid belts. It was a hostile star, unwelcoming to life of any kind, but it was the gateway to the Keith Cluster, a constellation of stars spanning a fertile pocket of space twenty-six light-years in diameter and containing at least one hundred other stars, the brightest of which were the nineteen red giants that had attracted the captain's attention in the first place.

They passed the red giant at a safe distance, keeping out of the way of turbulent solar flares, and pulling the shades over the portside windows to keep out the blinding light.

The cosmic rays emanating from the red giant were so frequent and fierce that the DNA of several passengers aboard the *Destiny Unknown* were significantly altered—forever changing the course of human evolution. Where the captain was concerned, the shower of cosmic rays only aggravated his dementia, and for several days he had to be locked in his room with Esmeralda. Meanwhile John Galt Ibsen, under the direction of Howard Oppenheimer, was enlisted to guide the ship out of the treacherous terrain.

John Galt demonstrated mastery at the helm. He pointed the bow of the ship away from the red giant, minimizing the impact of the cosmic rays and setting a course that would invariably take the *Destiny Unknown* past three smaller golden stars that might prove more hospitable to humans.

John Galt Ibsen calculated it would take at least 4,232 years to visit every star in the Keith Cluster, and since their food supply was running low, they would have to play a game of roulette, picking the stars most like the sun and searching their orbits for Earthlike planets.

This was the plan he presented to the captain when the demented old man was lucid enough to return to the bridge.

"A good plan." The captain nodded, aware that he was becoming less and less capable of inventing any plan of his own. "It looks like you have picked us three good ones," he added, noting the small triad of golden stars on the horizon, "Alecto, Megaera, and Tisiphone—the three Furies. How long before we reach them?"

"Two or three years, by my estimation," John Galt replied. "They are the nearest I could find."

"Very well," the captain said and added, "Hell hath no fury like a woman scorned." This was probably a crack at Esmeralda in her lair as much as an allusion to the three vengeful Furies of Greek lore.

Then he said to no one in particular, "Keep a hold of your head, Johannes. You lost it the last time we went ashore."

CHAPTER 27
YEARS 25-27

THE COMBINED EFFECT of cosmic rays and decades of space travel had taken its toll on a few of the more senior passengers. Raquel Muniz, the geriatrics specialist on the ship, rallied enough support to turn the fourth-floor living quarters into a senior center and transferred Martha Marigold, Richard Park, Arthur Stanton, and Howard Oppenheimer to cozy cabins with regular room service and on-site living assistance.

Marcus Fincus was allowed to remain in his stateroom since he was still pretending to command the ship. Esmeralda stayed, too, since she refused to be "hauled off someplace to rot."

Under Raquel Muniz's direction, the Sunny Side Senior Center flourished. Ruth and Olivia Perkins-Borges, having recently completed their studies with Margaret Frost, volunteered to assist Raquel Muniz, and together they succeeded in creating a comfortable space to which the aging passengers could retire when no longer fit to work.

They transformed Bartholomew's old cabin into a rec room replete with shuffleboard and bingo. There were weekly visits from Bobo the chimp, and the occasional sing-along led by Arthur Stanton and Amanda Sphinx. Meals were delivered to the residents' rooms if they weren't up to the half-mile trek to the mess hall. There were routine checkups and colon exams and scalp massages. And for some of the seniors on the ship, these were the best days they had known since they blasted off so many years ago.

One by one, the aging passengers fell prey to the lure of the senior center, to the lure of Yahtzee and Parcheesi and miniature golf in the hallways, to an easy retirement and breakfast in bed, until at last every person over sixty had taken refuge in what Raquel Muniz was calling the Palm Springs of deep space—everyone except the captain and his wife.

And who was running the ship? Why, the fifteen young men and women who had spent their childhoods running through its halls and playing hide-and-seek in its endless corridors. Whenever someone retired, someone younger came along to take his or her place. Margaret Frost took over for Martha Marigold teaching classes. Robert Stowe took over for Richard Park in the labs. Melanie Lorne suffered a minor stroke, and Deidre Hundt was promoted to chief engineer on the bridge. And soon the captain, holding fast to his captainship, was like a rotting stump in a forest of freshly grown sprigs; when he looked about him to see who remained of the crew he had mustered at the beginning of the mission, he saw only strangers—young, disrespectful, and brash.

It didn't help that he was becoming more forgetful by the day. Sometimes his dementia transported him back to the Moon Wars, when he commanded a fleet of seventeen ships and took orders directly from the president of the United States—then he would shout for more nukes and scream, "Fire! Fire! Fire!"

Sometimes the captain did not recognize his own wife. He'd open the door to his cabin, see a strange woman lying in the bed, and conclude he had the wrong room. Then he would close the door, wander up to the bridge, and fall asleep in the captain's chair.

Raquel Muniz tried some memory exercises with the captain. Marcus Fincus succeeded only in recalling that he was a notorious Casanova and tried to unhook Raquel's bra strap with one hand.

Raquel was happily engaged to Eric Yen, a thirty-seven-year-old engineer and one of the original children to board the ship twenty-seven years ago. When she told Eric how the captain had behaved, Eric raged and stamped and vowed to make the captain pay. Raquel reminded her jealous fiancé how easily Marcus Fincus could have mistaken her for any one of his dozens of mistresses and made Eric promise to forget the whole thing.

On the bridge the next day, when the captain asked Eric to check the stabilizers, Eric Yen said nothing, turned his back on the captain, and picked at his nails until John Galt Ibsen reissued the order. Only then did Eric Yen check the stabilizers.

It was then that everybody knew John Galt Ibsen was in charge.

***

The next week, they ran out of toilet paper. All able-bodied passengers were issued cotton rags. The residents in the senior center had it easier—they were given adult diapers so they could go whenever (and wherever) they pleased.

Marcus Fincus refused to wear a diaper. He was insulted that anyone would even suggest such a thing to a renowned space captain—even though he needed a diaper more than anyone. Esmeralda was repulsed by the captain's declining state, and whenever he made a mess in his pajamas, she would kick him out of bed and scream like a madwoman until somebody came to change the sheets.

On one such night—the captain had retreated to the bridge in exile—the *Destiny Unknown* detected an object floating in space a few million miles dead ahead.

The ship's autopilot, which usually steered the ship at night, had been disabled because Marcus Fincus thought he might have to nuke a Canadian fighter craft at any moment—he was reliving the Moon Wars all over again. And while all the passengers and crew members slept, the captain peered into the darkness, hands on the controls, searching for enemy spies.

Even though the ship's autopilot had been disabled, the supercomputer remained wide awake, running the engines, balancing the thermostat, converting CO_2 into oxygen, and probing space with its radar. That's when it spotted something bobbing noiselessly out in the void. The supercomputer was an expert at judging distances, and it calculated that the *Destiny Unknown* and whatever this thing was would collide in fifty-seven seconds.

So the supercomputer did exactly what it was programmed to do. It launched the alarm sequence. There were bells and whistles and an ominous robotic voice counting down over the PA: "Fifty-seven seconds to impact; fifty-six seconds to impact; fifty-five seconds to impact," and so on. The captain sprang out of his seat, certain that the Canadian reconnoiters had him in their sights. He pushed all sorts of buttons—buttons that might have effectively maneuvered an American V3 Starfighter. But this wasn't an American V3 Starfighter, of course—it was a B78 Interstellar Space-Ark, the first of its kind, with controls unlike anything the captain had seen in his military career. The countdown continued: "Forty-nine seconds to impact. Forty-eight seconds to impact."

Elsewhere on the ship, the passengers were roused by the

alarm. Those who had trained on the bridge immediately registered the danger they were in. If the *Destiny Unknown* collided with a comet or an asteroid at 0.876 times the speed of light, they would be shredded to pieces. Deidre Hundt and George McGraw and Eric Yen leaped out of bed and sprinted for the bridge.

John Galt Ibsen, who had been studying late in the library, was the first on the scene. He burst into CC just as the robotic voice warned, "Nineteen seconds to impact." He pushed past the old man who was fumbling with the controls and, without hesitating, slammed his palm down on a big yellow button.

The engines shifted into reverse and began backpedaling to counter their forward momentum. There was a creaking and a groaning, as if the ship were splitting in half. Still the ship careened onward.

"Thirteen seconds to impact."

The rest of the crew arrived on the scene, breathless and terrified. The whole ship rattled.

The object, whatever it was, appeared out of the darkness, a twinkling speck smaller than a pinprick, illuminated by the headlamps of the ship.

"Five seconds to impact."

John Galt tried to gauge the size of the object. Was it a faraway planet? A nearby comet? He steered the ship half a degree to the left, the maximum rotation the ship could handle without splitting into pieces. The whole vessel bucked violently.

The captain was ejected from his chair—he flew through the air and slammed into the viewport. There he stayed, plastered against the glass, as the ship groaned and grumbled to a maddening halt.

"Three seconds to impact."

Nobody had ever heard the captain scream so loudly as he braced himself for the collision.

"One second to impact."

The object was on them, at one moment no bigger than the eye of a needle and the next, the size of a house. Then the entire ship heaved and sighed, the engines powered off, the lights flickered, and they came to a halt, mere inches from the deadly object.

The captain slid down the windowpane, the side of his face imprinted on the cold glass.

Before them, glowing blue in the blinking lights of the *Destiny Unknown*, was escape pod A. Its hull was covered in icy barnacles. Its engine was idle. The little pod revolved slowly on its axis, its viewport just sliding into view.

And there was Jason Fincus, staring right back at them.

CHAPTER 28

YEARS 27-28

THEY DOCKED ESCAPE POD A and ushered Jason into the infirmary. His muscles were atrophied. His pulse was weak and arrhythmic. And throughout the entire examination he said nothing; he just cradled his knees in his arms and shivered under the stethoscope.

For him, forty-three years had elapsed since he had left the *Destiny Unknown*. For everyone else it had only been twenty-one years.

So when Barbara Chatsworth, the psychiatrist, asked Jason his age, Jason replied, "Fifty-nine," when he should have said, "Thirty-seven." That made Jason just seven years younger than his mother, Esmeralda Fincus, who had just turned sixty-six.[21]

---

[21] This discrepancy did not concern Barbara Chatsworth. She knew all about Einstein's theory of relativity, which proved that objects moving at speeds close to the speed of light will experience time more slowly than

Marcus Fincus did not recognize his son. He raised all hell because he believed that Jason was a Canadian spy from the enemy camp. So Elijah Perkins-Borges crumbled a few sleeping pills into the captain's astronaut paste and deposited him in bed next to his wife.

"I don't want him anywhere near me," Esmeralda snorted, regarding the captain's limp body with disgust.

"Well maybe you'd like to come out and see your son, then," Elijah said.

"My son is dead."

"We found him. He's in the infirmary now."

Esmeralda stared hard at Elijah. Then she turned on her side and closed her eyes.

Esmeralda did not appear in the infirmary until many hours later. By then, Jason was fast asleep. She stood over his bed and fingered the edges of the sheets while Elijah Perkins-Borges adjusted Jason's IV drip.

Esmeralda returned to her room before Jason awoke. She did not go again to see Jason for many weeks.

***

objects at rest. So while Jason Fincus was putting around at forty-four miles per hour, time on the *Destiny Unknown* was ticking away at about half the rate of time on escape pod A, which made Jason Fincus twenty-two years older than he would have been had he remained on the ship going 0.876 times the speed of light.

The next day Jason Fincus told them the wild story of his journey through space. It came out in jumbled, broken spurts, for Jason had not spoken to another human being in forty-three years.

He claimed to have spent fifteen years searching endlessly for Earth or the *Destiny Unknown* or any other sign of human civilization. He told them how he had won at solitaire a million times, and how he had uncovered two albums uploaded to the escape pod's database—Cyndi Lauper's *She's So Unusual* and *The Very Best of Sting & The Police*—which he had played over and over until his ears bled. He talked of stars that blinked and fluttered like fireflies and buzzed around his ship until they made him dizzy.

When Barbara Chatsworth asked him what had happened after the first fifteen years, he shivered uncontrollably and started crying, and then rolled into the fetal position on the floor and hummed "Girls Just Want to Have Fun."

Barbara Chatsworth prescribed Xanax to treat his anxiety and agreed to continue psychiatric treatment after Jason regained some of his physical strength.

Elijah Perkins-Borges conducted a full exam. While sifting through the tangled mop of hair, Elijah discovered a festering tattoo behind Jason's left ear. It looked like a postal stamp. Elijah snapped a few pictures of the tattoo and treated the inflamed skin with antiseptics.

He asked Jason if he had done the tattoo himself.

Jason replied, "*They* did it to me."

Robert Stowe, Richard Park's replacement, took a sample of skin cells from around the tattoo to the lab for testing. The results were conclusive: the ink had come from a NASA-brand Zero-Gravity pen. They found the pen lying on the floor of escape pod A.

"Why would you do this to yourself?" Barbara Chatsworth asked Jason the following week. "Were you trying to hurt yourself?"

"I told you," Jason said. "I didn't do it."

Switching tactics, Barbara Chatsworth asked, "How did you end up in the Keith Cluster? You were only traveling forty-four miles per hour, were you not?"

"*They* brought me here," he said.

"Who are *they*?" Barbara Chatsworth asked.

Jason barked, "Back off, lady!"

Barbara Chatsworth prescribed several more medications and diagnosed Jason with a severe case of schizophrenia characterized by jumbled speech, false memories, and a propensity to hear voices in his head.

Over the next few weeks, Jason's behavior was extremely erratic. He would sleep all hours of the day. When he was awake, he hardly moved at all, except to scream or cry. His speech was highly impaired—he would say whole sentences out of order, spouting off nonsensical strings of words. When he did make sense, he claimed to be an ambassador from Prague whose divine purpose was to keep the moon from falling onto Earth.

He obviously didn't remember that the moon had been destroyed in a nuclear war several years before he was born—and that Prague had been destroyed in a nuclear war, too.

***

Jason became a permanent fixture in the infirmary, where he underwent extensive physical therapy to rebuild the muscles in his arms, legs, and lower back. The medications calmed him some, and on good days he could hold a conversation without screaming or crying or carrying on about the moon.

But he became agitated when Barbara Chatsworth pressed him for more information about his harrowing experience.

"Why don't *you* tell *me* what's been going on around here?" he retorted. "Where are my mother and father? Why haven't they come to see me?"

Barbara Chatsworth looked away guiltily, not knowing what to say.

"Are they dead?" Jason demanded, his voice rising to a dangerous level.

"No," Barbara Chatsworth assured him. "They are not dead."

"*Then what?*" Jason screamed.

"I think that's enough for today," Barbara Chatsworth said. And then, turning to Elijah Perkins-Borges, she said,

"Double his dosage and note any changes in his behavior."

Meanwhile, the passengers aboard the *Destiny Unknown* were doing everything in their powers to prevent Marcus Fincus from visiting the infirmary. The captain was bruised and battered from his encounter with the glass windowpane at the front of the ship, and even though he had no memory of the incident, no memory of Jason Fincus or escape pod A, he remembered quite well that they'd captured a Canadian spy.

There was no telling what sticking Marcus Fincus and Jason Fincus in the same room would accomplish. And nobody wanted to find out.

***

Lydia Anne Greene had never met Jason Fincus. She was born after his mysterious disappearance twenty-one years before (forty-three years afor), and she was curious to meet the man that had become the source of so much gossip on the ship, the man who was also rumored to be her half brother.

One night, on some excuse of needing a Band-Aid, she visited the infirmary and peeked behind the curtain into the alcove where Jason Fincus lay convalescing. It was late, and she expected him to be asleep. But the lamp on his bedside table was on, and he was sitting up, reading a book.

Jason looked up instantly when Lydia Anne came in, his

head snapping up like a startled animal's. Lydia Anne Greene jumped back with a muffled "I'm sorry." But Jason was in one of his milder moods, and he assured her that she was not bothering him in the least, and that he could use some company.

When she pulled back the curtain a bit and took a few steps into the light, Jason saw that she looked remarkably like Emma Greene, the woman he had fantasized about so often when he was a boy. When she told him her full name, Jason said, "Your mother must be Emma?"

"She died," Lydia Anne said and then changed the subject. "What are you reading?"

"It's an old Stephen King novel, *The Dark Tower*. Not my first choice, but it showed up one morning. I guess somebody here remembers I like Stephen King."

"I've read it," Lydia Anne Greene said. "I think I've read almost every Stephen King novel there is. They have them all in the library. I can get you another one."

Jason Fincus nodded. He couldn't take his eyes off Lydia Anne. She looked so much like Emma Greene—the way he remembered Emma Greene, anyway. Emma had been about Lydia Anne's age when Jason ran away. The last time Jason saw Emma, she was in the service closet with his lumpy old father. The memory made him flush. That day, that moment when he opened the door to the service closet, had cost him forty-three years of his life.

He had no idea that same moment had given birth to the

girl standing before him now. Jason Fincus had never been good at putting two and two together.

"Well, I just wanted to introduce myself," Lydia Anne said. "I'll let you get back to your reading."

And she turned to go, swinging the curtain shut behind her.

"Hey!" Jason called out.

Lydia Anne pulled the curtain back a few inches and poked her head back in.

"Will you bring me another book tomorrow?" Jason asked. "I'll be done with this one by morning."

Lydia Anne nodded.

She was about to close the curtain when he stopped her again.

"Wait! Why haven't my mom and dad come to see me?"

"I'll bring the book tomorrow," she replied and slid the curtain back into place.

Lydia Anne headed for the library where John Galt Ibsen was studying Heisenberg's uncertainty principle. When she sat down, John Galt barely murmured a hello, so immersed was he in his studies.

Not even a hello, Lydia Anne thought.

After pretending to study for a few hours, Lydia Anne stood to leave. John Galt didn't even look up. And he certainly didn't pay her any mind when she crossed over to a familiar bookshelf and stuffed a Stephen King novel into her knapsack.

***

By the time the *Destiny Unknown* reached the first of the three stars—Alecto, as Marcus Fincus had dubbed it—Jason Fincus could move about on his own. But his muscles were weak, and he was still having trouble making it very far past the infirmary. So he spent the majority of his time behind his curtain, reading whatever Lydia Anne Greene brought him.

The system of planets surrounding the star Alecto proved to be uninhabitable—composed mainly of Jovian gas giants several times the size of Jupiter, whose gravitational pulls threatened to crush the *Destiny Unknown* and all its crew members if they ventured too close.

When they got to the star Megaera many months later, they found a solar system so young that the planets were nothing more substantial than loosely connected clouds of molten rock and debris.

Tisiphone was a disappointment as well, having no planets at all.

This was a major blow to John Galt Ibsen, who had so easily won the confidence of the crew with his ready calculations and smooth handling of the ship. And although they began to question whether it was wise to let a sixteen-year-old—for he had just turned sixteen—run the ship, they were still willing to follow his lead when he turned the nose of the vessel fifteen degrees starboard and four-and-a-half degrees skyward and set out for the next nearest star, which they called Elpis after the Greek goddess of hope.

CHAPTER 29

YEARS 28-29

THEN ONE DAY Marcus Fincus stubbed his toe on the steps leading up to the bridge, and he insisted on being taken to the infirmary for stitches. Elijah Perkins-Borges offered to patch him up on the spot—a trip to the infirmary wouldn't be necessary. But the bleeding was so bad, so profuse—Marcus Fincus was on blood thinners for clotting—Elijah finally ordered a bed made up for him in the infirmary. Thither the captain hobbled, George McGraw supporting him on the left and Deidre Hundt on the right.

When they arrived, the curtain was drawn about Jason Fincus, and the prodigal son was fast asleep, having taken a heavy dose of sedatives only moments before the captain arrived. A cot was readied on the opposite end of the room, and there they stopped the captain's bleeding and tucked him in for the evening.

In the middle of the night Jason Fincus woke up, as he

was prone to do, and when he heard somebody snoring on the other side of the curtain, he threw back his sheets and hobbled out of bed. With some effort, he parted the curtain and crossed over to the lumpy form sleeping noisily on the neighboring cot.

Then he recognized his father.

He tapped the captain gently at first and whispered, "Dad?"

But when Marcus Fincus merely grunted and rolled over on his side, memories of fatherly neglect came flooding back to Jason, and he roiled into a violent fit, slugged his father hard in the shoulder, and cried out, "Hey, you! Wake up!"

Marcus Fincus sprang to life, reaching instinctively under the pillow for a pistol. Finding none, he cowered helplessly in the corner of the bed and stammered, "Who the hell are you, and what do you want?"

Whether the captain didn't recognize Jason because of how old Jason had become—Jason was sixty and Marcus Fincus was seventy—or because his memory was so far gone, it is hard to say.

Jason, having blamed his father for everything bad that had ever happened to him in his life, was incensed. He took one look at the captain's swollen toe. "So that's the reason you're here." He launched onto the captain and bit the toe clean off. The captain screamed in horror and started banging on the call button. Jason spit the toe onto the floor and retreated to his side of the room.

Lydia Anne Greene, having heard the captain's cries from her compartment down the hall, arrived first on the scene. Seeing the two old men huddled in their respective corners, Jason talking to himself and Marcus Fincus fumbling around on the floor for his missing toe, Lydia Anne concluded that the dangerous confrontation everyone had been hoping to avoid had finally occurred.

She pulled the curtain closed between the two invalids and managed the captain's bleeding until help arrived. Then she went in to see Jason. He was lying facedown, trying to suffocate himself with a pillow. Whenever it seemed he must finally be dead, he'd turn over, gasp for air, and then try again.

Lydia Anne watched this ridiculous charade for some time before deciding to intervene.

She grabbed Jason's wrists with her two delicate hands and made him sit up and face her. Then she explained, "Your father is suffering from dementia. He doesn't remember any of us anymore, or where he is, or what's going on."

Jason stared ahead, refusing to meet Lydia Anne's fierce gaze.

"You've been wondering why he wouldn't come to see you. Well, there it is. He is very ill, and there is no way of making him understand where you'd disappeared to for twenty-one years."

"Forty-three years." Jason scowled. Then he shuddered, as if remembering something very painful.

Lydia Anne placed a small hand on his trembling shoulder, and Jason fell against Lydia Anne's bosom and sobbed. She held him there until he fell asleep. Then she tucked Jason into bed and returned to check on the captain, whose foot would have four toes from then on. The captain had passed out when Elijah had tried to cauterize the wound. Lydia Anne noticed how similar the captain and Jason looked, sleeping fitfully on opposite ends of the ward.

She sat down in a chair in the middle of the room and dozed, keeping a loose watch on the two invalids for the rest of the night. In the morning, before Jason awoke, she helped Elijah transfer the captain back to his cabin, where Esmeralda accepted him grudgingly and complained of the stink of urine, which was not a hallucination, seeing as the captain had just wet his pants.

The next day Jason made no mention of his father. In fact, he seemed quite chipper. He participated eagerly in his morning exercises and made extraordinary progress.

When Barbara Chatsworth asked him, "How did you feel when you found out your father has dementia and has no memory of your existence?" Jason Fincus merely said, "Can you ask Lydia Anne to bring me another book? I'm done with this one," and he shoved *Animal Farm* at the psychiatrist.

"Did seeing your father again bring back any old feelings?" Barbara persisted.

"Two feet are better than four," Jason said.

"Excuse me?"

"Have you read *Animal Farm*?" Jason asked.

"No."

"And you call yourself a psychiatrist!"

Jason chortled and rolled over on his side. He switched off the bedside lamp, indicating that they were done for the day.

Barbara Chatsworth left the room in a huff, and later that night she read the first ten pages of *Animal Farm* and dismissed the book as "rubbish."

***

Esmeralda had gone to see her son several times since his incarceration in the infirmary but always while Jason slept. Whenever she visited, Esmeralda tidied up Jason's little alcove as he lay there snoring like his father. She left long before he awoke, fearing he might see her and blame her for his unhappy fate, as she blamed herself.

So, for many months, as far as Jason knew, Esmeralda was inexplicably absent from his life. Then late one night as Jason lay fast asleep, Esmeralda dropped a dustpan, and it clattered noisily on the floor.

Jason stirred and Esmeralda froze. It seemed as though he would sit up at any moment and catch her standing there.

When Jason did not wake, Esmeralda finished sweeping and hurried out of the room.

All the while Jason watched her through a thin slit in his eyes. He was frightened by how much older she looked. She was heavier than he remembered and graying, and her face was wrinkled and pruned. But she was still beautiful, he observed.

He could not bring himself to confront her. She was too much of a stranger now. He remembered all the movies where mothers and fathers were reunited with their long-lost children, and the first thing they did, those people in the movies, was wrap one another in a warm embrace and say, "I love you."

But Jason couldn't imagine hugging his mother any more than he could imagine hugging his psychiatrist, Barbara Chatsworth. He couldn't imagine hugging his father, either. He could imagine *punching* his father. That made a hell of a lot more sense to him than all those warm embraces in the movies.

He *wanted* to hug his mother. But there were so many years between them now that all he could do was pretend to sleep while Esmeralda tiptoed around his room rearranging the books and the magazines. They would never say another word to one another, and when Jason moved out of the infirmary, he never ventured near her stateroom. And she, in her turn, would never go out, except late at night when she could gaze on her sleeping son without being caught.

***

Within a few months, Jason was strong enough to move back into his old cabin. He continued psychiatric treatment with Barbara Chatsworth, and he continued to have schizophrenic episodes that posed a threat to the other passengers.

One day, when Jason was suffering from a searing headache, brought on by what he claimed to be a million people rambling on and on just behind his eyeballs, Barbara Chatsworth handed him a sheet of butcher paper and an eight-pack of Crayola markers and asked him to illustrate the cacophony in his head as best as he could.

Jason, wishing to do anything to relieve the pain, emptied the pack of markers onto the floor and began scribbling a series of lines and swirls. He covered every square inch of paper, front and back, like a regular Jackson Pollock.

When all the ink had run dry, Jason Fincus looked up at Barbara Chatsworth. "They've gone away, the voices."

Then Jason calmly rolled up the parchment and took it away to his room.

The migraines did not stay away for long. In fact, in later months they became so frequent that Barbara Chatsworth prescribed whole spools of butcher paper—as well as the ship's entire supply of Crayola markers—to ease Jason's suffering. And Jason, in schizophrenic fits, would lock himself in his room and churn through spool after spool, producing elaborate renderings of the violent visions in his head.

Little by little, Jason became progressively private about

his drawings. And after Barbara Chatsworth commented on their "provincial aesthetic," he refused to let her see them again.

Jason was his sanest with Lydia Anne Greene. She had a soporific effect on him. So Lydia Anne became his primary nurse, spending more time on Jason than on all of her other patients combined. She did not mind so much. It reminded her of the hours she had spent caring for her mother, Emma Greene, after the Gzorazkians had removed parts of her brain.

However, where her mother's behavior had been calm and predictable, Jason's was wild and erratic. He could be a smiling charmer one day and a tempestuous ass the next. But even on his darkest days, he made an attempt at good manners whenever Lydia Anne was around. He complained less of the voices in his head. He made some effort to eat. And if she promised to visit again the next day, he promised to take his medication.

And every so often, when he was feeling particularly garrulous, Jason shared some of the adventures he'd had over the course of forty-three years alone in space with Lydia Anne. His stories were outlandish and strange, and Lydia Anne had no choice but to chalk them up to psychotic fantasies.

Jason explained that he had kept track of the days by drawing little circles around the page numbers in *Moby Dick*.

"Whenever I got to page three hundred sixty-five," he

said, "I went back to the beginning and drew a new circle around page one, so that I could measure the years in space like rings on a tree."

Lydia Anne searched escape pod A and couldn't find a copy of *Moby Dick*.

"Even after they caught me and tagged me and put me under a giant microscope," Jason said, "I still managed to keep track of the days because they let me keep my copy of *Moby Dick*. Then one day, they flashed a super bright light in my eyes, and all of a sudden I could remember the exact number of days and years all on my own. I used to have a terrible memory. Ask Miss Marigold! But ever since they flashed that light in my eyes, I haven't been able to forget a single thing."

"And yet you still forget to take your medication," Lydia Anne replied.

***

There was no doubt—Jason's memory had improved over the last twenty-odd years (forty-odd years afor). Jason's father, however, was having no such luck. The journey to the star Elpis took a little less than a year, more than enough time for the captain to forget almost everything except the most colorful memories of his youth. He still remembered Esmeralda, only he remembered her as she was fifty years ago when he was a teaching assistant at Caltech and she was the prettiest girl in the freshman class. With each passing day, as the captain's mind shut out more and more of his past, he became increasingly devoted to Esmeralda, pulling out all the stops to win her heart.

Esmeralda played as hard to get as she had fifty years ago, reprising her role as the standoffish socialite, which had won her the title of "Ice Queen" among her peers. She ignored Marcus Fincus and his advances with a calculated precision that drove him into a mad frenzy of desire.

And in his passion to secure her affections, Marcus Fincus quickly and noiselessly ended his affair with Margaret Frost and swore his allegiance to one woman and one woman alone: his wife.

Margaret Frost was distraught. Her self-worth had grown increasingly dependent on the captain's midcoital expressions of adoration. Now that the captain had returned to the bed of his wife, Margaret's sexual appetite raged. Yet no one else on the ship was patient enough to make love to a woman who talked between kisses and made long sentences out of every passionate cry.

Her students noticed the change in her disposition. She was frazzled and unprepared, and at the end of the quarter, everybody was getting As in all subjects, even though most of them didn't deserve them.

Margaret Frost tried to rekindle her relationship with the captain, but it didn't take. He couldn't even remember her name anymore. And whenever she cornered him alone in the hallways or in the stairwells and tried to take off his clothes as she used to do, one button at a time, he would push her away with a strength surprising for a man of his age, point to his wedding ring and shake his head.

Margaret Frost was desperate. She longed for the company of a man. She did not eat except when it was necessary to survive. She slept long hours. And whenever she tried to pleasure herself in the shower, she could not bring herself to climax.

Then one afternoon she had a novel idea. She had seen Jason Fincus eating alone in the cafeteria a few times, and she had been surprised at how much he looked like his father. He had inherited his father's deep-set brown eyes, strong jaw, and full head of hair. And although Jason was a schizophrenic recluse with a reputation for violent outbursts and erratic behavior, Margaret wondered fleetingly if he had inherited his father's sexual prowess, too.

She took no time finding out. One night, when everyone else on the ship was asleep, she crept down the corridor to Jason's room and tried the door. It was unlocked. Margaret entered, wearing only a thin nightgown that did nothing to disguise the outline of her bosom.

Jason, a chronic insomniac, was sitting up in bed reading Tolstoy's *War and Peace*. He was stark naked himself, preferring to sleep in the nude. As soon as she stepped into the room, Margaret saw his member rise to welcome her, and she noticed how similar it was to the captain's in length and girth, and in the pattern of pubic hair that crept up to his bellybutton.

Without so much as a word between them, which was a first for Margaret Frost, she walked over to the bed, mounted him, and rode him to climax.

Margaret did not speak the entire time. She was terrified—she had heard that the slightest word could set Jason off. And Jason said nothing, because this was his first time with a woman and he didn't want to screw it up.

When they had finished, she left him lying there beside the dog-eared copy of *War and Peace*.

They did not see each other again for a fortnight. Then, as before, she entered his room at exactly two in the morning and repeated the same wordless performance from the previous fortnight. Jason had been waiting for her to reappear. He had not slept a wink in the intervening weeks. After she left his room the second time, Jason slept sixteen hours straight.

Their affair continued unabated for many weeks, always with Margaret entering at two in the morning, and with Jason Fincus lying naked on his back to greet her. And not until they reached the star Elpis did he even discover her name.

Only after she told him a second time did Jason remember the chatty girl from grade school with the matted hair and skinny legs—the girl who had been sent to detention for talking out of turn more times than anyone could count.

Yes—she was *that* Margaret Frost.

CHAPTER 30

YEARS 29-34

ELPIS CAME AND WENT, despite its implicit promise of hope; it was no more habitable than any of the other systems they had explored since their departure twenty-nine years ago. Although John Galt Ibsen was already setting the coordinates for the next star on the list, the passengers decided to give up on naming the stars they visited. The recurring letdown was too much for their fragile psyches.

Shortly after they left Elpis, Barbara Chatsworth performed a long-overdue psychiatric evaluation of each passenger aboard the *Destiny Unknown*.

This is what she concluded: due to a combination of malnutrition, inactivity, and psychological trauma, nearly 86 percent of the ship's population suffered from mild to severe depression; just about everyone had begun taking psychotropic medications—benzodiazepines being the community favorite—and the supply of prescription drugs was fast becoming as scarce as the food.

The search for a life-sustaining planet was proving to be a much more difficult task than anyone had expected. John Galt's sure and steady leadership had led everyone to believe that salvation was just around the corner. Nevertheless, John Galt had always known that their chances of finding anything habitable in the Keith Cluster were slim, and that doing so before their food supply was exhausted was as likely as winning the lottery on Gzorazki.[22] But he also knew the only chance they had of surviving was to visit as many solar systems in the Keith Cluster as they could in the short time they had left. The more planets they visited, the more probable the chance of finding one with oxygen to breathe and water to drink and soil to till. And John Galt Ibsen also knew that having a star—any star—to focus on gave the crew hope. So each new star in the distance acted as a placebo to stave off madness and, heaven forbid, mutiny.

However, the last thing on anybody's mind was mutiny. The passengers had already had their mutiny, silently and peacefully, when they stopped taking orders from Captain Marcus Fincus and yielded command to his brilliant young successor. Nobody was sorry for the change. They clung to John Galt Ibsen with an unwavering trust that bordered on worship.

As a courtesy, and because nobody could explain it to

---

[22] The Gzorazkian National Lottery is one of the most luckless lotteries in the universe, sometimes going a century without a winner.

him any other way, the passengers continued to refer to Marcus Fincus as "Captain." And John Galt Ibsen merely went by "sir" or, more commonly, "Mr. Ibsen, sir."

The only person who called him anything else was Lydia Anne Greene, who had been calling him Johnny ever since she could remember. And with each passing day she found herself more and more confused by her feelings for him. As his responsibilities grew, their study sessions in the library became less and less frequent, until Lydia Anne found herself hoping for a glimpse of him in the hall or in the dining room. But his daily duties, his constant plotting and mapping of stars, and his never-ending search for a new world kept him at the helm of the ship for nearly twenty hours a day.

Whenever she did see him, it was always in public while he was briefing the crew on the status of their mission or reassuring the passengers with words of optimism and hope. He was a young leader, only seventeen, but he had the intelligence of his father, the wisdom of his mother, and a tenacity all his own that bent minds and hearts in his favor.

Never once did his conviction falter in the presence of his crew. He was always calm when he arrived on the bridge in the morning, and that same steadfastness persisted well into the evening until he finally dismissed the crew for the night. Only then, when he was completely alone, did he heave a sad, lonely sigh that betrayed his many doubts and misgivings. And in the silence of a dreaming ship, John Galt Ibsen would collapse into the captain's chair and stare pleadingly at the taciturn stars.

***

Emmett Greene, at eleven years old, idolized the new captain. He focused all his young energy on being wherever John Galt was going to be whenever John Galt was going to be there, so much so that for a while Emmett would cut class just to sit outside the bridge and listen to the muffled sounds of John Galt's voice within.

Emmett had to be warned personally by John Galt Ibsen himself that to amount to anything whatsoever in life he was going to have to attend school *rain or shine*. Emmett Greene had no concept of rain or shine, but the antiquated expression had somehow survived in the weatherlessness of space, and he knew exactly what it meant.

"That's how I got to where I am," John Galt Ibsen added on a somewhat softer note.

And with that, Emmett Greene applied himself rigorously to his studies and fast became the top student in his class.

They chased stars for more than four years without success, always finding planets ravaged by comets or dry and parched from orbiting too close to their suns or shrouded in poisonous gases that no human could hope to survive.

Emmett Greene graduated early, at the age of fifteen, showing remarkable skill in the fields of planetary physics and interstellar navigation. He was assigned an apprenticeship on the bridge, where he trained directly under the aging Howard Oppenheimer.

Ever since Johannes Levi lost his head in a Gzorazkian laboratory, the *Destiny Unknown* had flown without a first mate. Emmett Greene put an end to that. Possessing a knack for being exactly where John Galt Ibsen needed him to be at precisely the right moment, Emmett Greene was named de facto first mate and successor to the headless Johannes Levi.

Emmett wasn't yet sixteen.

***

As Emmett saw more and more of John Galt Ibsen, Emmett's sister, Lydia Anne, saw less and less of them both. So she sought solace in her friendship with Jason Fincus. They spent long hours reading together in the library and swapping book recommendations. At one point, they even tried to write a book of their own. It was about a series of homicides that takes place on a cramped spaceship during a long journey to a distant star. The frightened crew, rapidly dwindling in number, tries to deduce the identity of the murderer and, after accusing and executing several innocent passengers, discovers, to their ultimate shock and dismay, that it was the ship's supercomputer doing the killing all along.

They were going to call it *Instructions to Kill*, and they were just getting to the good part, where the supercomputer poisons the water supply, when eighty-year-old Martha

Marigold, the retired schoolteacher, was diagnosed with ovarian cancer. Lydia Anne was needed in oncology.

The cancer metastasized within weeks. They administered radiation and chemotherapy. But new tumors kept popping up all over the place.

The book about the murderous supercomputer was forgotten—Lydia Anne had her hands full tending to the suffering schoolteacher. Once again, Jason Fincus found himself alone.

Yes, he still consorted with Margaret Frost, and together they staved off their respective demons with multiple orgasms. But their relationship remained purely carnal. If Margaret Frost had ever developed any emotional feelings for a man, they were for Jason's father. And Jason reserved what sincere affection he was capable of feeling for Lydia Anne Greene.

In Lydia Anne's absence, Jason found himself falling back into despair. He began flushing his medication down the toilet, and he craved another of his father's million-dollar cigars. He spent hours plotting to get into the cryogenic storage chest in the captain's stateroom without being seen.

Then he discovered, through a conversation with his interim nurse, Raquel Muniz, that his mother took her bath at precisely six o'clock every night, at which time his father was usually ushered from the room because Esmeralda refused to be seen naked by anyone, especially her husband.

So when Esmeralda was scrubbing the soles of her feet

with a pumice stone, Jason Fincus crept into the captain's stateroom and stole the remaining stash of million-dollar cigars.

He retreated to his old haunt in the downstairs service closet and was looking for a place to hide the cigars when he discovered a loaded pistol stashed inside a box of laundry detergent. That was how Jason Fincus, a schizophrenic off his meds, came into possession of the most dangerous weapon on the ship.

***

That was about the same time the Montgomery brothers—the five surviving children of Hannah Montgomery, each of whom was born on the planet Gzorazki—on the advent of their mutual sixteenth birthdays, and in celebration of passing their exams, endeavored to throw a private party in the hull of the ship. That year didn't just mark the sixteenth birthdays of the Montgomery brothers—it marked the sixteenth birthdays of all fourteen youngsters born on the planet Gzorazki.

The party invitation spread by word of mouth and was extended only to those who could be trusted not to spoil the fun. The students either graduating or preparing to graduate that year from Margaret Frost's classroom were the first invited. The Perkins-Borges girls—attractive, silly twenty-somethings—were then added to the guest list. Through them, some of the more eligible gentlemen were invited: Ricky Mancini, age forty-six, bachelor; Rico Torres, age forty-two, bachelor; and Robert Stowe, age forty-four, married once, to Drey Marlow, divorced. And Robert Stowe, who was working in the infirmary one day, invited Lydia Anne Greene.

Lydia Anne Greene wasn't surprised to learn that her own brother, who had grown up alongside the Montgomery boys, was not invited to the party. Everybody knew that whatever Emmett knew, John Galt Ibsen knew, too. And certainly John Galt Ibsen would not approve of *this* kind of party.

However, John Galt Ibsen already knew about the party. In fact, he had been the one to plant the idea of it in the Montgomery boys' heads. He had caught the Montgomery brothers whispering excitedly in the cafeteria on the day of their exams, and in response to the guilty silence that resulted in John Galt's passing by, he said, "Your sixteenth birthdays are just around the corner, aren't they?"

"Yes, Mr. Ibsen, sir," the boys responded.

"I hope you boys aren't planning some kind of party."

"No, sir."

That had done the trick. It had never occurred to the boys to throw a party. And now that they knew they *shouldn't*, they couldn't help themselves.

Of course, it wasn't long before Margaret Frost caught hold of a note as it was being passed around during one of her tedious lectures. The note was written entirely in code, and Margaret frowned when she found she couldn't make heads or tails of it, much to the amusement of her students. She took the crumpled note to John Galt Ibsen, and it took him two minutes to break the code. That's how he came to know the particulars of the party.

John Galt Ibsen had no desire to break up the merriment. He believed the youngsters (which is how he thought of them, even though he was only twenty-two) were entitled to their fun. What he didn't know was that the Montgomery brothers had figured out how to make vodka from the seeds in the hull of the ship. Mixing wheat grain with pilfered yeast cultures, which grew in abundance in the labs, the resourceful offspring of Hannah Montgomery were able to produce a crude form of vodka—hard to swallow but entirely effective.

***

Lydia Anne Greene stopped by Jason Fincus's room on her way to the party. He was in bed reading *To Kill a Mockingbird* and comparing himself to Boo Radley, the friendless, misunderstood hero of the novel.

When Lydia Anne stepped into his room, he had a tear in his eye for Boo Radley. Jason cried often and easily, especially when he was reading something particularly sad.

Seeing him there with a box of tissues and sparkling eyes, Lydia Anne Greene did something she had not expected herself to do. She invited him to the party.

"So that's why you're all dressed up," Jason said, sniffing. "I was wondering."

"I'm not dressed up," Lydia Anne said. "Just a little makeup, that's all."

"Ho-hum. Is that all?"

Lydia Anne blushed, and to cover it up she turned toward Jason's wardrobe and stuck her head inside of it. When she came out she had a clean white dress shirt and a pair of pleated slacks. She tossed them on the foot of the bed and told him to change.

Then she stepped into the hall to wait.

When Jason Fincus appeared in the doorway, his hair slicked back, his shirt tucked in, his chin cleanly shaved, he looked so much like his father—their father—that Lydia Anne shuddered.

From the second-level stairwell they could hear the reverberation of the party down below. The bassline of the music pounded through the ship like a migraine.

Someone had moved the movie projector into the stowage bay and was playing a colorful array of clips from Andy Warhol films, which flashed and throbbed like a disco strobe light. A space had been cleared among the sacks of seeds to make room for a dance floor.

The stowage bay was packed shoulder to shoulder, and Lydia Anne and Jason were whisked in opposite directions almost as soon as they stepped inside. Lydia Anne groped for Jason's hand in the darkness, felt it clasp hers, clammy and wet, and then it slipped away as somebody shoved between them.

A moment later Jason reappeared with two glasses of homemade brew. Lydia Anne sipped the putrid concoction reluctantly and felt its effects in a sudden rush of dizziness.

She clung to Jason for stability, but he was little help. He had already downed a second glass and was exhibiting the tolerance of a teenager. Together they stumbled onto the dance floor and tripped the light fantastic like a couple of drunken monkeys.

Nobody was surprised to see Jason Fincus at the party. He was the embodiment of rebellion for the younger generation—the only person to have ever escaped the *Destiny Unknown* and survived. The Montgomery boys hooted and hollered their approval when Jason arrived, and they showered him with the kind of affection usually reserved for an older, cooler brother. They made sure to refill Jason's cup and Lydia Anne's the whole evening, which explains how Jason and Lydia Anne came to be alone at four in the morning in the downstairs service closet smoking the captain's million-dollar cigars, utterly wasted.

The beat played on down the hall. Inside the service closet, it sounded as if an entire rock concert had been stuffed inside a pillow. And upstairs, alone in the infirmary, Martha Marigold, in the midst of chemotherapy, dreamed there was a hammer knocking out every tooth in her skull.

Lydia Anne had never noticed the service closet before, had never thought to open the door, and had never been inside—except as a fertilized egg.

Jason lit another cigar. "This is where I grew up."

Then he leaned in and kissed Lydia Anne full on the lips, blowing a puff of cigar smoke out of his nostrils.

Lydia Anne breathed the heady scent of fermented tobacco, tasted it on Jason's lips, and closed her eyes for a dizzying moment. Then from out of the haze of drunkenness came a shining kernel of nauseating truth: *Jason Fincus was her brother*.

She reeled back and shook loose the disorienting fog of drunkenness. "I'm your sister," she blurted out, pushing him away. And in response to his confused expression she explained, "*Half* sister. Your father is *my* father."

This shocking news affected Jason in two ways. Foremost, he was furious at his father for ruining his chances with yet another Greene girl. At the same time, he felt betrayed by Lydia Anne Greene. Why had she waited so long to tell him this essential bit of information?

Down the hall, somebody broke a champagne glass. Upstairs, Martha Marigold awoke in a cold sweat, heaved onto her side, and pushed the call button.

***

The call button sent a wireless signal to the pager that

Lydia Anne Greene always wore on the waistband of her pants. The pager went off like a screaming banshee in the awkward silence of the service closet.

It came as a great relief as far as Lydia Anne was concerned. She did not want to discuss her relation to Jason Fincus any further, did not want to recount the circumstances of the imprudent kiss, did not want to breathe the stench of fermented tobacco ever again.

And for the rest of her life the smell of cigar smoke would make her retch.

She gave Jason a pitying glance and explained she had to go. Just as she was leaving, she turned around and said, as she did routinely, "Remember to take your medication, Jason." And then she was gone.

When Lydia Anne, still tipsy, arrived at Martha Marigold's bedside, the ailing schoolteacher was unconscious with one arm dangling over the side of the bed and the other slung across her forehead.

Lydia Anne attempted to resuscitate Martha and pumped her body with epinephrine, and when the old woman went into cardiac arrest, Lydia Anne pounded on her chest with closed fists and blew air into her lungs. She would remember only snippets of the sobering moment when she realized Martha Marigold was dead. Elijah Perkins-Borges would find Lydia Anne asleep on the bed next to Martha's lifeless body the next morning.

He would never mention to anyone that Lydia Anne had

reeked of vodka and cigar smoke when he found her in bed with Martha Marigold's corpse that morning. Indeed, after performing a routine autopsy, he would later confirm what he initially suspected, that no amount of epinephrine or CPR would have revived the schoolteacher.

Meanwhile, downstairs in the storage closet, Jason fingered the barrel of the gun he had discovered in the box of laundry detergent. It was loaded. He casually switched the safety on and off, like a light switch. Then he stuffed the gun into the waistband of his khaki slacks. Whether the safety was on or off at this point, he couldn't say. He went straight to his bedroom, cleared all the bottles of medication off the nightstand, and emptied them into the toilet.

***

For a *Homo sapiens*, the line between love and hate is so fine, so paper thin, that being in love is always one step away from madness. It is not uncommon for such a human to cross back and forth, skipping lithely from one side of the line to the other, as many as twenty times a day. So Jason went back and forth like that for hours. And sometimes, Jason stood squarely in the middle, walking the fine line between love and hate. It is also possible for a *Homo sapiens* to experience both feelings at precisely the same moment, to balance precariously on the tightrope that is the boundary between passion and loathing.

Did Jason resolve anything by flushing his medication down the toilet? No. Did Jason plan to use the gun? God knows. He seemed to have forgotten it completely in his quest to purge his nightstand of antidepressants, anti-psychotics, and mood stabilizers, all of which reminded him of Lydia Anne Greene, *his sister*.

When he did finally collapse on the bed, he felt the cold muzzle of the pistol against his skin. If he could have flushed the gun down the toilet, he would have. If he could have flushed the whole goddamned ship down the toilet, he would have done that, too.

But since neither was an option—at least not in the three-dimensional universe in which humans currently live—Jason hid the pistol under his pillow. It was an instinctive decision, and it would have infuriated Jason to know his father would have done exactly the same. Marcus Fincus, for the better part of his life, had always kept a pistol under his pillow.

Humans have a funny expression still in use today: "The apple doesn't fall far from the tree." That's what someone would have said if anybody had been around to see Jason Fincus stuff the pistol under his pillow. And they probably wouldn't have known what they were talking about because the last apple fell from the last apple tree over two million years ago.

***

Jason no longer left his cabin. He had stashed away enough astronaut food to last him a lifetime. And in a state of insanity, he pledged never to come out again. The only person he admitted was Margaret Frost, who, despite Jason's declining state, still visited every night. Jason always unlocked the cabin door just after midnight so Margaret could come and go without a sound. And although Jason played at being sane whenever they made love, Margaret noticed the wild look in his eyes, dodgy and suspicious, like a rabid dog; it scared her.

And then she found the gun stashed under his pillow. He was in the bathroom performing his postcoital ablutions when she overturned the pillow and saw the barrel of the gun, gleaming like a pool of liquid mercury. Upset and unnerved, she replaced the pillow, patted it gently as if she were patting an atom bomb, and tiptoed out of the room. Little did she know the last thing she would ever see was the dusky barrel of that very gun.

CHAPTER 31

JOHN GALT IBSEN was no closer to finding a life-sustaining planet than when he had first taken charge of the ship. Discreetly, he began work on the first superspectrum x-ray telescope, a project he had been contemplating for many years: a telescope capable of seeing infinite distances, an instrument capable of discerning even the faintest objects in God's great universe, an invention capable of detecting all known wavelengths of light and gravity and sound.

He would never complete the superspectrum x-ray telescope. Stranded as he was aboard the *Destiny Unknown*, he didn't have the resources for such a project. But it was something to which he could bend his powerful mind during those long empty years. The preliminary blueprints he drew up would win him acclaim posthumously some two million years later when a man by the name of Archibald Ibsen, a descendent of John Galt, would work from them to create the first functional superspectrum x-ray telescope in human history.

Archibald Ibsen would win the Vestan Prize in physics, reaping the seventeenth Vestan Prize in Ibsen family history.[23] Such is the great legacy of the Ibsen bloodline. A bronze statue of Austin Ibsen stands at the Webber Street entrance to the Ibsen Museum of Human History in New Chicago on the planet Vesta. A marble statue of Amanda Sphinx stands just inside the front doors in an alcove on the right-hand side of the entry. Amanda is standing with her palms open in saintly welcome. A third statue towers in the lobby. It is none other than John Galt Ibsen, who stands like an eighteenth-century sea captain, compass in hand, looking up at the skies.

***

John Galt Ibsen died a virgin. How is it then that there came to be so many children descended of him, children who begot children who begot children for hundreds of thousands of years until at last Archibald Ibsen was begotten?

Herein lies part of the solution to that very puzzling conundrum.

In an attempt to secure the fate of the human race, Dr.

---

[23] Archibald Ibsen would win a second Vestan Prize in biology some years later for inventing microscopic robots that, when injected into the bloodstream, slowed the aging process. Humans from thereafter would live upward of two hundred years.

Robert Stowe collected sperm samples from all the virile men aboard the *Destiny Unknown*. There was some concern that the diet of nutrient-deficient astronaut food and the increased exposure to cosmic rays had resulted in sterility among the male population.

This theory was supported by the simple fact that no woman aboard the ship had become pregnant in over fifteen years, which was certainly grounds for investigation. It turned out to be a false alarm. The men on the ship tested at such high levels of fertility that condoms were distributed in abundance. What Dr. Robert Stowe hadn't considered was that perhaps there wasn't as much intercourse going on aboard the ship as one might suppose. And this was, in fact, the case. Most men aboard the *Destiny Unknown* suffered from such severe levels of depression that impotence turned out to be the primary suspect in the case of the missing babies, not infertility.

The semen samples were kept on file in the freezers in the laboratory, neatly labeled with the name of the donor on each vial. When they landed on the planet Vesta the freezers were cleared out and most of the contents, including the semen samples, were dumped into a ditch with all the other trash accumulated over the decades—the beginnings of what would become the first landfill of the new world—a clear marker that humans had arrived.

When they emptied the freezers' contents into the open ditch, they failed to notice one sample was missing—the sample belonging to John Galt Ibsen.

***

Another uninhabitable star came and went. Then another. A few minutes past midnight on the morning of November 5, thirty-six years into their journey, Captain Marcus Fincus awoke with a bladder near bursting. He rolled over in bed, saw Esmeralda lying asleep, mistook her for a Canadian prostitute, and wondered momentarily what he owed her for her services. Then he climbed out from beneath the covers and went in search of a bathroom.

He had the choice of two doors: one leading to the toilet and another leading to the corridor on level four. As fate would have it, Marcus Fincus chose the door to the corridor on level four. There he wandered up and down, holding his crotch like a five-year-old child, trying doors along the way and finding them all locked. Then at last, he opened the door that would seal the fate of poor Margaret Frost.

Marcus Fincus had stumbled upon his son, Jason Fincus, lying naked in bed, awaiting the ritual arrival of his midnight mistress. When Jason Fincus saw his father standing there in the doorway, something in his brain snapped like a cold piece of celery. While the bewildered ex-captain tried to find the bathroom, Jason Fincus drew the pistol from under his pillow and aimed it directly at his father's chest.

The present danger brought Marcus Fincus out of the

NICHOLAS PONTICELLO

depths of his delirium for a single lucid moment, and when Jason Fincus pulled the trigger, the captain leaped aside, narrowly avoiding a quintessentially Oedipal death.

There came a scream, clear and short, like the whistle of a train.

It was Margaret Frost. She had just entered Jason's room. And the bullet that had missed its target had found her instead.

She went down instantly.

The gunshot woke Deidre Hundt, whose cabin was one floor below. She rushed to the bloody scene in time to see Jason trying to stuff the gun back under his pillow.

Deidre Hundt set to work at once trying to revive Margaret Frost. Meanwhile, Marcus Fincus made his way to Jason's private washroom and proceeded to urinate in the bathtub. Jason Fincus, wide-eyed and frantic, darted out of the room.

The gunshot had awakened others as well. A handful of passengers arrived on the scene and gathered around Deidre and the bloody corpse.

Margaret's body was removed to the infirmary, where it was covered with a white sheet. It was propelled into space the following morning.

As for Jason Fincus—he was nowhere to be found. He had fled in escape pod B, taking with him a year's supply of food for fifty people, or fifty years of food for Jason alone. However, Jason living out those fifty years in space was doubtful. Recall that escape pod B had the faulty moleculator that was pronounced dead twenty-four years ago.

When they realized that Jason had run off in an escape pod again, there was some discussion as to whether he should be recaptured and brought to trial for his crime or left to suffocate alone in deep space.

John Galt Ibsen ordered the *Destiny Unknown* onward.

"Let him be," he said. "I cannot think of a more elegant solution."

***

I have not placed an asterisk by Jason's name on the ship's manifest in the appendix of this dissertation because I do not claim to know whether Jason did in fact die alone in space three days after the murder of Margaret Frost, as was predicted by John Galt Ibsen and the rest of the crew—or if, perhaps, he went on to have adventures of his own. I did not continue to follow Jason's trajectory with my superspectrum x-ray telescope, so I do not presume to know his ultimate fate. Nor do I dare put my faith in the odds, which were stacked heavily against poor Jason Fincus from the beginning. I would like to remind my readers that Jason Fincus was a human being and, as I have observed, where human beings are concerned, the odds, no matter how heavily stacked they may be, tend to shift and bend like light in a prism whenever a human has the common sense to hope.

So even if Jason Fincus was *likely* to die of asphyxiation three days after the murder of Margaret Frost, there is no guarantee that he did.

***

In an improbable chain of events, the death of Margaret Frost led to the salvation of the entire human population. Here is how it happened.

After Elijah Perkins-Borges carried away Margaret Frost's stiff body, Anita Lund arrived on the scene to scrub away all traces of the bloody crime. In the midst of flipping Jason's mattress, which had been splattered with blood, she uncovered Jason's collection of drawings in Crayola Marker on butcher paper—the tortured ramblings of a schizophrenic madman.

Anita Lund passed the sketches on to the only person she remembered having anything to do with Jason: Lydia Anne Greene.

When Lydia Anne Greene saw the drawings that Jason had been so careful to hide, she recognized in them something more than the tortured ramblings of a schizophrenic madman. Lydia Anne believed she had come into possession of a series of detailed star charts. And she had the good sense to pass the so-called ramblings on to John Galt Ibsen—who, she knew, could interpret star charts better than anyone else.

John Galt Ibsen took one look at the tortured ramblings of

the schizophrenic madman and felt in his heart that miraculous human condition—hope.

***

John Galt Ibsen eased the *Destiny Unknown* to a stop, idled the engines, and locked himself in his cabin for three days with nothing to entertain him but the prolific works of Jason Fincus. When he emerged, he had read and reread the ramblings of the schizophrenic madman enough times to convince himself that what he was reading was, in fact, a detailed treasure map leading to a life-sustaining planet on the outer edge of the Keith Cluster, a mere seven light-years away—an eight-year journey.

What made the drawings of Jason Fincus so credible?

Well, this is what convinced John Galt Ibsen, anyway: from the moment Jason Fincus had rejoined the crew of the *Destiny Unknown*, he had kept an accurate record of every mile they had traveled and every star they had visited. When asked how he could have managed such a feat with so little knowledge of space travel, Lydia Anne Greene recalled Jason's story about aliens flashing lights in his eyes so that he could never forget a single thing as long as he lived.

"Maybe he just remembered it all." Lydia Anne shrugged.

Jason's treasure map led to what he described in one of his doodles as "a green-and-blue planet more beautiful than Earth ever was."

Jason Fincus wrote, "This I know, for I have seen the maps of the ones who call me *human specimen zero*, and damned if they don't swear by their maps."

That was enough to go by. Eight years, in the scheme of things, wasn't so long. And if the green-and-blue planet Jason waxed lyrical about didn't exist, then it would only prove that Jason was indeed as crazy as everybody thought he was.

And if the green-and-blue planet did exist...

Another entry, scrawled across his mysterious star charts, described in further detail those enigmatic beings that referred to Jason Fincus as human specimen zero:

> They call themselves interstellar biologists. They roam the galaxy, tracking all manner of creatures from the Hublinoid starchasers to the Jovian amoebae that, incidentally, account for 98 percent of all dark matter in the galaxy. They mark their specimens with tattoos, usually inked onto the backside of the ear, or in the case of creatures with no ears at all, in an armpit or on the bottom of a foot. In the case of the Jovian amoebae, which are too small to tattoo, they don't mark them at all. They simply stick a beaker out in space and scoop up whole fistfuls for their terrariums.

Here Jason included a picture of what looked like an aquarium with pink dots swimming around.

They called me human specimen zero. They refused to call me Jason. They took pictures of my brain with a giant camera that could see inside my head. The side effects of brain imaging with the giant camera, I was told, are nausea, headaches, fatigue, and remembering for the rest of your life every little thing that you ever see or hear again. After having the pictures of my brain taken, I was able to memorize Newton's *Principia*, which was stored in the database of escape pod A. Consequently, I have mastered the fundamentals of Newtonian physics. I made it halfway through Hathaway's *Expert Guide to Deep-Space Travel*, also in the database, which means I am about halfway through understanding everything there is to know about getting around in space.

There was no telling how much of what Jason reported was true. But there was no denying that some of the elements of Jason's story checked out. It was true that each escape pod was equipped with a digital library that included both Newton's *Principia* and Hathaway's *Expert Guide to Deep-Space Travel*. It is also true that much of the universe is made up of dark matter, for which humans at the time had no explanation.

John Galt Ibsen set aside work on the superspectrum x-ray telescope and turned all his attention to decoding Jason's star charts. And soon the course was set. John Galt Ibsen pointed the muzzle of the ship at a pinprick of light so faint it could very well have been a speck of dust shimmering in the headlamps of the ship. The passengers were skeptical but hopeful. All they had to do was survive long enough to reach the green-and-blue planet and see for themselves.

***

Esmeralda Fincus, feeling the loss of her son as acutely as she had the first time he ran away, claimed that none of what Jason wrote in Crayola markers could be taken as truth. "He is a very sick man," she told Anita Lund one afternoon while Anita was tidying up, "just like his father."

She demanded Anita stop whatever she was doing and sit on the edge of the bed to hear her better.

"I used to visit him," Esmeralda went on. "I used to go in very late, sometimes as late as three in the morning. And do you know what I would do? I would clean up after that poor sick boy."

And here she started to cry. "I didn't want him to see me. I was afraid he would blame me for his miserable fate."

Then Esmeralda wiped away her tears. "I think his sickness is genetic. Things like that can be genetic, you know. His father's family has a long history of insanity. Why, Stella—Marcus's mother—wore a lampshade for a hat."

Anita Lund blinked, and Esmeralda shifted her gaze to the floral pattern on the rug.

"One night I walked in, and he was in bed with a girl. I

can't be quite sure who she was. I didn't stay long enough to find out. I can only remember her hair—dark, wavy hair—like mine."

Here Esmeralda corrected herself. "The way my hair used to be, anyway."

She went on. "After I saw him with that woman—the woman with the hair—I never visited again. It is a horrible thing to walk in on two people making love—especially if one of those people is your own dear child."

Here there was such a long pause that Anita Lund was compelled to speak.

"I can only imagine," Anita offered.

"I have no friends," Esmeralda said.

"Madam?"

"I have nobody to tell these things to." At this point Esmeralda closed her eyes and, with a single flick of her wrist, motioned Anita out of the room.

***

There was much speculation as to whether the star charts Jason Fincus had left behind were authentic—if the speck-of-dust star to which they were headed was the fulcrum of a green-and-blue planet capable of sustaining human life.

Some people worried that John Galt Ibsen was staking eight years of astronaut food on the tortured ramblings of a schizophrenic madman. Then there were those who swore by the maps, who saw how precise Jason's calculations had been, and who couldn't believe that a man who had tested at an IQ of eighty could come up with such elaborate blueprints without the help of aliens—of interstellar biologists.

Such debate had not divided the passengers since the great typhus outbreak when Esmeralda Fincus and Richard Park had argued over the existence of rats aboard the ship.

Richard Park had won that round. And now, at the venerable age of seventy-five, he was unconcerned as to whether the green-and-blue planet really existed. What mattered was that it gave them somewhere to go.

"As long as we have a destination," he said, "I'm willing to stick around in this mortal hell."

***

That year they didn't celebrate Christmas. The only person who bothered to remember was Lydia Anne Greene, who had always held Christmas dear as it was also her mother's birthday. And she observed the holiday with a solemnity befitting a funeral. She locked herself in her room for the duration of the morning, skipping breakfast and lunch, and came out only to give John Galt Ibsen his Christmas present, which was a poem that went like this:

> He was a boy
> Born out in space

Amid the Milky Way.
She thought he had a handsome face,
Although she'd never say.
And as a child he never cried;
In Gzorazkian he'd croon.
As a man he walked with pride
And made the ladies swoon.
And then one day he took the helm,
And although he'd never flown,
He saved the fifty-something crew
Of the *Destiny Unknown*.

When she gave John Galt Ibsen the poem, she didn't say "Merry Christmas" because she figured John Galt was too serious to remember Christmas.

John Galt Ibsen was amused. The poem was good, and in sixty-eight words it told the story of his life. As a thank-you, he wrote a poem in response, mimicking her arrangement. He slipped it under her cabin door.

She was a girl
Born out in space.
Growing up they played.
She had an even handsomer face,
At least that's what they said.
She grew up quick; she grew up wise;
She studied, learned, excelled.

She was invited to the Montgomery party,
While John Galt Ibsen was expelled.
And while she led a fruitful life,
Shining like a star,
He remained distant and aloof,
Admiring her from afar.

PS—I'm afraid it doesn't rhyme as prettily as yours.

It was a rare display of John Galt's sillier side. Lydia Anne framed the poem and mounted it on her wall. Now it hangs in the Ibsen Museum of Human History alongside a fountain pen that Lydia Anne was said to be fond of. The poem Lydia Anne wrote to John Galt has since been lost, as have many of the personal effects *he* was said to be fond of.

That is because John Galt Ibsen wasn't quite fond enough of anything to hold on to it for very long.

CHAPTER 32

YEARS 37-44

THE *DESTINY UNKNOWN* stayed its course. For eight long years the flagging crew peered out at the tiny yellow dot that promised to be their last hope of survival. They were running out of time. Their food supplies would last them no more than two or three years on the green-and-blue planet— enough time to plant a few crops, if they were lucky. If the green-and-blue planet proved to be a fantasy of Jason's mind, then they could dig into the seed stores, maybe— extend their time on the ship a year or so more—but the likelihood of reaching another star with a habitable planet in that short time was slim. This one had to be it.

The maps Jason had left them proved to be astonishingly accurate. As they closed in on the yellow star, they measured its brightness and mapped the relative positions of the neighboring stars. Everything was *exactly* as Jason had described. And sure enough, when they entered the gravitational field of Amalda—the name they had chosen for the star—they were able to make out the outline of a tiny blue dot in orbit around the sun. The planet came to be called Vesta.

The planet was Earth-size, its surface a mosaic of frothy cerulean seas, sandy yellow beaches, leafy emerald forests, and frosty mountaintops. Fluffy white clouds sailed across the oceans and broke against the cragged highland peaks like great waves. Blue rivers crisscrossed the valleys like veins, supplying an endless flow of freshwater to the verdant continents. At the equator, a torrential tropical storm churned the air like a giant blender, and to the north and south, great snowy icecaps reflected the yellow light of the sun back into space where it nearly blinded the weary passengers of the *Destiny Unknown*.

The excitement on the ship was palpable. For those born on the *Destiny Unknown*, Vesta was a sight to see—they had never seen a planet so welcoming as this one. And for those old enough to remember Earth, this new planet reminded them of home.

Two moons circled Vesta. The *Destiny Unknown* fell into step beside them, letting the gravity of the planet carry them in orbit like the current of a river. They observed the planet from all angles, searching for a site with plenty of water and rich soil and flat ground on which they could build their homes and plant their crops.

Judging from the light reflecting off the surface of the planet and the accumulation of clouds in the sky and the density of the greenery below, they were able to guess what kind of climate each region offered: arid and dry, cold and wet, icy and frozen, warm and moist. And they likened these regions to places that had once existed on Earth, places that had been destroyed by rising temperatures: the Sahara Desert, the British Isles, the Arctic, the Amazon.

Then they found it: a lush valley not far from the sea, separated from the coastline by a long row of hills and protected from inclement weather on all sides by a network of mountain ranges that stood like bulwarks flanking a palace courtyard. The valley was checkered with small lakes fed by lazy freshwater streams. To the north stood a sprawling deciduous forest that promised fruit and lumber and game.

At the age of seventy-two, Earl Updike, resident poet laureate, was so struck by the beauty of this new world that he picked up his pen—although he had given up writing many years ago when he could no longer find inspiration in the stars—and he wrote this sonnet:

Oh, Earth, if you were to us a nurturing mother
And the sun was to us a father and friend,
Then let us plead guilty to seeking another:
A new mother to plunder, a new father to rend.
You see, Mother, she loved us straight into the ground,
And Father was so thirsty he drank every drop.
So we tiptoed away without making a sound
And flew forty-four years with scarcely a stop.

Then out of the darkness came a whisper of light
That shone ever brighter as onward we flew—
A star like the sun, only younger and sprite,
And a stepmother world covered in blue.
By God, you are beautiful; pray, tell us your name.
Then give us the chance, and we'll destroy you the
same.

They chose a patch of flat land in the middle of the valley, not far from the convergence of two fast-flowing rivers,
and called it Dos Rios. It was to become the first interstellar
colony in the history of humankind. They would later learn
that Dos Rios flooded during the monsoon season, and they
would migrate north to higher ground. Archaeologists have
since dug up the remains of Dos Rios, and among them they
found the bones of Bobo the chimp, an antiquated cigar box,
and a ditch full of human semen samples. All the artifacts
from the excavation are on display in the Ibsen Museum of
Human History in New Chicago.

***

When the base-camp site was finally agreed on and the
course set, the crew readied for landing. John Galt Ibsen
issued a series of commands, first to the chief mechanical
engineer, who surveyed the landing gear and shouted "Aye-
aye," then to the sailing master, who punched a set of coor-

dinates into the mainframe, and finally to the first mate, who sounded the all clear.

The engines fired, and they began their descent.

Then, in another instant, the ship bucked and screeched to a halt. The engines sputtered, the lights flickered, and power all over the ship went out.

There was a collective cry of disappointment, and then, as weightlessness took over, nobody moved, not a finger, not a step. Their bodies floated in the air and bobbed like ice cream in soda.

John Galt Ibsen was the first person to recover from the shock. And while he searched around for a flashlight, the rest of the crew stared longingly out the windows at the green-and-blue planet as if it were a mirage, an ethereal paradise, never to be.

When at last he found a flashlight, John Galt Ibsen left the bridge, left all of the catatonic passengers peering hopelessly out into space, and went to find Lydia Anne Greene.

She was in the library. She, too, was staring dreamily out of the giant glass skylight at the green-and-blue planet. John Galt Ibsen shook her from her stupor and asked if she would accompany him to the hull of the ship. He needed someone to hold the flashlight while he fiddled with the fuse box.

They were just about to leave when something banged on the glass ceiling above.

They looked up. Outlined against the starry sky was the figure of a man, lying facedown on the glass dome. He was wearing a white space suit and helmet. Through his tinted visor they could see his face. It was Marcus Fincus.

The space suit was attached to the ship by way of a long nylon cord that extended from the air lock and stretched a distance of four hundred feet.

At the first sign of power failure, Marcus Fincus, who had been in the middle of a bath, climbed into one of the space suits and clambered out onto the roof of the ship to see what was the matter.

The matter was this: Marcus Fincus was a demented old man, and he didn't know the difference between a light socket and a screwdriver. What he thought he was doing on the roof was anyone's guess.

He had tripped over one of the crossbeams and fallen against the glass dome. That was the bang they heard. Once he had recovered from the fall, he moved on, each step sounding on the roof with a hollow thud.

The glass dome bulged out just enough for Lydia Anne Greene and John Galt Ibsen to follow the captain's progress. And as the captain made his way across the roof of the ship, he clung to the nylon cord as if it were a lifesaver.

A crowd was gathering in the library now to see what was going on overhead. The sight of the captain bumbling along the surface of the ship was more amusing than alarming, seeing as they couldn't think of anything he could do to worsen their situation. They were already stranded in space without power. What else could possibly go wrong?

Then the captain came to a point where the cord would stretch no farther. He fumbled with the clasp for a few minutes, and the cord came loose. It snapped back and whipped around like a fire hose.

Marcus Fincus forged onward, clinging to rungs welded onto the side of the ship. Just as he was nearing the portside gunwale, he pounded a fist on the bulwark, and a maintenance hatch popped open.

The captain climbed inside and disappeared from view.

John Galt Ibsen was confused. What could the captain possibly hope to accomplish? The only components in that particular hatch were the—

Then it came to him.

"I'm going out there," he told Lydia Anne Greene. "Whatever you do, don't take your eyes off me for a second. If anything goes wrong, watch for my signal."

And John Galt Ibsen was out the door in a flash.

Lydia Anne Greene and the rest of the crowd stayed on to see what was going to happen next. And sure enough, Marcus Fincus reappeared a few minutes later, this time cradling something in his arms.

It was an opaque cube about the size of a tissue box. There was a murmur among the passengers. Nobody had ever seen the cube before, and nobody could think of what it was.

Then Lydia Anne Greene remembered a conversation with John Galt Ibsen some years back.

He had said what a wonder it was that a ship as big as the *Destiny Unknown* could be run by a square cube no bigger than a human brain and weighing about the same.

Marcus Fincus had in his hands the motherboard of the supercomputer, the brain of the ship.

The captain clambered across the surface of the ship, carrying the cube under one arm and keeping balance with the other. And with each step he became more hesitant, more unsure.

In the distance, the nylon cord trailed like a kite tail, and Marcus Fincus looked at it longingly.

Then John Galt Ibsen appeared on the opposite side of the glass dome.

Marcus Fincus spotted him and froze. And there he stayed for some time, hugging the cube to his chest, his eyes darting from John Galt Ibsen to the nylon cord to the black void surrounding them.

Then John Galt Ibsen put out a gloved hand to Marcus Fincus, coaxing him forward.

The captain took a step, and then another, and slowly he made his way across the rooftop. When he came to the glass dome, he looked down at all the people below, their faces glowing in the starlight—he was so agitated by their horrified expressions that he forgot to watch for the crossbeams. The toe of his boot caught sharply on a ledge, and he went tumbling outward into space.

There was a collective gasp among the crowd. Marcus

Fincus flailed for a handhold, and the opaque cube rocketed out of his arms.

At that very moment the nylon cord whipped around and smacked the captain across the face. He grabbed hold of it with both hands and reeled himself in. Meanwhile the opaque cube spiraled into the void, its outline growing fainter and fainter until it was one with the darkness.

John Galt Ibsen didn't even hesitate. He unfastened himself from his safety belt and dove after the cube.

The crowd drew a collective breath. John Galt Ibsen flew past Marcus Fincus, past the tip of the nylon cord, and out of reach of anything that might bring him safely back again.

Lydia Anne tracked John Galt Ibsen until he was swallowed by the void, and even then she did not take her eyes off the spot where he had disappeared.

And then Amanda Sphinx appeared at the door to the library. She had been in her room reading Chaucer when the power went out. It had taken her some time to adjust to the weightlessness, and to find a flashlight. And she had made her way down the long corridors of the ship, following what sounded like footsteps on the roof.

She came into the library in time to hear a collective gasp, which was the sound of the crew reacting to the sight of John Galt Ibsen fading into infinite darkness.

She floated to the ceiling, saw Marcus Fincus clinging to the nylon cord, saw only one person where there ought to have been two, and sensed right away that her son had done something incredibly reckless.

"What happened?" she demanded. "Where is he?"

"He dropped it," somebody said, nodding toward the captain, "and Mr. Ibsen went after it."

She followed Lydia Anne Greene's gaze to the point in space where John Galt Ibsen had vanished. And together they stared fixedly into the emptiness that had engulfed the one man they both loved.

Then a light blinked on in the darkness. Lydia Anne was the first to see it: a tiny flash in the void.

John Galt Ibsen had brought the flashlight with him.

It flashed an SOS, and Lydia Anne suddenly remembered they still had escape pod A. The escape pods were designed to operate independently of the ship. So even though the *Destiny Unknown* was without power, there was the possibility escape pod A still worked.

She hurried downstairs and burst through the air lock. Someone had gotten there before her. The engines were already running, and her brother Emmett was sitting in the driver's seat.

"Close the air lock," he shouted.

She secured the door and took a seat beside him.

"Do you know how to fly this thing?" she asked.

"Sure," he said. "We had to learn in school."

"I don't remember any of that stuff."

"Fasten your safety belt."

Then the escape pod broke away from the *Destiny*

Unknown and zoomed into space. Emmett Greene switched on the headlights and steered the vessel toward the pinprick of blinking white light in the distance.

When they reached John Galt Ibsen, he was floating on his back with the black cube resting on his chest. With the flashlight in one hand, he was flicking it on and off with his thumb.

The escape pod circled him twice. On the second time around, John Galt Ibsen caught hold of a rung on the starboard side, and they carried him back to the ship.

CHAPTER 33

YEAR 44

THEY MADE THEIR FINAL DESCENT in the dead of night. A fine mist wafted off the rivers and cloaked the valley in darkness. John Galt Ibsen ordered the passengers to remain on board until he could run a full diagnostics test on the atmosphere to guarantee their safety. Even then, John Galt Ibsen insisted Bobo be the first to breathe the Vestan air.

Given the darkness and the unfamiliarity of the terrain, everyone agreed that nothing could be done until sunrise. The planet would still be there tomorrow, they assured one another nervously.

But one man could not wait until tomorrow. That man was Arthur Stanton. He was 104 years old, and he didn't have time to waste. While the others were sleeping, he sneaked into the air lock and peered out the porthole at the misty valley bathed in the blue light of two gibbous moons.

If he died, he thought, at least he would die on solid ground. And if he lived—

The air lock opened with a hiss. Cool, wet air poured in. For a moment, Arthur Stanton held his breath. Then, slowly, he inhaled the Vestan air.

Arthur grinned like a baby. It was air! Sweet, fresh air— and not the recycled kind that came from moleculators.

Arthur Stanton closed the air lock behind him, tightened the laces on his boots, and strolled into the mist. He walked until the sun peeked over the hills. And he discovered many things. He discovered that the life-forms on this planet were primarily carbon based, seeing as he could eat the fruits that grew on the trees. He discovered that the water was potable, since he could drink freely from the streams. And he discovered that humans were not the first intelligent species to set foot on this planet.

Someone else had been there, too.

This he knew when he came upon the carcass of what looked very much like a New England cottontail. Its insides had been devoured by some Vestan beast. Only the tail, feet, and head remained intact. On closer examination of the carcass, Arthur Stanton found a very familiar marking behind its right ear: a tattoo about the size of a postal stamp, the same tattoo Jason Fincus had had imprinted behind *his* ear.

Arthur Stanton wrapped the carcass in his sweater and carried it back to the ship.

***

Meanwhile, the bridge crew assembled and ran the final tests on the Vestan atmosphere. They found it contained no traceable toxins, and it was nearly identical to Earth's atmosphere, with four parts nitrogen to one part oxygen. The temperature throughout the night had fluctuated between sixty and seventy degrees Fahrenheit, and the atmospheric pressure was 101,132 pascals, a little less than on Earth. The weather was mild, and the gravity appeared to be only slightly weaker than on Earth.

It was a veritable Eden.

The last test was to see if Bobo could survive in the Vestan atmosphere. They didn't know Arthur Stanton was already tromping around the countryside without a space suit.

When all the tests were complete, Elijah Perkins-Borges reluctantly retrieved Bobo from his cage and carried him to the air lock, where John Galt Ibsen was waiting to see him off. Elijah Perkins-Borges hugged Bobo good-bye, and John Galt Ibsen shook the chimp's furry hand. And they nudged him out of the ship.

Bobo took a few steps into the grassy field, paused to scratch himself, and then, having not died of asphyxiation or chemical poisoning or any other disaster, began picking at bugs in the grass.

John Galt Ibsen declared the planet habitable. And as the passengers gathered near the air lock to disembark, Bobo feasted on crawly things in the grass and strayed farther and farther from the ship.

An argument broke out over who should be the first human to set foot on the new planet, initiated by none other than Esmeralda Fincus, who had roused herself for the occasion. She was just making a case that Marcus Fincus, the rightful captain of the ship, should be the first to touch alien soil when Arthur Stanton appeared on the horizon with the rabbit carcass slung over his shoulder.

Bobo ambled over to Arthur Stanton and climbed into the old man's arms. Then the air-lock doors slid open, and the passengers poured out to greet the first man to ever set foot on Vestan soil.

They would never be able to make heads or tails of the tattoo behind the rabbit's ear. But everyone agreed it looked remarkably like Jason's tattoo.

***

The first Vestan child was born to a virgin mother. The child's name was Rhea Silvia. Her mother was Lydia Anne Greene. Rhea Silvia was born four months after they had established the colony of Dos Rios. As the resident obstetrician, Lydia Anne Greene had no trouble artificially inseminating herself with John Galt Ibsen's frozen sperm. And when asked about the father, she always blushed and said what her mother, Emma Greene, had said about her: "She has no father."

Little Rhea Silvia loved her mother's stories about the *Destiny Unknown* so much that when she grew up she wrote them all down in a book. That book is called *New Genesis* and is often regarded as the most thorough account of the maiden voyage of the *Destiny Unknown*.

But no account is more accurate than the one I have just given you.

And decades later, on a planet very much resembling Earth—its atmosphere four parts nitrogen to one part oxygen—the Vestan colonies would develop the technology to broadcast a message back to their boiling ancestors trapped under layers of CO_2 and dirt. This is what the message said:

We made it.

APPENDIX

THE SHIP MANIFEST

A SHIP IS A SHIP IS A SHIP. And that is what the *Destiny Unknown* was: a ship. A spaceship, to be exact, carrying fifty passengers from Earth to Vesta on a forty-four-year mission—carrying the forefathers of humankind. Every human being alive in the universe today is descended from the passengers of that ship.

Here is the manifest from the *Destiny Unknown*, giving the name of each passenger and his or her station and age at the beginning of the trip. The original manifest is proudly displayed in the Ibsen Museum of Human History on the corner of Webber and Third Streets in the city of New Chicago on the planet Vesta. A copy was also displayed in the Smithsonian Museum in Washington, DC, on Earth until the sun swallowed the planet in AD 5.52 billion.

I have made a few changes to the original manifest for the benefit of the reader. I have indicated those who died serving

NASA's New World Population Project with an asterisk to commemorate their bravery. And since the original manifest does not take into account the children born in transit, I have added those names in an addendum following the original fifty names.

The Original Manifest

Marcus Fincus, *Captain* (age 42)

* Johannes Levi, *First Mate* (age 23)

Howard Oppenheimer, *Sailing Master* (age 36)

Melanie Lorne, *Chief Mechanical Engineer* (age 35)

* Maurice Yanne, *Signals Specialist* (age 46)

* Bartholomew Barbate, *Chief Electrical Engineer* (age 38)

Deidre Hundt, *Associate Mechanical Engineer* (age 25)

George McGraw, *Midshipman* (age 22)

Percival McQueen, *Midshipman* (age 17)

Edith Young, *Midshipwoman* (age 20)

James Nguyen, *Midshipman* (age 22)

* Dr. Myles Jamison, *Chief Surgeon* (age 48)

Elijah Borges, *Veterinarian* (age 26)

Maisey Perkins, *Dental Surgeon* (age 32)

*Barbary Montclair, *Head Chef* (age 48)

Tyson Summers, *Sous Chef* (age 28)

Greta O'Hare, *Sous Chef* (age 34)

Ginger Martin, *Plant and Cell Biologist* (age 32)

Richard Park, *Immunization Specialist* (age 40)

Fred Garrity, *Chemist* (age 25)

Pierre Tulare, *Physicist* (age 29)

Thelma Watson, *Lab Technician* (age 22)

Jacob Mulholland, *Lab Technician* (age 20)

Barbara Chatsworth, *Psychiatrist* (age 35)

* Martha Marigold, *Schoolteacher* (age 46)

Arthur Stanton, *Songwriter* (age 60)

Pearl Hart, *Painter* (age 36)

Earl Updike, *Poet Laureate* (age 28)

Albert Morris, *Director of Clean Space Janitorial Services* (age 31)

* Emma Greene, *Clean Space Janitorial Staff* (age 20)

Anita Lund, *Clean Space Janitorial Staff* (age 18)

Esmeralda Fincus, *Passenger* (age 39)

Jason Fincus, *Passenger* (age 10)

* Austin Ibsen, *Passenger* (age 12)

Amanda Sphinx, *Passenger* (age 15)

* Brandelyn McCormack, *Passenger* (age 8)

* Margaret Frost, *Passenger* (age 8)

Kelsey Holmes, *Passenger* (age 8)

Hannah Montgomery, *Passenger* (age 8)

Robert Stowe, *Passenger* (age 10)

Raquel Muniz, *Passenger* (age 9)

Harvey England, *Passenger* (age 13)

Frances Dillon, *Passenger* (age 10)

Drey Marlow, *Passenger* (age 8)

Eric Yen, *Passenger* (age 10)

Ricky Mancini, *Passenger* (age 12)

Rico Torres, *Passenger* (age 8)

* Dog, *Canis lupus familiaris* (age 1)

* Bill, *Psittacus erithacus erithacus* (age 6)

Bobo, *Pan troglodytes* (age 2)

Manifest Addendum

Lydia Anne Greene (born year 7)

Molly Perkins-Borges (born year 7)

Maggie Perkins-Borges (born year 8)

Olivia Perkins-Borges (born year 10)

Ruth Perkins-Borges (born year 11)

John Galt Ibsen (born year 12)

Ryan Hollander (born year 18)

Regina Lund (born year 18)

Graciella Lund (born year 18)

Derek Lund (born year 18)

Javier Lund (born year 18)

Yolanda Lund (born year 18)

Frank Lund (born year 18)

Mitchell Xavier Montgomery (born year 18)

Jesse Montgomery (born year 18)

Nicholas Montgomery (born year 18)

Joseph Montgomery (born year 18)

Daniel Montgomery (born year 18)

* Reginald Montgomery (born year 18)

Emmett Greene (born year 19)

ACKNOWLEDGMENTS

THANK YOU to my parents, Nick and Shelly, without whom I could not have been born in the year AD 1984 on the planet Earth, in the form of an advanced primate. To Joey, who said he liked this book more than my first one. To Danny, who has been reading my work since he was fourteen years old. To Tyler Thompson and Kelly Tsou, two of the earliest readers of *The Destiny Unknown*. To Victoria, my line editor, who likes my space-related similes. To Jo, my copyeditor, who saved me from professional embarrassment. And, finally, to the Monkey, who is a hell of a lot smarter than any *Homo sapiens* I know.

ABOUT THE AUTHOR

NICHOLAS PONTICELLO is a high-school mathematics teacher and STEAM (Science, Technology, Engineering, Art, and Mathematics) coordinator at Flintridge Preparatory School in Los Angeles, California. Mr. Ponticello graduated from the University of California, Berkeley, with degrees in mathematics and astrophysics and was awarded a certificate in sustainability from University of California, Los Angeles, Extension. His debut novel, *Do Not Resuscitate*, received honorable mention at the 2015 Green Book Festival, which spotlights "books that contribute to greater understanding, respect for and positive action on the changing worldwide environment" and was a semifinalist in the 2015 Kindle Book Awards for Literary Fiction. Mr. Ponticello resides in Los Angeles with art historian Nico Machida and their six freshwater fish.

For more titles by this author, please visit www.booleanop.com.

Made in the USA
San Bernardino, CA
20 April 2017